DON PENDLETON'S

STONY

AMERICA'S ULTRA-COVERT INTELLIGENCE AGENCY

MAN®

SEASON OF HARM

Recycling programs
for this product may
not exist in your area.

First edition February 2010

ISBN-13: 978-0-373-61989-4

SEASON OF HARM

Special thanks and acknowledgment to
Phil Elmore for his contribution to this work.

Printed in U.S.A.

THE GUNSHIP GAINED ALTITUDE

Grimaldi allowed the deadly machine to crest the rise at the far end of the now-burning poppy field. Below, in the depression beyond, sat the camp and heroin-processing center. Phoenix Force would be moving in from the perimeter just now; Grimaldi would, therefore, fight from the center of the camp, moving outward. He overflew the camp, chose his spot and yanked hard on the controls, making the gunship shudder and dance as it dumped its velocity. He brought the killing snout of the helicopter around in a slow arc.

"G-Force is all go, twice," he said aloud. "Heads down, gentlemen."

The M-28 turret's twin M-134 miniguns began spitting 7.62-millimeter death. The slow arc of the chopper fanned the slugs out as Grimaldi picked his targets, centering on the small, prefabricated, corrugated metal buildings closest to the center of the camp. Men carrying Kalashnikovs began running for their lives. Something volatile within one of the buildings exploded, throwing shrapnel and flames in every direction. Grimaldi kept the pressure on, his gunship's inventory ticking down in his head, the chopper wreaking havoc in the enemy's midst.

He began whistling "The Battle Hymn of the Republic," smiling faintly as the Triangle drug plant slowly disintegrated at the touch of his trigger finger.

SEASON OF HARM

CHAPTER ONE

Camden, New Jersey

Agent Marie Carrol surveyed the decaying buildings and littered streets through the passenger window of the SUV. The city of Camden always depressed her. It wasn't simply that the Bureau had repeatedly ranked the city of nearly eighty thousand people as one of the most dangerous in the country. No, what bothered her about Camden was the crushing sense of hopelessness. Like Newark, Camden was also one of the poorest cities in America, but she'd seen both crime and poverty before. Something about Camden was different, as if a cloud of misery hung over the place, and could not be dispelled even by the sights and attractions of the relatively prosperous waterfront. She'd seen it all before, from the Adventure Aquarium to the USS *New Jersey,* and she wasn't impressed.

Ironically, the warehouse to which their small convoy traveled was in the Urban Enterprise Zone, whatever that was supposed to mean. She had no doubt that their quarry had a bustling urban enterprise under way. Too bad that it was completely illegal.

Carrol looked at her reflection in the tinted window glass. She wasn't doing too bad, she thought. Not yet forty, her auburn hair still all her own color. Smooth features, a few laugh lines. She filled out her suit fairly well, too, if she said so herself; the time in the gym every other night was paying off. The ring still on her finger was a sore point with her mother, who told her she was clinging to the past; Jim was gone and the divorce was long final. There was no point dwelling on it, her mother kept telling her. Well, she'd come to terms with it in her own way, and on her own time. Carrol sighed as she watched the streets of Camden slide past.

"You've been awfully quiet," said her partner, Agent Michael McCray. McCray, as the senior agent with the task force, was in charge of the operation. He drove with casual ease. They had two trucks of FBI agents behind them, not to mention plenty of guns, and Carrol felt absolutely ridiculous. All this hardware and all these agents to take down a room full of DVD pirates. It was obvious to Carrol that McCray wasn't worried, and why should he be? He knew as well as she did that this was about making an impression, about looking good for the cameras. They didn't have any press with them, but that would change as soon as they secured the warehouse and spread the loot out to make a good show for the press conference. It was the usual dog and pony show, and if the tables were piled high with cocaine or guns, the display made sense enough. It was hard to think they were really keeping the homeland safe from organized crime, however, by busting traffickers caught red-handed with illegal copies of *Showgirls*.

Public relations, that's what it was. The word had come down from above that they were to keep an eye open for the on-camera benefits, generate some positive press for the Bureau. With half the nation downloading movies illegally, Carrol wondered what taking down a room full of old-style DVD burn-and-bootleggers was going to accomplish.

"Marie?" McCray prodded. "What's the matter, not talking to me?"

Carrol turned to him and frowned. She sighed again. "No, Mike." She shrugged under her seat belt. "It's just… you know. The assignment."

"I know it's not terribly exciting," McCray said. "But indications are that this is just the tip of the iceberg. You know that. We take down the crew here in Camden, see who rolls over and then take the investigation up the chain. Eventually we get them all."

"In theory," Carrol said. "But they're still just movie pirates."

"What's the matter," McCray said, chuckling, "do you wish they were heroin smugglers?"

"I'd feel like we were doing something more important."

McCray nodded. "Well, I suppose we would, at that." He shifted in his seat. The senior agent was a big man with snow-white, close-cropped hair, craggy features and a tie cinched tight around his thick neck, over a shirt whose collar appeared just a bit too small. "But this is an important assignment. This bootlegging ring has its fingers in several different industries, if the preliminary reports are correct. They're taking in what could be *millions* of dollars. That's no small thing, no matter how dull the operation itself might be."

"I know, Mike." Carrol nodded. "Just permit a little griping ahead of time."

McCray chuckled again. "Fair enough," he said. "Look at it like a wedding you don't want to go to. You'll be glad you did when it's over. And it'll take longer for the photos afterward than for the ceremony itself."

Carrol laughed despite herself. "Okay, Mike."

"At least I'll be home at a decent hour," McCray said. "Ellen has really been riding me about the overtime."

He picked up the walkie-talkie in the cup holder in the center console. "McCray to Two and Three," he said. "We're a block away. Everybody get ready."

"Two, ready," came one response.

"Three, roger," came the second.

"Ready to do some good?" McCray winked at Agent Carrol.

"Let's not get carried away," Carrol said. She laughed again; McCray's sense of humor was hard to resist.

Agent McCray brought the SUV to a halt along the curb fronting the warehouse. The half-dozen FBI agents who made up the rest of the task force piled out of their trucks, some toting AR-15 rifles, some carrying Glock pistols. Two of the agents carried a portable battering ram. Doing her best to keep her expression neutral, Carrol joined McCray as the two walked purposefully up the cracked asphalt walk to an access door at the side of the warehouse. Both agents drew their Glock sidearms.

"Do it." McCray nodded.

The two agents with the battering ram took position, braced themselves and swung the heavy metal cylinder.

The door lock broke easily and the agents swarmed in. The two lead agents dropped the ram and let their fellow agents cover them, drawing their own weapons as the team spread out to control the space within.

"FBI! Nobody move! Federal Bureau of Investigation!" the agents announced themselves. Men and women froze, putting up their hands and staring in confusion.

The warehouse was a large rectangle, with tall, painted-over and dirt-smeared windows dominating the long ends of the box. A catwalk and what was apparently a partial upper level ran along the outer perimeter. Carrol spotted a metal staircase at the back of the warehouse floor that led to the upper level.

The floor itself was a maze of tables and benches. On each of these were piles of DVDs in various states of packaging. Carrol recognized a set of burning machines on a table at one end of the room. The machines were humming away, still automatically copying whatever disks were placed within them. On other tables, color-photocopied labels were being cut and placed in plastic sleeves on clamshell DVD cases. Cardboard boxes were everywhere, piled two and three deep under the tables and next to them, forming narrow aisles through which the workers had to navigate.

The workers blinked in confusion as the FBI agents moved among them, searching and securing them. Most of them did not appear to speak English. A few spoke in Spanish or broken English; Carrol wondered what a background check would turn up.

"Bonarski, Gerdes," McCray ordered. "Up the stairs and secure the upper level."

"Sir," another agent called. He had opened one of the cardboard boxes stacked under the table closest to him.

"What is it, Harney?" McCray asked.

"Sir, I knocked over that plastic bin of DVDs. Look what was inside it…and inside *this*." He pointed at an overturned plastic container and at the cardboard box just unsealed.

McCray came over and peered inside the carton.

"Holy shit," he said.

The box was full of large plastic zipper-lock bags stuffed with white powder. McCray bent, removing a small pocket knife from his suit jacket. He snapped the blade open and poked it into the bag. Careful not to inhale the powder, he raised the coated blade to his nose and let its odor travel to his nose.

"Heroin," he said. He looked up. "Watch them," he ordered the agents, indicating the confused workers. "And check those other boxes."

"Here, too, sir," Agent Harney called. "Packed full. Every box."

Agent Carrol looked around the warehouse in amazement, counting the cardboard packages. "Mike, if every one of these boxes is full of heroin…"

"Still think a DVD piracy ring isn't worth busting?" McCray grinned back at her. He lowered his Glock as she did the same. "This has to be *millions* of dollars of heroin. Maybe more. I've never seen so much in one place."

Suddenly, Carrol felt very anxious. "Mike, what have we stumbled onto here?" She scanned the room, her fingers clenching as she half raised her weapon once more.

"Easy," McCray said. "Easy, now. Sometimes luck just works on our side. Relax, Marie."

"I know, I know," Carrol said. She couldn't help it; she couldn't shake the feeling something was wrong.

"Bonarski! Gerdes! What have you got up there?" McCray looked up to the catwalk. When there was no answer, he called again, "Gerdes? Agents Gerdes and Bonarski, report, damn it."

The only response was a corpse that came flying over the catwalk.

Carrol felt her heart leap into her throat. The body that struck the floor, scattering workers and bringing up the heads of the workers and the assembled FBI personnel, was that of Agent Gerdes.

The ghastly expression on his face left no doubt that he was in fact dead. His throat had been cut from ear to ear.

"All agents—" McCray began to order.

"That," a voice shouted in accented English, "will be quite enough!" Punctuating the words were the sounds of a dozen assault rifles being cocked. The barrels of the Kalashnikov rifles suddenly appeared over the catwalk railing, wielded by small, deadly-looking men who appeared more than ready to use them.

"Drop your weapons!" McCray ordered.

"You," said the man who had spoken previously, "are in no position to make demands." He appeared at the railing, holding a gun to Agent Bonarski's head.

He was a small man, perhaps five feet, four inches, with a swarthy complexion and vaguely Asian features. To Carrol he looked Filipino, or maybe Thai. He was dressed much the same as the other armed men now looking down from the catwalk, sporting a mixture of civilian clothes and castoff military uniform. Specifically, he wore cut-off BDUs, unlaced combat boots and an open and very faded olive-drab fatigue blouse over a Rock-and-Roll Café T-shirt. A red-and-white bandanna was tied over his skull, knotted above his forehead. He was chewing an unlighted cigarillo. The hammer of the .45-caliber pistol in his hand was jacked back, and a very nervous Agent Bonarski was sweating as the barrel was jammed into his temple.

"Do not hurt that agent!" McCray commanded. "Identify yourself!"

"You may call me Thawan." The man smiled, his face a mask of petty cruelty. "And you may also call me master of your fate. Drop your guns."

"I can't do that." McCray shook his head. "I'm ordering you to stand down, mister!"

"Such arrogance," Thawan said. "It does not surprise me. Do you, American, have any idea what you have walked into this day?"

"I've got an idea," McCray said. "Now put down those guns!"

"No," Thawan said. He chewed on the cigarillo, switching it from one side of his mouth to the other. "You are about to die, American. It can be quick and clean. It can also be very, very messy."

"Sir…" Agent Bonarski said.

"Silence!" Thawan hissed. He pressed the .45 more tightly against Agent Bonarski's head. "American," he said to McCray, "think carefully about the choice I give you."

"Drop your weapons!" McCray ordered again. "I am an authorized representative of the federal government and I will not tell you again!"

"You poor, sad little man." Thawan's smile broadened. "Messy, then."

The .45 went off, and Agent Bonarski's suddenly lifeless body fell from the catwalk.

Hell erupted.

The agents on the warehouse floor began firing their weapons as the men above held back the triggers on their Kalashnikovs. Full-auto weapons fire echoed through the cavernous space, drowning out all other sound.

The wave of heat and light and pressure broke over Agent Carrol as the gunfire surrounded her. Time slowed. As she moved, raising her Glock and firing round after round, she felt as if she were trying to move through water, her every action encountering impossible resistance. Her eyes widened in horror as she watched blood blossom on Mike McCray's chest. He staggered under the onslaught of dozens of rounds, dropping his weapon and falling to the floor.

Carrol acted on instinct. She emptied her Glock in the direction of the catwalk as she ran for the cover of the nearest benches, diving beneath one and colliding with the cardboard cartons of drugs and DVD cases. She grunted as her shoulder hit the stack of boxes, then rolled, bullets tearing up the table above. Several rounds struck the cartons, scattering fine white mist in every direction as the bags of heroin were punctured.

From her position, Carrol could see the exit, the very door whose lock the team had broken so casually just minutes before. It was so close and yet so impossibly far. With bullets striking the table, the floor, and burning through the air all around her, she pushed herself to her feet and ran for the door, her Glock useless and locked open, no thought of reloading or fighting back. Blind flight instinct kicked in as the chaos around her became total. She saw another of the armed agents die scant feet away as she ran.

If only she could make the car. If only she could get to the radio. If only she could call for backup. There was still a chance.

The hammer blow to her chest felt like a cinder block against her ribs. Her knees buckled. She felt herself falling, the floor taking a thousand years to come up, everything happening so slowly…

She saw stars in her vision as the floor hit her face. The pain was a distant sensation, hardly significant. Some part of her was able to process that she had been shot. How many times and how badly she didn't know. She felt warm blood on her cheek; she tasted it in her mouth. She thought, as she floated, disconnected from her body, that she had broken her nose in the fall. She tried to push herself to her feet and could not. She couldn't feel her legs.

The agent who had gone down in front of her stared back at her, eyes glassy in death. Carrol tried desperately to think, to act, as her mind clouded over with pain and then numbness. Her hand struggled to find the inner pocket of her suit jacket.

The gunfire died away. Thawan's men filed down from the catwalk and began moving from body to body. A single shot rang out, and then another, from opposite sides of the warehouse. The shooters were killing the survivors. Those workers unharmed in the gunfight were being herded to one side of the workspace. The wounded workers were shot dead with the same casual disregard the gunmen had shown the FBI agents.

"Now, move, move," Thawan was ordering the remaining workers, who looked at him with wide-eyed terror. "Collect the boxes. Collect the drugs. Everything must be packed and made ready for shipment. Gig!"

One of the gunmen, an even smaller, misshapen man with a scar across his face, hurried forward, cradling his Kalashnikov.

"Yes, boss."

"Call for the trucks. We must move up the timetable."

"That will take time, boss. The schedule is complicated. We will have to rearrange the drops."

"Gig Tranh," Thawan said with an exaggerated sigh, "did I ask for your opinion?"

"No, boss."

"Then do as I tell you!" Thawan shouted, waving his .45 to punctuate the point.

"Yes, boss." The small man scuttled off, pulling a wireless phone from his BDU jacket as he did so.

"You and you," Thawan pointed to the nearest frightened workers. "Come here. You will help me search the bodies. We will take everything of value. Guns, ammunition. Their wallets. Their watches. Also, I want their badges. One never knows when such things will be of value."

Agent Carrol, against the increasing, crushing weight of her limbs, managed to drag her own wireless phone from her jacket. Thawan was moving back and forth across the hazy field of her vision. She had one chance. She could feel her life slipping away; could feel her hold on consciousness ebbing. From what little she could see from the floor, it did not appear that any of the other FBI agents had survived. If they had, they would be killed. It was only luck that nobody had gotten to her yet.

She had to live long enough to let someone know, to get out word of what had happened. If only Thawan would move back into view…

Thawan stopped, turned and looked straight at her.

She snapped the picture with her phone's camera option.

"Well, well," Thawan said. He walked to her deliberately, not hurrying, seemingly not at all concerned. "What do you think you are doing?"

Carrol could feel her vision turning gray at the edges. The sound of Thawan's voice was hollow in her ears, as if he spoke through a metal pipe.

She hit Send, transmitting the MMS message to the first contact in her phone's address book.

Thawan reached down and snatched the phone from her. He took notice of the empty Glock still clutched in her other hand. Contemptuously, he kicked her pistol aside. Then he examined the phone.

"Well," he said, shaking his head, "it appears you will not be calling for help. Even if you had, pretty lady—" he smiled, showing rotted, uneven teeth "—it would do no good. We will be gone before anyone arrives. You have died for nothing." He dropped the phone to the floor and stomped it with one booted foot. It took several tries, but he was finally able to crush the phone, snapping it into several pieces.

"You…" Carrol managed to say, her breath coming in short rasps now. "You…won't…"

"Won't what, pretty lady?" Thawan smiled. "Won't get away with it? Won't escape? Won't walk over the bodies of your dead fascist pig brothers and escape? I will, and more." He squatted and took her face in his left hand. His right still held the .45. Holding her chin and jaw, he moved her head from side to side. "Such a shame. Such a waste. You are really not so bad-looking, you know? We could have had some fun, my boys and I. But no," he said and let her go. She collapsed, now staring directly at the ceiling. "No, you are too far gone. But not so far gone that I will not help you there."

The last thing Agent Carrol saw was Thawan standing over her, the barrel of the .45 impossibly large as he aimed it between her eyes.

The muzzle-blast was very bright.

CHAPTER TWO

Stony Man Farm

In the War Room at Stony Man Farm, the stern-looking and apparently disembodied face of Hal Brognola stared from one of the plasma wall screens, twice as big as life. Across from the screen, seated near one end of the long conference table, Barbara Price tapped keys on a slim notebook computer.

"How about now, Hal?" she asked.

"Yes, I can hear you." Brognola nodded, his disembodied voice amplified by the wall speakers positioned around the room. Price tapped a key to lower the volume slightly, bringing the big Fed's virtual presence to something closer to normal. The microphone on Brognola's end of the scrambled connection was producing some feedback, which Price eliminated with the stroke of a key.

"You forgot," Aaron "the Bear" Kurtzman said, rolling into the room in his wheelchair, "to ask him to say, 'Testing, one, two, three.' Hardly a dignified state in which to find the director of the Sensitive Operations Group."

"What can I say?" Brognola said, his voice dry. "I'm a man of the people."

Price nodded. The big Fed was broadcasting from his office on the Potomac, roughly eighty miles away in Washington, D.C. Even through the scrambled link, she could tell that Brognola was forcing the humor. The strain was visible around his eyes. It would not be the first time she had seen his image on the screen and worried for his health. Brognola drove his people hard, but he drove himself much harder.

Kurtzman rolled into position next to Price's chair and put his heavy stainless, industrial-size coffee mug on the conference table. "It's a mystery to me," he said, "how the settings on that connection change from conference to conference."

"Goes with the territory, Bear," Price said. "The first rule of technology is that anything that can malfunction will do so just before the meeting."

"Sounds familiar, at that," Kurtzman grunted. The head of the Farm's cybernetics team—not to mention a computer genius in his own right—took a long swallow from his mug of coffee.

The rest of the computer support team filed in, heralded by the dull roar from the MP3 player whose headphones were jammed into Akira Tokaido's ears. The young Japanese computer expert was, as always, listening to heavy metal at eardrum-bursting decibel. He wore a leather jacket and an eager expression.

After Tokaido was Carmen Delahunt, who looked unusually somber this morning. Price knew why; the normally vivacious redhead was formerly with the FBI. She was speaking in hushed tones with fellow cybernetics team member Huntington "Hunt" Wethers. The refined, graying black man said something to which Delahunt only nodded. The pair took seats on either side of Akira, making way for the personnel crowding the corridor behind them.

Phoenix Force was first into the room, led by David McCarter. The lean, hot-headed Briton was sipping from a can of soda and muttering something under his breath. It was, Price thought, probably a complaint of some kind that he would be more than happy to air during the briefing.

The former SAS operator was followed by quiet, solid demolitions expert Gary Manning. The big Canadian and former member of an antiterrorist squad with the Royal Canadian Mounted Police was in turn chatting with Cuban-born guerilla expert Rafael Encizo. The deadly Encizo moved with a quiet grace that was an interesting counterpart to Manning's comfortable, solid gait.

Behind the two men, Calvin James, the dark-skinned, wisecracking product of Chicago's South Side, said something Price couldn't hear that made Manning smile and caused Encizo to laugh out loud. The former SEAL and expert knife fighter had a cutting sense of humor, as he was fond of saying. It was an old but dependable joke. James was followed by former Ranger and born-and-bred Southern boy T. J. Hawkins, whose easygoing manner and comfortable drawl masked a dynamic and keen-minded soldier.

Together, the five men of Phoenix Force were the Farm's international warriors, taking the fight for justice from America's shores to the rest of the world. The three men of Able Team, Stony Man's domestic counterterrorist operators, were close on their heels. The trio took the remaining seats around the now-crowded conference table.

Blond, crew-cut, bull-necked and ever gruff, Able's leader, Carl "Ironman" Lyons, looked to be in a typically cross mood. Lyons had little patience for these briefings, which Price knew usually reminded the former L.A. police officer of the bureaucracy he'd left behind so many years before. Next to him, trying and failing to banter with him, was Hermann "Gadgets" Schwarz. Schwarz was an electronics expert whose devices and designs had supplemented the Stony Man teams' gear on more than one occasion. Schwarz was more than an electronics whiz, though; he was also an experienced counterterror operative and veteran of countless battles.

Quietly considering all assembled was Rosario "Politician" Blancanales. The normally soft-spoken Hispanic was a former Black Beret and an expert in the psychology of violence and role camouflage. As such, Price had noted many times before, he tended to hang back, observe and gather data before saying anything. When he finally spoke, it was normally worth listening to him.

"All right," Price said. "Hal, you're ready?"

"Yes, go ahead." Brognola nodded on the plasma screen.

Price touched a key on her notebook computer. The plasma screen opposite Brognola, visible to all at the table, came to life. The image it displayed was that of a small, dark-skinned man wearing an open BDU blouse over a novelty T-shirt. He carried a .45 in one hand. The image was somewhat grainy and had clearly been enhanced, but the face of the man—and the cruelty evident on it—was clearly visible.

"This," Price said, "is Mok Thawan. This photo was taken seconds before Thawan executed a gravely wounded FBI agent."

Delahunt swore under her breath. The rest of the Stony Man personnel nodded or simply took in the image, saying nothing.

Price pressed another key. The image changed to that of a large interior space littered with empty tables—and dead bodies. "Camden, New Jersey," she said. "This warehouse was the target of an FBI task force pursuing what is believed to be one of the largest retail piracy rings operating in the United States. According to the data assembled by the task force members beforehand, this site was a clearinghouse for the smuggling of illegally manufactured and copied DVDs."

The image changed again as Price touched the key once more. She scrolled through several photos of the dead FBI agents, whose bodies had been marked with evidence tags. Empty shell casings littered the floor.

"What is that dust everywhere?" McCarter asked, sipping his Coke.

"That," Price said, tapping a couple of keys and bringing up some close-up shots, "is heroin."

"Bloody hell," McCarter said.

"Not long after the shoot-out," Price explained, "local police responded. They found what you see here. Dead FBI agents, stripped of their weapons. An empty warehouse. And heroin residue everywhere." She entered something on the notebook computer and scanned the file on her screen. "The police reports indicate that all of the agents were shot except one, who had his throat cut. There was nothing else in the warehouse except a few empty boxes and several shattered plastic DVD cases. Whoever was operating there, whatever the extent of their activities, they pulled up stakes and got out of there fast and completely."

"So the Bureau raided what they thought was a fairly tame retail piracy operation," Blancanales said, "and instead got heroin smugglers?"

"That's just the beginning of it," Price said. She switched the image on the plasma screen back to that of Mok Thawan. "Thawan is a known quantity, with an Interpol dossier a mile long. Specifically, he figures prominently in organized crime centered in southern Asia. He's an enforcer for a group that calls itself the Triangle."

"The Triangle runs heroin from Thailand and Burma to the United States," Brognola said. "Just about every major law-enforcement agency, foreign and domestic, is aware of its activities, but precious little has been done about it up to now."

"Why is that, Hal?" Schwarz asked.

"A combination of factors," Brognola said, sounding weary. "Corruption in the local governments, especially in Thailand. There is some evidence that the Burmese government is directly involved, too, but it's less overt, which might mean it's even worse."

"If they bother hiding it, there's something to hide," Encizo said.

"Exactly." Brognola nodded. "The Triangle is also incredibly violent. They respond with ruthless, overwhelming force whenever threatened. This bloodbath in New Jersey is nothing compared to the slaughter of government troops in Thailand last year, when a joint DEA-Interpol task force got close to the Triangle's operations there."

"If they're so big a problem," McCarter interrupted, "why haven't we targeted them before now?"

"Until recently," Brognola said, "they've been ghosts. International law enforcement has been a step behind the Triangle for the past three years. Several attempts to penetrate the organization with undercover agents have also failed."

"Every one of the agents has turned up dead or gone missing entirely," Price explained. "Interpol claims to have at least one agent unaccounted for, but nobody's heard from him or her for at least six months."

"Likely swimming with the fishes," McCarter concluded.

"The massacre in New Jersey has the Man agitated," Brognola said, "and for good reason. The sad but direct fact of the matter is that we cannot allow government agents to be killed en masse on U.S. soil, not without mounting a response."

"You don't mean to tell me this is about making a statement?" McCarter demanded. "Bloody Christ, Hal! Is that what we've come to now?"

"You know better than that, David," Brognola said sternly. "There are certain political realities, yes," he explained, "but what's changed is that we finally have a way to track the Triangle and get out in front of their operation."

"Bear and his team—" Price nodded to Kurtzman, Tokaido, Delahunt and Wethers "—have conducted an extensive investigation into financial accounts and networks known to be linked to the Triangle."

"By 'extensive,' she means 'illegal,'" Wethers said with a faint smile.

"Very." Price glanced at Brognola, whose expression had gone sour. "Using Interpol and U.S. federal agency records as the jumping-off point, we've gotten to know the Triangle intimately, exposing portions of its operation, identifying links in the poppy production and heroin trafficking, and discovering certain key facts." She looked to Delahunt.

"First," Delahunt said, "the Triangle operates a conventional bootlegging ring that appears to smuggle several different consumer products. Counterfeit designer clothing, the DVDs found in New Jersey, consumer electronics... it's very extensive, perhaps the biggest ever to operate internationally."

"The Triangle is piggybacking the distribution of the heroin on the smuggling of their retail goods," Price said. "They're using the same network, but sheltering the more serious criminal activity with the bootlegging."

"It's brilliant," Blancanales put in. "Vice is always easier to understand than legitimate commercial activity. It offers a unique shield, for if the smuggling is discovered, those exposing it will be tempted to stop at the piracy, thinking they've found what there is to find."

"Bloody right," McCarter said. "Nobody trusts a guy who says he's got nothing to hide. But if you think you've found him out—"

"You stop looking for whatever else he might be doing," Blancanales finished. "Multiply that across an entire organization and you have a very clever strategy for covering the true depths of a criminal enterprise."

"Trickery of that type goes only so far, of course," Brognola said. "That's why the Triangle is so ready and willing to do violence to shield its activities. When discovered, they immediately hit, and hit hard, then fade from view. The method has served them well until now."

"What's changed, Hal?" Schwarz asked.

"I'll answer that," Price said. She tapped a couple of keys and an exploded-view mechanical drawing of a satellite appeared on the plasma screen opposite Brognola. "This," she said, "is NetScythe. It's an experimental military spy satellite developed by DoD in conjunction with some of the more brilliant boys and girls at NASA."

"What does it do?" Schwarz asked.

Price nodded to Tokaido.

"It is really very amazing," Tokaido said, pointing to the plasma screen. "NetScythe uses a combination of fuzzy-logic algorithmic processing, digital satellite imaging and an advanced telescopic array very much influenced by the Hubble Space Telescope. This allows it to track targets on the ground, very specific targets that correspond to complicated threat or interest profiles developed by analysts on the ground." He pointed to himself, to Wethers and to

Delahunt. "By inputting our target criteria and our warning flags, we can have NetScythe track Triangle assets on the ground, from space. When those assets move, be they people, vehicles or people and vehicles moving to and from specified target profile locations, NetScythe's heuristic meta-analysis can predict where those assets may move to next."

"Bloody hell," McCarter said. "The thing predicts the future?"

"In a way, perhaps," Hunt Wethers said. "It's a bit more complicated and not quite as definitive as that, but essentially, it will tell us how to get ahead of the Triangle's operatives in order to target components of its organization. Much more important, analysis of the target assets may tell us where the links in the Triangle's chain are located. We can use what we know to learn what we don't know. With several Triangle assets designated, we can find others of which we were previously unaware."

"It's the break we've needed to dig into the Triangle and root it out," Brognola said. "But there are other considerations at play."

"Which brings us to the second very important piece of information we uncovered." Price nodded once more to Delahunt.

"The Triangle is funneling money, and large quantities of it, through several holding companies and multiple banks," Delahunt said. "The money is finding its way to Aleksis Katzev."

"*That* Aleksis Katzev?" Blancanales asked.

"The same," Price said. She touched a key and the image of Russia's strong-man president appeared on the plasma screen. "Aleksis Katzev. President of Russia. Former KGB operative, rumored to have Spetsnaz special forces training. Also linked to the deaths of several political rivals, often by poisoning, none successfully traced to Katzev or his operatives."

"In other words," Encizo said, "not a very nice man."

"No," Brognola put in. "Specifically, Katzev has been rattling sabers for months now, talking about recovering the glory days of the Soviet Union, and using the United States as the scapegoat that will pull the Russian people back together against a common foe. We believe Katzev is receiving funding from several known terrorist organizations, in fact, though the Triangle is by far his biggest investor."

"What do you mean by 'rattling sabers,' Hal?" T. J. Hawkins asked.

"Russian naval assets and air power have been buzzing U.S. planes and ships in international waters off Russia for some time now," Brognola said. "The hostilities are growing. Katzev gives a fiery speech just about every week on state television out of Moscow, too, usually working in references to the Great Satan that is the United States."

"Sounds like an old script," Calvin James said.

"But it works," Brognola said. "Tensions between the U.S. and Russia are at an all-time high, and diplomatic relations are getting very close to breaking down. There's some chance that this will subside after the elections, but there are no guarantees, and if Katzev secures another term, we have no way of knowing just how far he'll take this."

"The Triangle," Delahunt said, "apparently hopes to expand its operations farther into Russia, which is what it gains by funding Katzev. Katzev has strong ties to the Russian *mafiya,* and the Triangle won't make any inroads without their say-so. They're violent, but the *mafiya* are no strangers to protecting their turf. We all know just how interwoven organized crime is with Russian society. We're basically seeing the opening steps of a business merger in the making."

"That's a merger we need to prevent," Price said. "There is, however, some hope that Katzev's hold on Russia can be broken. He faces a hard fight in the country's imminent national elections." She tapped a key, and another man appeared on the plasma screen. He was younger, perhaps early forties, and dressed in a neatly tailored suit. "This is Yuri Andulov," Price said. "He's an experienced diplomat and a known friend to the West. He's got a growing base of support in Russia. Polling data is unreliable and shows heavy favoritism to Katzev, the incumbent, but we believe Andulov may very well be slightly ahead."

"The problem," Brognola said, "will be keeping him alive until the elections occur. Katzev's enemies have a way of dropping dead from mysterious food poisonings or other ailments. One got cancer rather suddenly. Another disappeared completely, along with his family. Katzev plays for keeps, and it seems very doubtful he intends to go head to head with Andulov at the ballot box—not if he can take him out before it comes to that."

"More than one attempt has been made on his life, in fact," Price said. "To now, his bodyguards have kept him out of harm's way, but the assassins only have to succeed once."

"I don't have to tell you," Brognola said, "that Katzev's term of office has marked very difficult U.S.-Russia relations. Andulov could turn that around, normalize things between the two countries, and bring Russia back from the brink of open war with the West. Another Katzev term, by contrast, will very well take us to that precipice."

"Are you saying we've taken an active interest in eliminating Katzev?" McCarter asked.

"No," Brognola said, "only in exposing Katzev's link

to the Triangle. The rest will take shape on its own, provided Andulov isn't murdered before he can take office."

"It smacks of nation-building, Hal," McCarter said.

"No." Brognola shook his head. "That is *not* what we do. But Katzev is an active threat to United States' interests, and he is linked to a violent criminal organization. If that link comes to light, if Katzev's activities are exposed and if we can put a stop to whatever he might be doing in conjunction with those activities, it is in everyone's best interests that we do so."

"Fair enough," McCarter said. He traded glances with Carl Lyons, his fellow team leader. Lyons frowned and nodded.

"I do not have to point out," Brognola said, "the potential for an international incident that this raises. We cannot afford to enflame an already difficult situation where Russia is concerned. Plausible deniability must be the order of the day, even if they know we're only making a show of it, and we know that they know. The situation in Thailand and Burma might get tricky, too—no government official likes to be accused of being in bed with international organized crime or terrorism. You can count on no local support abroad."

"Bloody wonderful," McCarter groused. "Can I assume we will be traveling sterile?"

"You will," Brognola said. "Your personal weapons, if you have a preference, should prove no problem in the case of sidearms, but use your best judgment. You'll be issued other operational gear that cannot be traced directly to any specific distributor."

"Gadgets has consulted with our technical team," Price said, nodding to Schwarz, "and we will be issuing both Able and Phoenix several pieces of microsurveillance and hacking equipment that should prove useful in your mission. There's something else, however." She looked to Tokaido once more.

"We will also be providing all of you with these," Akira said, holding up a small breathing mask. "It contains microfilter technology. You may encounter very large quantities of drugs and fumes from drugs, especially if destroying caches of narcotics. These masks will protect you from the fumes and filter out the toxins, enabling you to breathe without difficulty."

McCarter reached across the table for the mask. Tokaido gave it to him, and McCarter turned it over and over in his hands thoughtfully, examining it.

"I want you all to draw equipment from Cowboy and assemble within two hours," Price directed, referring to John "Cowboy" Kissinger, the Farm's expert armorer. "Phoenix, we have the first target for you in Thailand. Jack Grimaldi is ready to provide air support and will meet you on the ground there. He's coordinating the transportation of certain assets." Grimaldi was Stony Man's veteran pilot, a capable operator of almost any flying machine, from fighter jets to helicopters.

"And us?" Carl Lyons asked.

"We've traced the Triangle's financial records and uncovered a second facility owned by the holding company that held the lease to the Camden warehouse," Price told him. "It's a casino in Atlantic City. You'll start there."

"Sounds like fun," Schwarz said.

"It won't be," Lyons said dourly.

"All right, people," Brognola said. "This is an important operation. The stakes are high. The price paid already…well, it's been too high. We're on the job to stop this before it goes any further. A lot is riding on this. The Man has made this our highest priority. Do what you do."

"Let's move, everyone," Price said.

CHAPTER THREE

Atlantic City, New Jersey

"Kind of out of the way, isn't it?" Schwarz said from the passenger seat of the Chevy Suburban. Next to him, Carl Lyons was replacing the magazine in his Daewoo USAS-12 automatic shotgun. He chambered a heavy 12-gauge buckshot round with a heavy clack of the charging handle. The 20-round drum magazine in place on the massive weapon was supplemented by the 10-round box magazines Lyons carried in the pockets of his heavy canvas vest. The vest also covered the .357 Magnum Colt Python in a shoulder holster under Lyons's left arm.

Lyons sipped from a disposable cup of fast-food-chain coffee and eyed the front of the casino. The street was busy enough; cars moved past in both directions, and plenty of pedestrians bustled by. The gambling house itself, the Drifts, was not too far from the old Sands building, but still not exactly located in prime real estate compared to its competitors. It was as out of the way as a casino in Atlantic City was likely to be, Lyons thought. He looked at Schwarz and grunted, taking another long sip from his coffee cup.

Like Lyons, Schwarz wore casual civilian clothes. His dark blue windbreaker concealed the Beretta 93-R, custom-tuned by Cowboy Kissinger, that he wore in a shoulder rig of his own. On his belt under the windbreaker he also carried several small grenades, most of them flash-bang and incendiary charges.

"You know, it occurs to me that we spend a lot of time waiting in the truck while Pol gets to go out and have fun," Schwarz said, ignoring Lyons's attempt to shut down the conversation before it could begin.

"He gets shot at more, too," Lyons said.

"Like I said," Schwarz confirmed. "All the fun."

Lyons ignored that. Each member of the team wore a microelectronic earbud transceiver in his ear. The little devices transmitted to each other on a tight frequency and had an automatic cutoff for sounds above a certain decibel level. This allowed the team members to stay in constant touch with each other without relaying deafening gunfire over the channel. Through this link, they both heard Pol Blancanales say quietly, "Let's not wish any undue excitement on me, gentlemen." Schwarz smiled at that, but Lyons didn't react.

The fact was, for all their banter, Blancanales was indeed in a precarious position. Before Able Team could roll through the Drifts with guns blazing, they had to determine exactly what was going on inside. If the Triangle owned an interest in the casino but was running no significant smuggling or trafficking operations within, Blancanales's quiet reconnoiter might best be followed up with another soft probe in which they raided local documents, file cabinets and computers, looking for additional hints to the Triangle's operation. It would prove dull and disappointing, given the mission parameters and their desires to bring the Triangle's people to justice, but it would be the only way to handle such a scenario.

On the other hand, if Blancanales found himself surrounded by enemies who were trying to kill him, it would pretty much be open season.

"All right, guys," Blancanales said quietly. "I'm in position."

"Roger," Schwarz said. He took the small video unit from the dashboard and adjusted the frequency. On the color screen set in the handheld unit, a picture appeared, showing the inside of the casino at chest level. The video stream was being transmitted by a tiny camera set within the belt buckle Blancanales wore. The video captured from it would give Able Team a visual record they could review later, while giving Lyons and Schwarz a real-time briefing of what they faced within should the situation get ugly.

Lyons leaned over to get a better view. Schwarz held the video unit up between them. Blancanales's words, and some of the ambient noises around him, were transmitted to both men's earbud transceivers, just slightly out of the sync with the picture.

Blancanales was moving through the main lobby of the casino, headed toward the slot machine pits. The crowd looked like the dregs of Atlantic City, the sort of regulars, drifters, grafters and barflies who would gravitate to one of the seedier establishments among the many gambling houses. Schwarz spotted several hookers working the crowd. Lyons ignored him until he started counting them off, then told him to shut up.

"Thank you," Blancanales said softly. It wasn't clear whether he was expressing his gratitude to Lyons or to the cocktail waitress who had just offered him a bottle of sparkling water.

Blancanales worked his way around the room, blending in as one of the customers. The nondescript outfit the Politician had chosen for this little run included a tan button-down shirt open, dark slacks and a leather blazer that had seen better days. In short, Blancanales looked just like one of the nightcrawlers gambling at the Drifts, which was exactly what he'd wanted. The Politician could blend in anywhere, anytime. It was one of the things that made Blancanales so effective an operative in these scenarios.

He was moving through the slot machine pit now, dodging lifers of all ages transfixed by the one-armed bandits. Lyons was amused to see the magnetic cards being swiped through the machines. He supposed a lot had changed since the last time he'd been in a modern casino, but it didn't seem the same to him: waiting to hit the jackpot so you could increase the balance on your gambling card, rather than filling a plastic cup with metal tokens. It was all fool's gold, he supposed, but that didn't make it any less amusing. He and Schwarz watched as Blancanales passed row after row of desperate players swiping those cards and pressing push-button gaming screens instead of yanking on metal handles.

As the two other Able Team members watched, Blancanales made a slow, careful circuit of the entire main level of the casino. While not the largest or the nicest gambling house in Atlantic City by any means, the Drifts was still a fairly elaborate establishment. It took some time, and Blancanales knew his work well enough not to push too hard. Hurrying would look suspicious. He had to search the casino without looking like he was searching the casino, being careful not to raise any suspicions.

"There," Lyons said finally. "There's another one."

"Another one?" Schwarz asked, looking at him.

"Pol," Lyons instructed, "without looking like you're doing it, back up three paces and slowly pan right."

Blancanales took his time. He managed to make the move look natural, from what the two in the truck could see. The scan from his camera eventually took in what Lyons had noticed. He pointed to the screen.

"That guy?" Schwarz queried.

"That guy," Lyons said. "That's the second big mother in a black turtleneck and black jeans I've seen tonight, just standing around. They're not dressed like casino security." They had seen the official security guards working the casino; those guards wore matching maroon blazers.

"Sure looks like a guard," Schwarz agreed. "What's he guarding?"

"Pol, can you tell what he's pretending not to cover?" Lyons asked.

Blancanales moved around slowly, taking in the guard from two different angles, then moving farther down the corridor just off this corner of the casino. Finally he found a remote corner where, Lyons figured, there was no one to overhear.

"There's a fire door at the end of the hallway, opposite the guard," he reported, whispering. "There's also a camera focused on that door."

"Take another look around," Lyons said. "Let's be sure."

Blancanales did so. He worked his way across the casino again, paying special attention to the darkest corridors and corners. When he was satisfied that the door he'd seen was the only one guarded in that manner, he reported as much. Lyons nodded to Schwarz. During Blancanales's sweep, they had counted a total of three of the black-clad incognito guards. Two of them were surreptitiously guarding the front and rear entrances, in both cases doubling up on the more overt casino security personnel. The lone guard in front of the camera-equipped door was therefore unique.

"How do you—" Blancanales said, then stopped. Schwarz and Lyons watched as a pair of women in micromini black dresses flounced past him.

"Not bad," Schwarz remarked.

"Hookers," Lyons said.

"As I was saying," Blancanales said once they were out of range, "how do you want to play it?"

"I'd like to know what's beyond that door," Lyons said, "but I'd rather not tip our hand just yet."

"All right," Blancanales said. "But we'll only get one shot at this. It might get hairy on the way out."

"If it does, so much the better," Lyons said. "We'll back you up."

"Easy for you to say, Ironman." Schwarz poked him in the ribs.

"Zip it," Lyons growled.

The two watched as Blancanales moved along the corridor, essentially flanking the lone guard while staying out of what was likely to be the mounted camera's field of view. He affected a drunken stagger, if the sudden swaying of the video feed was any indication. Then he was stumbling into the guard.

"Hey," the guard said, sounding disgusted. "Get the hell off me, asshole."

"Whereza baffroom?" Blancanales slurred.

"Not here, stupid." The guard reached out to give Blancanales a shove. To Lyons and Schwarz it looked as if he was reaching right for the camera.

Blancanales lashed out with a sudden, vicious edge-of-hand blow to the side of the man's neck, staggering him. Blancanales followed up with a knee to the man's groin and then a relatively light blow to the back of the head. The guard dropped like a stone.

"Remind me not to piss off Pol," Schwarz cracked.

"I said shut up," Lyons said absently. It was an old act between the two of them, and one neither man had to think about consciously.

Blancanales dragged the guard into the corridor he was guarding, careful to stop short to stay out of the mounted camera's field of view. Lyons and Schwarz watched as their teammate quickly searched the man, after first checking his pulse.

"He's not dead, is he?" Lyons asked.

"No," Blancanales said quietly.

"Proceed," Lyons instructed.

Blancanales found a 1911-pattern .45-caliber pistol in the man's waistband, under his turtleneck. He also found a key card. He tucked the .45 into his own waistband, where Lyons knew it would keep Blancanales Beretta 92-F company. Then he moved quickly to the door, swiped the magnetic key card and popped the door open.

"Go fast, Pol," Lyons said. "Whoever's watching knows you're not supposed to be there." He checked the loads in his Colt Python before replacing it in its shoulder holster. "Get ready, Gadgets."

"Roger," Schwarz said. He set the video unit on the console between them and drew his 93-R. Then he checked the machine pistol's 20-round magazine.

On the small color screen, Blancanales was making his way down a stairway. It was dimly lighted by small red light bulbs set within metal grates along the cinder-block wall. All pretense of the supposedly lavish gambling establishment had been dropped here. Whatever this was, wherever it led, no attempt had been made to disguise it.

Blancanales stopped at the bottom of the stairs. He was facing a pair of metal double doors. Pushing past these, he found himself in an empty anteroom. There was another set of doors. These were locked, but the electronic lock pad on the wall matched the one that had been installed at the top of the stairs. Blancanales used the key card again, sliding it through, and was rewarded with the metallic click that signaled the door unlatching.

He pushed the door quietly open.

At least a dozen men looked up at him.

On the screen, the scene was clear enough, in the split second Lyons and Schwarz had to observe it. The basement, which was lighted by overhead fluorescent lights, was filled with long, low tables. Men sat at these tables, weighing and dividing individual portions of white powder into smaller plastic bags. Several other men holding shotguns and rifles, a mixture of Mini-14s, AR-15s and even Ruger 10/22s, stood around the room at intervals watching over the process.

"Who's he?" one of workers asked.

"Hey, that's not—" another said.

Blancanales ran for it.

The first bullets struck the doors behind him as he cleared the next set of double doors.

"Go, go, go!" Lyons ordered. He grabbed the Daewoo shotgun as he piled out of the truck. Schwarz was close behind with his 93-R. The two men ran through the traffic outside the Drifts, dodging honking vehicles as they made for the entrance to the casino.

"I'm coming up the stairs," Blancanales reported through their earbud transceivers. "The sewing circle I just interrupted is hot on my trail." There was some static, suddenly, over the connection.

Gunfire.

Schwarz and Lyons burst through the front doors of the casino, Lyons leading the way with his Daewoo at port arms. Customers scattered. A woman screamed at the sight of the big Able Team leader with the massive automatic shotgun in his arms.

"Stop!" a uniformed security guard yelled. He walked up to Lyons. "You there, you can't come in here with that!"

"Buddy," Lyons growled, "you'd best back up."

The security guard reached out, placing a hand on Lyons's shoulder. "I said stop!"

Lyons butt-stroked him, lightly, slamming the Daewoo's stock into the side of his head. He folded over with a grunt. "Told you," Lyons said.

Schwarz had the 93-R in both hands and was covering the crowd. "Everyone out!" he said. "Proceed to the exits in an orderly fashion! We are federal agents!"

The casino's patrons didn't need to be told twice. They started hurrying toward the main exit, giving the Able Team commandos a wide berth. A couple of the uniformed guards looked as if they wanted to say something, but they were apparently unarmed and seemed to Lyons to be just what they were supposed to be—civilians hired to watch for pickpockets and roust the occasional drunk.

"Gadgets," Lyons said, bringing the Daewoo up to his shoulder as they approached the corridor Blancanales had entered, "find me those other covert guards."

"On it," Schwarz said. He broke from Lyons and began sweeping the wing they had just passed.

As Lyons neared the hallway, he fought the urge to react as Blancanales came bursting through the fire door. Blancanales had his 92-F in his left hand and the captured 1911 .45 in his right. As the fire door slammed, bullets ricocheted from the opposite side. They did not go through.

"You all right?" Lyons asked calmly.

"Never better." Blancanales smiled. "But we've got a nest of hornets down below."

"Positions?"

"Bottom of the stairwell." Blancanales jerked a thumb toward the fire door.

"Good," Lyons said, hefting the Daewoo. "Get ready on the door."

Blancanales stowed the 1911 and transferred the 92-F to his right hand. "You sure?"

"Yes," Lyons said. He grinned. It was not a pleasant smile.

Somewhere behind and to the left, they heard a shotgun blast, followed by the chatter of Schwarz's 93-R.

"That'll be Gadgets ferreting out our friends," Lyons said. "Back him up after I go."

"Will do," Blancanales said. "Triangle operatives, you figure?"

"Doesn't matter," Lyons said. "Triangle or not, they've got a heroin distribution center in the basement."

"Could have been baking powder."

"More power to them if it was," Lyons said. "Okay, in three."

Pol nodded and gripped the fire door's handle.

"Three…two…one…*now.*"

Blancanales ripped open the fire door and triggered several shots down the stairwell. Lyons dived through, flat on his belly with the Daewoo in front of him. He threw himself with such force that he slid down the steps, holding the trigger of the Daewoo back as he did so. The buckshot rounds ripped up the doors at the bottom of the stairwell, tearing through the gunmen who waited in front of them.

The gunners screamed and died horribly. Lyons was up and charging as soon as he hit the bottom of the stairs. He slammed a combat-booted foot against the double doors, mowing down a gunman with an Uzi pistol who was waiting in the anteroom. He dropped the now-empty drum magazine in his USAS-12 and swapped in a 10-round box.

Another kick parted the doors separating him from the basement area. He dived through the doors, narrowly avoiding the answering fusillade. The workers were running and ducking for cover, but the gunmen guarding them and the product on the tables were cutting loose with everything they had. Full-automatic weapons fire converged on Lyons's position. He surged to his feet and, in a half crouch, carved through the ranks of the enemy gunmen like a shark swimming through a school of fish.

Bullets raked the table to his left, shredding plastic bags of heroin before shattering a set of electronic scales. Lyons triggered a blast that knocked the gunmen down and out forever.

Moving heel-to-toe in a combat glide, Lyons kept up his pace, staying calm and deadly in the middle of the firestorm. Each time his shotgun blasts found an enemy, the remaining shooters were that much more demoralized, firing that much more wildly. Finally, as the second to last man fell with a load of double-aught buck in his face, the last of the guards cut and ran for the doors.

"Oh, no, you don't, you little scumbag." Lyons let the USAS-12 drop, since it was empty, and drew the Colt Python from his shoulder holster and leveled it at the fleeing man. "Stop! Federal agent!"

The running man paused, spun and brought up a snubnose revolver. Lyons double-actioned a .357 Magnum round through his chest. The dead man never got off a shot.

"Lyons clear. Basement secure," Lyons announced.

"Gadgets clear," Schwarz said.

"Blancanales clear," Blancanales reported. "Two down up here, Carl. We weren't able to take them alive, unfortunately."

"Understood," Lyons said. He surveyed the drugs scattered around the room, and the dead men among the living. "Everyone over there," Lyons directed, pointing with the barrel of the Python. "Against the wall."

One of the workers looked at him, wide-eyed, and said something in rapid-fire Spanish.

"Pol, did you hear that?" he asked. "I've got several prisoners down there. They look to be noncombatants."

"Just barely," Blancanales said. "He says… Well, he says a lot, but it boils down to, 'we just work here.'"

"Yeah," Lyons said. He herded the workers. "Come on, people. Go."

"I'm on my way down," Blancanales reported over the transceiver link.

"Good," Lyons said. "I could use a translator."

"I'll stay up here and mind the store," Schwarz said. "It looks like the Justice Department identification Hal gave us is going to get a workout." The sirens were barely audible over the transceiver link.

"All right," Lyons said. "Run interference with the Atlantic City PD for us. Pol and I will work our way through these jokers, see if there's anything to be found."

"Any computers down there?" Schwarz asked.

Lyons double-checked, scanning the room carefully. He retrieved his Daewoo as he did so, holstering the Python and swapping box magazines in the shotgun. "Doesn't look like it," he said. "We've got a pile of drugs, some dead guards and not much else."

Blancanales entered the room, stepping over the dead body near the doors. He took out his secure satellite phone, part of the standard kit issued by the Farm, and took a digital photograph of the dead man. He would do the same for the others; it was standard procedure. The photos would be transmitted to the Farm for analysis, run through international crime databases using facial-recognition software. Identifying the gunmen might give them some connection to the Triangle's operation.

"Dead end?" Blancanales asked.

"Dead *men*," Lyons corrected. He jacked a round into the chamber of the USAS-12. "But us? We're just getting started."

CHAPTER FOUR

Thailand

Jack Grimaldi whistled "Flight of the Valkyries" to himself as the Cobra gunship came in low and slow over the landscape, moving up on the isolated poppy field that was Phoenix Force's first target. As Grimaldi flew, he listened to the radio chatter over his earbud transceiver. The little device linked him via relay from the chopper's electronics to the rest of the team on the ground. Phoenix Force was moving into position to attack the camp located at the east end of the poppy field. From the satellite surveillance imagery provided by NSA security satellites as well as NetScythe, it was apparent the camp included a full processing facility. Hitting the field and the processing plant would deal the Triangle a significant blow, sending a clear message.

Insertion of the team, including acquiring the Cobra gunship and making sure it was in position, had been relatively easy. While there was no way to count on the support of the government, especially given the covert nature of the operation, the Farm had plenty of discretionary funds to throw around at times like these. The Stony Man team had bribed their way over the Thai border and easily past Customs. The chopper had been more difficult, but even that had not proved much of an obstacle. While old, the machine was in great shape, and the armament it carried was in top condition. Grimaldi had checked it out at the airfield himself. Then he'd made his way by air in support of Phoenix Force's ground insertion that was utilizing hired commercial trucks. If anyone had noticed him, by eye or by radar, nobody had challenged him. No doubt everyone and his uncle who could in any way be bought off had been paid well enough to look the other way.

Strange bedfellows, the pilot thought. If the men they'd bribed to drive them out here thought anything of the armed men seeking to tangle with the local drug lords, they hadn't commented on it. No doubt they thought they were pocketing the money of dead men. That was fine; it meant they'd be even less likely to speak of it after the fact, though they'd been bribed well enough for their silence.

It was all part of the shadow war, the type of conflict in which Phoenix Force specialized. Evil criminals of the type found in the Triangle organization were accustomed to preying on others. They did not deal well with coming under sudden fire; they did not grasp that they, too, could become the victims of seemingly random violence. When, suddenly, they found themselves attacked from what seemed all sides by a foe they could not at first identify, they became confused and afraid. For many of them, fear was a new sensation, and one the Stony Man pilot was happy to bring them.

I love the smell of terrified organized crime bosses in the morning, Grimaldi thought to himself.

The AH-1 gunship was a familiar aircraft, one that Grimaldi enjoyed flying. Once the backbone of the United

States military's fleet of attack helicopters, long since eclipsed by the AH-64 Apache, it remained a very dependable, very lethal aerial weapon.

He checked his chronograph, then his GPS unit. "G-Force," Grimaldi said over the transceiver link, "in position."

"Roger, G-Force," McCarter's voice came back to him. "By the numbers. One, two."

"One, two, roger," Grimaldi said.

He angled the nose of the Cobra, allowed himself to pick up more speed and began triggering the hellstorm under his command.

The twin rocket pods unleashed their 70 mm cargo of Mark 4 folding-fin aerial rockets. The M-156 white phosphorous rounds detonated across the poppy field, leaving actinic flashes in Grimaldi's vision. He worked the chopper back and forth in a zigzagging pattern, making sure his deadly payload did its gruesome work among the flowers.

"G-Force is all go, zero one," Grimaldi reported as he fired the last of his rockets. The explosions radiated heat; he gripped the controls firmly, controlling the gunship. "Good hunting, gentlemen."

"Roger," David McCarter's voice came through the transceiver link. "Start run two, G-Force. Repeat, start run zero-two."

"G-Force is go zero-two," Grimaldi reported.

The gunship gained altitude. Grimaldi allowed the deadly machine to crest the rise at the far end of the now-burning poppy field. Below, in the depression beyond, sat the camp and heroin-processing center. Phoenix Force would be moving in from the perimeter just now; Grimaldi would therefore fight from the center of the camp, moving outward. He overflew the camp, chose his spot and yanked hard on the controls, making the gunship shudder and dance as it dumped its velocity. He brought the killing snout of the helicopter around in a slow arc.

"G-Force is all go, twice," he said out loud. "Heads down, gentlemen. I repeat, heads down."

At Grimaldi's direction, the M-28 turret's twin M-134 miniguns began spitting 7.62 mm death. The slow arc of the chopper fanned the slugs out as Grimaldi picked his targets, centering on the small, prefabricated, corrugated-metal buildings closest to the center of the camp. Men in olive-drab fatigues, carrying Kalashnikovs, began running for their lives. Something volatile within one of the buildings exploded, shooting shrapnel and flames in every direction and throwing several of the running figures to the ground. Grimaldi kept the pressure on, his gunship's inventory ticking down in his head, the chopper wreaking havoc in the enemy's midst.

He began whistling "The Battle Hymn of the Republic," smiling faintly as the Triangle drug plant slowly disintegrated at the touch of his trigger finger.

"YOU HEAR THAT?" Calvin James said.

"Hear what?" Rafael Encizo asked.

"Nothing." James shook his head. "Thought I heard whistling. Faint, like."

McCarter chuckled but said nothing.

Phoenix Force waited from cover at the perimeter of the camp, southwest of Grimaldi's position. They were crouched behind an old bus that had somehow been trucked in and buried half in and half out of the ground to form a makeshift storage bunker. Now that bunker provided them with adequate concealment as Grimaldi softened up the camp.

"Masks on, lads," McCarter instructed. "The fumes will reach us any minute." The team members donned their breathing gear. The black plumes from the burning poppy field were visible far beyond the chopper. The staccato drumbeat of the gunship's nose cannons slapped echoes from the metal buildings around them. Return fire from within the camp was sporadic, but left no doubt that Phoenix Force would encounter armed resistance once they made their foray inside.

Per the mission parameters, they were dressed and armed for plausible deniability. The members of the team each wore Russian surplus camouflage fatigues. Some of their equipment was mundane and readily available on the world market, like their web belts and the Ka-bar Next Generation fighting knives they carried. Their sensitive surveillance, communication and breathing gear was custom-built but untraceable to the Farm or the United States. They also carried folding-stock Kalashnikov rifles. None of the team favored the weapons overmuch, but they were all very familiar with them. Despite their ergonomic flaws and generally sloppy tolerances, the rifles were serviceable, reliable and deadly in their trained hands. The fact that ammunition would likely be readily available in the field was another point in the rifles' favor, too.

If they needed the extra firepower, Gary Manning also carried a Heckler & Koch HK-69 40 mm grenade launcher and a bandolier of grenades. Each team member also carried a sidearm. Manning had his .357 Magnum Desert Eagle, and McCarter carried his favored Browning Hi-Power. Hawkins, Encizo and James all carried untraceable Glock 17 pistols. Each man's web gear was laden with a variety of grenades, smoke canisters, extra magazines and a variety of other tools of the trade.

"G-Force, all in, all in," Grimaldi reported.

"That's our cue," McCarter said. As the chopper rose

higher above the carnage its pilot had created, Phoenix Force moved in.

Without being told to do so, Encizo and James broke to the left, while Manning and Hawkins moved off to the right. They would skirt the perimeter and take their own paths toward the burning center. McCarter headed straight up the middle, splitting the difference.

It was a straightforward operation. While they would keep an eye out for any intel they might gather on the ground, there were no specific target objectives other than the destruction of this Triangle asset. It was a refreshingly direct drop and smash, McCarter thought. No hostages to rescue, no supersensitive electronic devices to recover, no nuclear warheads to disarm. Just walk in, run about and burn it down.

A gunman in the olive-drab fatigues that seemed to be the uniform of the camp came running headlong from the nearest metal shack, heedless of the danger and failing to look around himself. McCarter let him go right on by, drawing a bead with his AK and pressing the extended metal stock to his shoulder.

"Hey," McCarter called, his voice only slightly muffled by his breathing mask.

The gunman turned and tried to bring up a pistol. McCarter shot him neatly through the chest. Two more men, one carrying a shotgun and the other a Kalashnikov of his own, came fast on the heels of their dead comrade. McCarter snapped his AK to full auto, held the weapon low and squeezed off a burst that cut the men down in their tracks.

Gunfire was audible from several different parts of the camp now. There were more firefights, to McCarter's ear, than there were contingents of Phoenix personnel. That was good; it meant that the men guarding the camp were panicking, firing blindly around themselves without clear targets. Filling the environment with lead made it decidedly unsafe, but scattered, unaimed fire was something with which the team could easily cope. A disorganized enemy was no better than sheep, to be carved up and brought down by McCarter's wolves. They'd done it many times before.

A long metal Quonset-hut-style building stood in front of him. McCarter moved quickly to the heavy wooden door at one end. He tried it, but it was dogged shut from inside, apparently. He took one of the high-explosive grenades from his web gear, pulled the pin, let the spoon fly free and dropped the bomb in front of the door before moving around the corner of the building.

The explosion buckled the metal wall of the hut and splintered the door, which fell inward. McCarter plunged in after it, his AK spitting lead as several men inside opened up on him. Bullets tore through the bunks on either side of him; the former SAS commando had blundered into a barracks. He dropped first one, then another, then a third gunman.

"Report!" he said out loud, stalking from bunk to bunk, checking the bodies to make sure none of the fallen men was shamming.

"Found the processing plant," James said. After a pause, there was an incredibly loud explosion that reverberated through the camp, shaking the walls of the barracks in which McCarter stood. "Processing plant eliminated," James said. "It's snowing."

"Don't stand around with your tongue out," McCarter said.

"Clear here," Encizo reported. "Several shooters down."

The dull thump of another, smaller explosion reached McCarter's ears as he cleared the other end of the barracks and exited through that side. Through the twisted wreckage of several small metal huts, he saw another one burst apart. That would be Manning, with his grenade launcher.

"Mopping up," Manning's voice said in McCarter's ear, as if on cue. "No problems."

"Clear," Hawkins said.

The Cobra gunship continued to swoop low over their heads, making a series of lazy circles around the camp. The rotor wash swirled the smoke plumes, giving the scene a surreal cast.

"Form up at the center," McCarter instructed. "What's left of that wooden structure." The two-story building in the middle of the camp, which Grimaldi had used as his reference for the chopper run, was obviously older than the metal structures erected around it. It bore the sagging roof and sun-weathered beams of several years in the Thai sun. What was left of elaborate woodwork on the shutters was mostly chipped away, either by time or, in the past few minutes, stray bullets. McCarter nodded approvingly as the members of Phoenix Force emerged from the surrounding area as if they'd been invisible moments before.

He pointed to Hawkins, Encizo and James. "Perimeter," he instructed.

The three team members took up positions around the hut, like the posts on a three-legged stool, eyes sharp for enemy incursion. Thanks largely to Grimaldi's opening attack, but also because of the lightning-fast Phoenix Force raid, the camp had become a burning ruin in only minutes. It was far from a secure location, however, and there was no telling how many gunmen might still be running loose and looking for payback.

The old wooden building had one door, which was of the same heavy, sun-bleached wood as the rest of the structure. McCarter motioned for Manning to move in with him. The two men took positions on either side of that door.

McCarter knocked loudly.

The Briton had only moved his hand out of the way a split second before when a shotgun blast tore through the middle of the door. Without missing a beat, Manning pulled a stun grenade from his web gear, popped it and threw it into the ragged hole.

McCarter and Manning closed their eyes and turned away. The blast was loud even outside the building; inside, it would have been deafening. Manning slammed aside what was left of the door with one heavy kick.

"In we go," McCarter said. "Go high."

Manning nodded.

They burst through the doorway, weapons ready. A man on the floor was writhing in pain, holding his face. Manning quickly rolled him over and secured him with two pairs of plastic zip-tie cuffs at wrists and ankles.

"I'm headed upstairs," McCarter said. There was a rickety stairway at the rear of the building. The ground floor itself was one large room, with a wooden table and several metal folding chairs at one end, and a makeshift kitchen at the other. A pool table, one leg gone and replaced by a pair of cinder blocks, sat in the center of the space. The felt was badly ripped.

Three different refrigerators in the kitchen area were connected to a generator, which still chugged quietly in the corner. An exhaust hose led to the outside. One of the refrigerators had been popped open by the blast or simply left open by the man who was now Phoenix Force's prisoner; it revealed shelf after metal shelf of cold beer.

So it was a rec room, McCarter concluded as he took the stairs two at a time. To men like these, recreation had only a couple of forms. The first was the booze, and the second—

"Bloody hell," McCarter muttered.

The stained mattress and twisted bedclothes in the center of the floor still boasted human occupants. A gunman wearing only olive-drab fatigue pants stood in the center of the room, with a naked woman held in front of him. The gunner had one arm around the woman's throat and the barrel of a 1911-pattern pistol to her head. He spit something at McCarter that the Briton couldn't understand.

"Easy now," he said in a calm voice. "Let's not do anything we'll regret later, shall we?"

"English," the man said. The girl squirmed and he tightened his arm around her neck. She was wide-eyed with fear and looked badly used; there was an old bruise yellowing on her jaw. McCarter guessed her age at midtwenties, though it was hard to tell. She was probably a local hooker but could just as easily have been kidnapped for the sport of the Triangle gunmen.

"English," McCarter confirmed. "Speak the Queen's tongue, do you?"

"I speak." The man nodded. "You let me go."

"We might be able to work something out, at that," McCarter said. "But I tell you what, mate. I'll lower my gun here—" McCarter gestured gently with the Kalashnikov "—and you let that girl go. There's no need to hurt her. She's done nothing to you, now has she?"

"You let me go," the man said, pressing the pistol harder against his captive's temple. "I kill her. You see. I kill her."

"That's really not a good idea," McCarter said. He placed the Kalashnikov on the floor. "You see? Completely unnecessary. My gun is down. Nobody's trying to hurt you. Just let her go and you can walk downstairs."

"No," the man said. "You not alone. You *all* let me go."

"Bloody hell," McCarter muttered again. This one was not stupid, for all his other abundantly evident personal failings. More loudly, he said, "All right. Now look, friend, I'm sure we can come to an understanding—"

In midsentence, McCarter's hand closed around the butt of the Hi-Power in its holster on his web belt. The gun came up, rattlesnake fast, and McCarter snapped off a shot that took the gunman between the eyes. His head snapped back. The 1911, and the dead man, hung there for a moment as if gravity was suspended...and then both the corpse and the pistol in its hand hit the ground, leaving the shocked girl standing there without a stitch on.

It only took her a few seconds to start screaming.

"Easy," McCarter said again. "Easy. It's over. It's over." He grabbed her and pulled her to him. "It's all over now...."

The pearl-handled switchblade the girl had been hiding behind her back came up and snapped open. McCarter, who had been waiting for that, simply side-stepped and popped her under the jaw with a closed fist. Her eyes rolled up into her head and she folded, falling onto the now bloody mattress.

"David," Manning said from behind him. "Are you all right?"

"Right as rain," McCarter said, looking down and shaking his head. "Mind the girl, here. She's one of them, or near enough." He bent, folded the switchblade and pocketed it.

"I saw," Manning said. "How did you know?"

"Kept that one arm behind her back even after he went down." McCarter jerked his head to the dead gunman. "Probably figured to stick me after I gave in to his demands."

"Triangle operative, you think?" Manning asked.

"No," McCarter said, "not necessarily. Doesn't appear to have been treated like just one of the boys, now, does she?" He regarded the unconscious woman as Manning gently rolled her over, wrapped her in a sheet from the bed and secured her wrists and ankles with zip-tie cuffs. "Probably just a local. Threw in her lot willingly with this bunch. Doesn't matter. Let's see if there's anything to see."

They searched the structure, then paired off in teams while Hawkins guarded the prisoners. Two at a time, they searched what was left of the burning camp, moving as quickly as possible. They found drugs, weapons and paraphernalia relating to both, but no additional intelligence and nothing that could be used against the Triangle.

"All right, lads," McCarter said, signaling to Grimaldi, who was hovering around in close support. "Let's clear out. Burn as we go, by the numbers. Move."

Each team member had incendiary grenades. As they withdrew from the camp, they threw these into any structures not already on fire or otherwise destroyed. The dull, hissing thumps of the grenades going off was followed by the red-orange glow of the chemical flames they spread.

"Everyone to the evac point," McCarter said.

"Meet you at the airfield, gentlemen," Grimaldi said. He dipped the nose of the Cobra in salute once, then again, and then was flying away.

"Let's hope those truck jockeys are where we told them to meet us," Encizo said.

"Two to one says they've cleared out," James put in, "rather than get caught in whatever heavy stuff they'll figure is going down."

"No bet there." Encizo shook his head.

"Can the chatter, lads," McCarter said. "If they're not

there, we'll have a long hike to the airfield. Come on, people. Move."

"Great," Encizo said.

Manning smiled, shook his head and took off in the lead, setting a grueling pace.

"Well," James said, nodding after the Canadian, "you going to let him show you up like that?"

"Bloody hell," McCarter groused.

CHAPTER FIVE

The Southern Tier of New York State

The rutted dirt road turned and twisted, the rented Suburban bounced and jolted despite its heavy-duty suspension and four-wheel drive.

"We're approaching the target coordinates now," Lyons said into his secure satellite phone.

"I'm uploading all of the satellite imagery we have to your phones," Barbara Price told him. Mission data would be sent to each team member's wireless unit; they would study the satellite images before making their run.

"You're certain we're on the right track?" Lyons asked for the third time.

"Yes, Carl," Price told him. "NetScythe's analysis of satellite imaging of that area has resulted in several clusters of probable hits," she explained. "The chain is a long one and took several hundred hours of data mining to establish, but the Triangle is running at least one chain of drug shipments from New Jersey to the target location, and back again. Multiple distribution points run from that location, too. The satellite data definitely supports your location as a hub of the Triangle's network."

"And we're facing what in terms of opposition?"

"More than likely," Price said, "a local biker gang reportedly up to its chrome exhaust pipes in the local drug trade. The Grubs, according to what I have here. There have been quite a few reports fired at local, regional and state levels concerning them and their activities, but so far New York's attorney general hasn't managed to nail them down, and neither have the Feds."

"Grubs. Catchy name."

"Very," Price said.

"How big?"

"No definite numbers," Price said, "but there are quite a few bodies on the ground. Unless it's a racetrack or an amusement park, you can assume anywhere from a dozen to two or three times that number. Completely speculative."

"Wonderful," Lyons said. "All right. Just wanted to be sure. Give Hal my love."

Price laughed. "I might just do that."

"Able, out," Lyons said. He closed the connection.

"I always knew you two had something going on," Schwarz said absently. He was examining the data the Farm had sent to each man's phone. Blancanales was driving, so Schwarz quickly and quietly gave him a rundown of what they were facing. Lyons brought up the data on his own wireless unit and listened in as Schwarz spoke.

"Okay, Pol, we've got a main building here, a double-wide, in the center of this clearing," Schwarz explained. Lyons examined the photographs provided by the Farm. They were enhanced shots taken from space, the detail provided by NetScythe reportedly enhanced, according to the notation, using the amazing device's programming logic. "Outlying trailers here and here." Lyons found the two structures as Schwarz described them. "According to the heat-signature analysis, the double-wide is the cookhouse, almost certainly crystal meth, if local law-enforcement reports are any hint. One of the outlying trailers may be storage for drugs, or may not be. One of them is most certainly the primary residence, where most of the personnel on-site congregate during the evenings. That much is verified by the heat clusters."

"Bet it smells wonderful," Lyons grumbled.

"I'll bet it does, at that." Schwarz smiled then turned more serious, all business where the work itself was concerned. "How do you want to play it, Ironman?"

"You and Pol," Lyons said, "will use the cover of the trees surrounding the property, work your way around to either side. West and east. I'm going to take the truck straight down the middle, up the road and to their front door."

"Uh, Ironman..." Pol started.

"Yeah?"

"Won't that mean they'll start shooting at you almost immediately?"

"It might. So?"

"Well, all right. Never mind, then." Blancanales shrugged.

"On my go," Lyons said as if the interruption had never occurred, "you'll move in on the cookhouse. I'll try to recon the storage trailer and take out the residence trailer while you do that. Expect resistance around and in the cookhouse to be the worst. There'll probably be plenty of guards."

"Probably?" Schwarz asked.

"Shut up," Lyons said automatically. "All right, no sense delaying the inevitable. Let's hit it."

Blancanales sped up as much as he dared, bringing the Suburban through the curves in sprays of dust and gravel. When, according to their GPS unit, they were just short of the clearing in which the target trailers stood, Lyons signaled Blancanales to bring the truck to a stop.

"All right," Lyons said. "Everybody out."

Blancanales removed an AR-15 from the back of the truck. It would be his primary contact weapon for the operation. Schwarz checked the 20-round magazine in his 93-R machine pistol.

"Ironman," Schwarz said, looking up at the big blond former cop as the man took the wheel of the Suburban, "be careful."

"Never," Lyons said.

"One of these days," Schwarz started.

"One of these days, nothing," Blancanales shot back. "He's indestructible."

"Wish I was." Schwarz grinned.

"Go," Blancanales said. Schwarz nodded. The two men split up, working their way through the trees that surrounded the property.

"Wish I was, too," Lyons said to no one. He tromped the gas pedal and the Suburban shot forward, the big engine growling.

"Keep it tight, guys," he said over his transceiver link.

"Got it," Schwarz said.

"Will do," Blancanales acknowledged.

Lyons did not have to drive far before he cleared the trees. Emerging at the opening to the clearing, he was confronted by a pair of leather-clad bikers sitting on elaborately chromed choppers. The motorcycles were parked across the dirt road, nose to nose. The men sitting on them were in their midtwenties to early thirties, greasy and unkempt, but the predatory air about them was unmistakable. Lyons saw no weapons, but both wore leather jackets that could conceal just about anything short of a rifle or full-size shotgun.

One of them came up along the driver's side of the Suburban. Lyons rolled down the window.

"You lost, asshole?" the biker demanded.

"No," Lyons said. He was very conscious of the other man at the nose of the truck.

"Then you'd best turn your ass around and get the hell out of here, hadn't you?" the biker at his window said. He reached into his coat.

"You should probably get down on the ground," Lyons said calmly. "Your friend, too. I'm a federal agent."

"Oh, really?" the biker asked. He seemed to think that was funny.

"No, really," Lyons said conversationally. "I'm with the Justice Department." He held up the credentials he had plucked from his pocket while driving up. "See?"

"Oh, damn it all to—" He clawed a revolver from under his jacket, bringing it up to shoot Lyons in the head.

"Yeah," Lyons said. The big ex-cop was faster. His Python was already pointing out the window of the truck. It spoke once, with authority, and the biker fell dead with a .357 Magnum bullet hole in his forehead.

Lyons stomped the gas pedal to the floor. The big Suburban pushed the other biker over. He went down screaming, still trying to pull his own gun, as Lyons simply drove over him. The two choppers were more of an obstacle, but the big Suburban powered over those, too, leaving behind bent and twisted chrome as it fought for traction in the dirt.

"Shots fired, shots fired," Lyons said. "The Grubs drew down on me," he reported to his teammates, "so assume armed and dangerous. I've taken two and am headed toward the buildings now."

"Roger," Schwarz said.

"Coming at you," Blancanales said.

Lyons rolled up to the trailer designated on their intelligence files as the residence building. He leaped from the Suburban, his Daewoo USAS-12 automatic shotgun at the ready with a 20-round drum magazine in place. Several motorcycles were parked in front of the trailer, as well as an old Ford pickup. Lyons ignored the vehicles. With one combat-booted foot, he kicked open the door to the trailer.

The gunfire that poured out was so heavy that he was forced to leap away, landing on his back in the mud in front of the trailer door. The men rushing to kill him, bikers all, were so eager to shoot him that one of them managed to put a bullet in the back of another. That biker fell dead at Lyons's feet, the Grubs colors on his vest spattered red with his blood.

Lyons fired from his back, hosing the doorway with double-aught buckshot. Men screamed and died.

The big ex-cop pushed himself up and through the doorway, the shotgun leading. He poured on the fire as he encountered several more bikers, some only half dressed as they were roused from fetid bunks by the fighting. Return fire devastated the cluttered, garbage-strewed trailer all around him, but none of it found the Able Team leader. Yet another biker died as a result of friendly fire, however, when Lyons dodged his clumsy knife attack and then yanked the man in front of him to play the part of human shield.

"Knife to a gunfight, pal," Lyons muttered before firing out the drum of the USAS-12 from behind the dead man.

The small, dark-skinned man moved so fast that Lyons almost didn't see him until it was too late. Levering the corpse off himself and bringing the shotgun up to acquire the next target, Lyons felt the shock transmitted through his big hands as the smaller man dived from hiding behind one of the bunks that lined the walls of the narrow trailer. He slapped the barrel of the shotgun so hard that Lyons's palms stung. The weapon was levered from his grasp as the small man snapped a brutal kick into Lyons's shin and then unleashed a hail of blows with his fists.

Lyons released the shotgun rather than fight for it. He deflected most of the punches, though a few got through and very nearly rocked him. His opponent was small, but all wiry muscle, and he packed a hell of a punch in his small frame.

Lyons got a good look at the man's face as they fought. Thawan.

He'd had his doubts as to NetScythe's ability to point them to targets ahead of the curve. He'd even entertained the notion that they might have stumbled on a local meth gang completely unrelated to the Triangle. The presence of Mok Thawan here, however, clinched it. They were definitely dealing with the Triangle.

Lyons threw a powerful front kick that staggered Thawan. In that instance, Lyons knew that, ultimately, he could take the little bastard if it came to that. It wouldn't be easy, especially in this confined space, but he thought perhaps he could do the job. He came in, angling for a decent shot. Just one edge of a hand to the neck or a leopard's paw to the throat and Thawan would be on the floor of the trailer, fighting to breathe. That was all it would take.

The glittering blade of the balisong flashed out and nearly caught Lyons in the face. He fought for room to draw the Python. Thawan anticipated that and slashed him in the arm as he tried to draw the gun, slamming a vicious elbow into Lyons's midsection as he followed through. Then he was past Lyons and running from the trailer.

"I've got Thawan!" Lyons shouted. "He's running from the residence!"

"Tied up here!" Blancanales shouted back. Lyons could hear the gunfire coming from the cookhouse. The firefight sounded ugly.

"Pinned," Schwarz reported. "We can take them but we won't be able to get to you."

"On it," Lyons said. He was already running as they talked, scooping up the USAS-12 and bulling his way through the trailer door.

The flash of light that accompanied the blow to his face was so sudden he thought he'd been shot. As his vision turned gray and he began to feel himself falling off the edge of the world, he heard a mocking voice.

"Gun to a knife fight, pal."

He reached out, wanting to wrap his fingers around Thawan's throat, hoping to stop the man then and there despite whatever injury had felled him. Then everything was receding and he could feel and hear nothing more....

THE VOLATILE CHEMICALS of a meth amphetamine cookhouse, Schwarz knew, meant that a firefight in a meth lab was a very iffy proposition. Fortunately for him and Blancanales, however, they'd caught the bikers in between runs of the chemical. They had been transferring a completed batch from the cookhouse to the storage trailer when the two Phoenix Force soldiers initiated their hit.

"On your left!" Schwarz called out. He triggered a pair of 3-round bursts from the Beretta 93-R and watched as the two men converging on Blancanales's position fell where they stood. They were using the heavy workbenches in the cookhouse for cover, hoping that none of the chemicals or equipment on top of those benches suddenly exploded or set fire to the entire trailer. In addition to the bikers they'd seen and dispatched, there were several men who were clearly not Americans. Both Stony Man team members shot several operatives who, from their size and skin tone, could very likely be Triangle operatives from Thailand or Myanmar.

"Come on," Blancanales said, finally luring the last of the cookhouse guards into the opening and putting a 5.56 bullet in the center of the man's face. "We've got to help Carl!"

"I hear you." Schwarz nodded. The two men made a cursory sweep of what was left of the cookhouse trailer, making sure no armed men still hid within. They came under fire as soon as they tried to leave, however. There was a shooter on the roof of the residence trailer.

"Sniper!" Schwarz warned.

As bullets ripped into the front of the cookhouse around the door frame, Blancanales very calmly assumed a shooter's crouch on one knee. He brought the AR-15 to his shoulder and, very carefully, took aim. The gunner was just beginning to track his shots in toward Blancanales when the Politician's rifle fired. The single shot did its deadly work; the shooter on the roof grunted and was still.

"Let's go," Blancanales said.

They found Carl Lyons flat on his back in front of the trailer. Schwarz produced an ampoule from his first-aid kit and broke the glass vial under Lyons's nose. The big ex-cop drew in a ragged breath and then turned away.

"Jesus, Gadgets, that stuff stinks," he complained. "Get it away from me, damn it."

"Are you okay?" Schwarz asked. Blancanales, with his AR-15, adopted a protective stance in front of the two men, ready for trouble and looking for any other gunmen who might still be on the move around their position.

"I'm fine," he said. "Where's the Ford?"

"Ford?" Blancanales asked.

"The pickup, a beat-to-shit Ford pickup truck. Where is it?"

"Not here." Blancanales nodded toward the road. "Fresh tire tracks there, could be your truck, or could be that one."

"He got away," Lyons groaned.

"Who, Thawan?" Schwarz asked.

"Thawan." Lyons nodded. "Little bastard came out of nowhere. He's fast, too."

"You're lucky he didn't kill you," Schwarz said.

"I said I'm fine."

"You don't look fine," Schwarz said. "In fact, you look like you've been cut badly."

Lyons looked down. His arm was bleeding freely. Schwarz cleaned the wound and applied a bandage from the first-aid kit, clucking like a hen. "You were lucky, Carl," he said. "It's not too deep."

"Good," Lyons growled. "Now get off me."

"Uh," Schwarz said. "Carl, there's no easy way to say this but…"

"What?" Lyons demanded.

"You…you have a line across your face."

"What?" Lyons pushed himself to his feet and grabbed the mirror of the nearest motorcycle.

There was a tire iron lying on the ground not far from where Lyons had been attacked. That had obviously been what Thawan had used. Lyons looked at the long, straight red welt across his forehead.

"At least he hit you in a nonvital area," Schwarz said.

They took some time to secure the area as best they could. The local police had not arrived yet, and for that the team members were grateful. There would be time for that complication in due course; right now, they needed to see if there were any clues to the Triangle's activities among what was left of the meth lab and the surrounding buildings. Lyons and Schwarz went back out to the front of the residence trailer as Blancanales searched from building to building, Schwarz pestering Lyons to within an inch of his life.

"Seriously, Carl, you could have a concussion," Schwarz advised.

"Do I look like I do?" Lyons growled back. "I don't have time for this crap."

Schwarz examined Lyons again, checking his pupils and testing a few other vitals. "All right," he said, "but if you start to feel any dizziness, nausea or light-headedness, you sing out. Don't be a hero. I know that doesn't exactly come naturally to you."

"Whatever." Lyons frowned.

"Hey, guys," Blancanales said. "Look at this." He had in his hand what Lyons at first took to be a sheaf of papers. When Blancanales got closer, the big ex-cop realized the man held a badly folded road map.

"What have you got, Pol?" Schwarz asked.

"Not the most subtle encryption job." Blancanales grinned. He spread the map out over the seat of one of the parked motorcycles. A route was laid out in highlighter on the map, leading through New York State and beyond. At intervals, red marker had been used to flag certain cities. Numbers had been written in over these cities.

"You're right," Schwarz said. "I believe, with time, we can crack this code."

"Knock it off," Lyons grumbled. He put his hand to his face and then to the back of his aching head. "Analysis."

"Clearly drop points," Schwarz said. "Even better, turn it over."

Pol realized that Schwarz was looking at something on the curled corner of the map. He flipped it and they saw another set of notations written in the margin next to one of the street grid listings. It read, "Van 1, Van 2, Van 3." Under each of these headings was a list of product quantities with the letters *H* and *M*.

"Heroin," Schwarz said, "and meth."

"And three vans." Lyons nodded. He immediately regretted moving his head that much.

"Looks like we've got the route they plan to use," Blancanales said.

"And that's powerful information for NetScythe," Schwarz said. "We can use this to coordinate with the Farm and intercept those vans before they get where they're going."

"We know where they're going, don't we?" Lyons asked.

"Yes, but not when," Schwarz said. "We can use this data so Barb and NetScythe can help us figure out when they're likely to get there. Then we can arrange to be there right on schedule."

"That I like," Lyons said. "Call the Farm. Arrange for a cleanup crew out here. Let's police up what we can and get gone before the cops come and start asking us about the body count. And let's make sure this place doesn't burn to the ground while we're at it. No need to cause a forest fire." He paused, making a sour face. "Also, make sure Barb knows that I saw Thawan but he got away."

"Don't sweat it, Ironman," Schwarz offered. "We'll get him."

"Oh, we will," Lyons said. "And when we do, I owe him a nearly broken face."

"Payback?" Schwarz asked.

"Payback hell." Lyons shook his head, groaning. "That's just me saying hello."

"I'd hate to see you say goodbye, then," Schwarz said.

"So will Thawan," Lyons vowed.

CHAPTER SIX

Outside Yangon, Union of Myanmar

The slight Chinese man, gaunt and wiry even for an Asian, was dressed in a loose-fitting pair of drawstring cotton trousers and a rumpled, matching shirt with baggy sleeves. The flowing garment had not entirely concealed the butt of the stainless-steel revolver in his waistband, next to his skin over his appendix. McCarter had taken note of that when they met and exchanged code phrases at the airport. The Briton didn't know exactly how much in bribe money, international saber rattling or other geopolitical pressure had been brought to bear here in Myanmar. All that mattered was that the old Toyota Land Cruiser had been waiting for them, Customs hadn't met or searched their chartered plane and nobody had challenged the men of Phoenix Force, who were carrying weapons most certainly illegal to the mere mortals on the ground in what had once been Burma.

Yangon, for that matter, was better known to most people as Rangoon. McCarter did not care much for the way various parts of the world, and the former British

Empire, much to his chagrin, had been renamed, rebranded and repackaged in the past few decades…but then, nobody was asking him, and he had better things to be worrying about. He forced himself to focus on the task at hand.

The little Chinese man had introduced himself only as Peng. Price had transmitted a limited dossier from the Farm on the flight in. Peng's name had been offered by Interpol when a discreet query regarding local assets was made through the international intelligence community's various networks. The Farm had gotten word to Peng and he had simply turned up at a time and place specified, whereupon arrangements for his rendezvous with Phoenix were made. Supposedly he was intimately familiar with the Triangle's operations, though why that was the case was either classified or unknown. McCarter had to admit that knowing so little about their guide, the man who was supposed to be the key to getting close to and inside the Triangle's operation here in Burma, made him nervous.

Peng's exact governmental affiliation was unspecified in his dossier, which meant it was secret. That told McCarter the man was a double agent of some kind, probably tied to the local intelligence services while working for, and feeding intel to, the Central Intelligence Agency. The specific agency might vary and Peng's true story might be something else, but the Farm vouched for him as far as it could, which meant he was probably trustworthy.

Peng was Chinese Burmese, specifically, part of a community of Chinese immigrants to the nation, raised from childhood in Myanmar. From the look of him he might have been of mixed race; it would explain his skin tone, among other things. The Chinese Burmese population was widely known to be underreported in Myanmar. Standing officially at three percent, the true figure was probably much higher. That little factoid had been part of Price's electronic briefing package.

Peng's file also said that he spoke Burmese, Mandarin and English, as well as a couple of obscure dialects specific to upper Burma. He was supposed to be expert with small arms and no slouch with a blade—which, if McCarter's eyes did not deceive him, he carried on a metal ball chain around his neck under his shirt. The little man had said nothing after their initial exchange, simply pointing in the direction they were to take the Land Cruiser once Phoenix Force was aboard and ready.

Grimaldi had stayed at the airfield to guard the plane and keep it ready for a fast departure. While it would have been nice to have his air support for the mission, they had been unable to secure a suitable local equivalent to the Cobra gunship Grimaldi had flown in Thailand. Other choppers were available, but they were unarmed civilian models. To McCarter's mind the benefit of having Grimaldi's eyes in the sky was not sufficient to risk turning the pilot into a target, albeit an airborne and moving one.

Through whatever technology and magic the NetScythe satellite employed, the Farm had been able to identify a facility in Burma that was, if not the termination of a Triangle drug trafficking line between Thailand and Myanmar, at least a major spoke in the network. The exact nature of the facility was unknown; satellite thermal imagery registered that it was there, in an area thick with vegetation. That was why Peng had been drafted for this duty; he was their local guide. He knew the terrain, knew the landmarks and knew the local crime scene. He would, at least in theory, stop them from reinventing any wheels as they performed their mission. If he had any thoughts about where he'd rather be or whether he wanted to be helping the Stony Man commandos penetrate what was looking like an increasingly isolated location miles from Yangon, he was keeping that to himself.

As if reading McCarter's mind, Peng spoke up in English. His accent was noticeable but not impenetrable. "You will come to a fork in the road," he said. "Take the right fork, and move slowly. We will have to stop frequently."

"Stop for what?" T. J. Hawkins asked. He was driving the Land Cruiser. Peng was seated in the passenger seat. McCarter and the other members of Phoenix Force rode in the back of the big old SUV, whose suspension was functional but had obviously seen better days.

"We will need to stop to defuse each mine," Peng said calmly.

"Wait, what?" Hawkins said, his drawl shortening as he looked at Peng with concern. "There are mines?"

"Every mile or so." Peng nodded. "For the unwary."

"Bloody hell," McCarter muttered.

"So the Triangle are known by the locals to be operating here?" Encizo asked from the backseat.

"Of course," Peng confirmed. "The operation is large enough that it would be impossible to hide. They do not try to hide it. The police, the military…they are paid to stay away. The Triangle protects its holdings with violence so total that none dare oppose it."

From his seat between Encizo and James—Manning was sitting with the equipment in the rear cargo area—McCarter looked at Peng sharply. Something about the way the man had said that sounded bitter. The Briton found himself wondering precisely what the history between Peng and the Triangle might be.

"What's the Triangle's body count around here?" Calvin James asked.

Peng looked back over his shoulder at the black man. "Body count?"

"He means," McCarter said, "just how much damage do they do in the course of their operations? What price is paid to allow them to keep running?"

Peng was silent for a moment. He looked out the window as the scenery jounced past. "The price is high," he said finally. "High for some, at any rate. The Triangle cares little for human life. All who get in the way, or those who are no longer useful, are discarded. Removed, like vermin…or like garbage. Many die. Many more are never seen again, and must be dead, but none can say."

McCarter frowned. This was what they fought; this was the reason the trade in which the Triangle engaged was far from the victimless crime some would claim drug use to be. Demand for drugs in Western nations fueled regimes tolerant of this type of cancer. It supported murderers like the Triangle and, if McCarter was any judge of people, it led to the victimization of people like Peng, or of their friends and loved ones.

"Gary," McCarter said, gesturing to Manning, "give him a hand when it comes to it."

The big Canadian nodded. Peng made no comment. McCarter's motives were not altogether altruistic; Peng was trustworthy enough, or so the Farm said, but McCarter wanted someone from the team to keep an eye on him during any activities as sensitive as dealing with explosives that could kill them all. He didn't intend to let Peng out of their sight for the duration of the operation. Unless and until Peng did something that proved beyond a shadow of a doubt that he could not be compromised by the enemy, McCarter and the members of Phoenix Force would be careful around him. McCarter thought it unlikely that Peng would double-cross them, though. Unless he was an Oscar-caliber actor, his hatred for the Triangle was very real. That alone did not make him trustworthy, however. The former SAS commando had seen plenty of men lose their heads and do something rash out of blind hatred.

Hawkins guided the Land Cruiser through the ruts of the twisting dirt road. Tree and scrub cover closed in around them; the area had a lush, claustrophobic feel to it. They were on the cusp of the rainy season, which meant the temperatures weren't too bad, and the morning shower had already fallen. McCarter was familiar enough with the country to know to expect more rain that afternoon, most likely.

"There," Peng said, pointing to a hump of earth not far ahead. It looked identical to several other mounds they had passed or even driven over along the way.

"Why this one?" McCarter asked as Hawkins stopped the Land Cruiser.

"It is six," Peng said. It took McCarter a moment to realize what the smaller man meant. Peng had been counting the mounds.

I just hope he doesn't lose count as we go, he thought.

Peng climbed out of the Land Cruiser. Manning opened the rear hatch and climbed out over the gear, his Kalashnikov at the ready with the stock folded. McCarter watched as the big Canadian kept a close eye on Peng and on the surrounding area as Peng worked. The Chinese Burmese operative, using a small entrenching tool borrowed from the gear in the truck, dug out the end of the mound and exposed a large metal disk about the size of a dinner plate. A wire trailed from the center of the heavy disk and disappeared into the earth mound.

"There will be a string of these," Peng explained, "perhaps six or seven, through the length of the mound. Pressure from a vehicle will detonate the string."

"How powerful?" McCarter asked. He had gotten out of the truck and was standing by the passenger door.

"Powerful," was all Peng would say. That meant, to McCarter's thinking, that the devices were probably powerful enough to reduce their SUV to shrapnel, to say nothing of Phoenix Force inside it.

Peng used the tip of the knife in the sheath around his neck—a small stainless-steel fixed blade with a cord-wrapped handle—to pry open the cover on the back of the disk he was holding. He reached inside and did something that McCarter could not discern. Then he simply tossed the disk to the ground.

McCarter flinched. Nothing happened; no explosion came.

"We may go now." Peng shrugged. "You may drive over it."

"You certain of that?" Hawkins asked as McCarter, Peng and Manning climbed back into the truck.

"I am sure," Peng declared. "It is harmless now."

McCarter wasn't certain, but he thought he heard Hawkins let out the breath he'd been holding after they safely drove over the first clump of mines.

What could have made for relatively slow going proved not to be too bad, with Peng quickly and quietly defusing each set of mines when he reached whatever count he was keeping in his head. Phoenix Force, with their largely in-scrutable guide leading the way, managed to traverse most of the access road without incident. Peng finally called a halt, not more than one hundred yards after defusing what he said was the last set of mines, as they reached a sharp curve in the road. The dirt trail narrowed significantly here.

"We must get out here," Peng said. He climbed out and McCarter followed him. "Beyond this narrow part," Peng went on, "one half kilometer, is an opening. Machine-gun nests are there. The drug plant is beyond. It is surrounded by a pit dug for the length of its perimeter. Take the path on the right. There is a footbridge. Turn left when you see the shoe."

"The shoe? Peng, what—" McCarter started to say.

Peng nodded and, without another word, melted into the trees.

"Where's he going?" Calvin James asked as he walked up, carrying his Kalashnikov.

"Bloody well wish I knew," McCarter said. He swore softly to himself.

"Are we blown?" Encizo asked. Phoenix Force, weapons ready, assembled around McCarter, careful to watch the trees around them.

"We could be," McCarter said as he shook his head, "but I'm going to trust my gut on this. We go, lads. Keep it tight."

With McCarter in the lead, Phoenix Force moved out.

The reached the clearing Peng had warned them about. It was not just a natural clearing; it was a kill zone, from which brush and cover had been removed to give the machine gunners a clear field of fire. Encizo, with a pair of field glasses from his gear, paused to get a close-up look at the enemy.

"I've got two… no, three men in each nest." The machine-gun emplacements were pits dug into the ground, around which sandbags had been piled. Each nest also had a corrugated-metal roof set on four stout posts, probably to keep the rain off the guards inside.

"How alert?" McCarter asked.

"Not very," Encizo said. "But moving around enough. They'll see us if we try to rush them, I'd bet."

"Then subtle is out," McCarter said. He looked at Manning. The big Canadian nodded and deployed his 40 mm grenade launcher.

"Ready," Manning said.

"Do it," McCarter ordered.

As the other Phoenix Force team members spread out and took combat positions, Manning targeted the first machine-gun nest. He slowly and carefully checked his range and his angle…and then pulled the trigger.

The grenade was away and Manning was already reloading the launcher before the first round hit. When the explosions came, they ripped apart the machine-gun nests from within. Manning fired twice more, making sure, obliterating the nests and taking the gunners inside with them.

"Well, they'll sure know we're comin'," Hawkins drawled.

"Double time, men," McCarter said. "Let's get to that facility and keep the pressure on."

They found the path on the right. There was another path on the left. Both appeared to lead to the perimeter pit around the crumbling, two-story stone building sprawled ahead of them under the trees. From where they stood, the members of Phoenix Force could also see camouflage netting spread over trees and on posts jutting from the roof of the building, obscuring its outline from overhead observation by plane or satellite. Even had they not known what was likely inside, it would have been obvious to the Stony Man commandos that something of great importance was being protected.

A sign at the head of each path bore a crude painted image of an explosion with a stick-figure body in the air.

"More land mines?" Hawkins asked.

"Let's hope Peng knew what he was talking about," James said.

McCarter stepped onto the path first. He was the team leader; the decision to follow through with the mission, despite Peng's sudden disappearance, was his. If the man had walked them into a trap, McCarter would damned well be the one to trip it.

They followed the path without incident. The cover of the scrub and trees closed in again when they got closer to the building. The footbridge was an extremely heavy affair made of two shaved trees and a series of plywood planks. They crossed this and found another fork in the path.

"I'll be damned," McCarter said.

He was looking at an old, rusted metal shoe the size of a Volkswagen. The heavy three-dimensional sculpture bore several holes from where it had rusted completely through in the Burmese climate. The logo of a famous sports company was just barely visible in relief on its side.

"Well, we know what the building used to be," McCarter said. "Bloody sneaker factory. The only question is why the Farm had no record of this place being here."

"Might have been off the books," James said. "Sweatshop kind of deal. From the look of this thing—" he nodded to the metal sneaker "—it's been closed for a couple decades, at least. Could be the company cut its losses, or closed the plant out of political pressure, and then did its best to forget it was here."

"Political pressure?" Hawkins asked.

"You know, man," James said. "Kids making sneakers at three cents an hour, that kind of thing."

"Right." Hawkins nodded.

"Well, the only business we're interested in is drugs, lads," McCarter said. "Come on. Let's follow Peng's directions." They turned left, spreading out as they headed down the path. The former shoe factory loomed above them now. It seemed strangely quiet.

"Funny that those explosions didn't alert them to—" Encizo started to say.

The wail of a hand-cranked siren somewhere inside the factory cut him off.

"You were saying, man?" James grinned, hefting his Kalashnikov.

"Now, lads!" McCarter said. "We breach the factory and take them down, on the double!"

The men of Phoenix Force wasted no time. McCarter let the much larger Manning shoulder his way through the access door ahead of them, smashing aside the old, rusted door as if it weren't there. Men inside were running this way and that through the corridors, carrying weapons, shouting to each other, but unaware that the enemy had already found their doorstep.

"Is that…?" Encizo asked.

"Christ," McCarter said. "They're shouting in Russian."

The first of the armed men rounded the corner and faced McCarter and his team in the corridor. He paused, looking confused. The members of Phoenix Force were wearing surplus Russian military camouflage and carrying AK-pattern weapons. The guard struggled to reconcile these familiar touches with the fact that he had never seen their faces before.

McCarter raised his Kalashnikov, ending the man's confusion. "On the ground!" he ordered.

Screaming something in Russian, the man brought up his own AK. McCarter shot him. "Go, go, go," the Briton ordered.

Phoenix Force split at the end of the corridor. Manning and Encizo went left, while James, McCarter and Hawkins went right. The corridors in which they traveled were perimeter hallways, skirting what would be the big, open factory floor at the center of the old plant. It was a common enough layout for an industrial facility of this type, and there was no reason the Triangle would have changed it significantly.

They encountered several more men in Russian military fatigues, carrying standard-issue Russian weapons. Surprise, and the initiative they had seized, served Phoenix Force well. They easily met and gunned down the resistance offered, sweeping into the factory floor almost simultaneously from two sides.

"Everybody down!" McCarter ordered.

Encizo repeated the order in Spanish, for all the good that was likely to do here in Burma. There were workers, mostly old men and women, moving in and around the stations spread out on the old shoe factory floor. McCarter recognized some of it as chemicals and distillation equipment; they were refining heroin here, if the smell was any indication.

"Masks on, lads," McCarter said. Stray gunfire had already hit several of the countless kilos stacked here and there on tables and on the floor among the distillation, refining and weighing equipment. "Check for hostiles!"

Hawkins secured the prisoners, herding them all to one side of the heroin plant. Manning and Encizo began checking the floor, moving in and around and behind the equipment there, checking for guards in hiding.

"Anything?" McCarter asked.

"Clear here," Encizo reported.

"Clear," Manning said.

"I don't get it," James said, looking at some of the tubes and burners arranged on the nearest table. "They're running the heroin from Thailand and it's getting here. What are they doing with it here? It was already processed."

McCarter looked over some of the chemicals, household and otherwise, sitting on another table. He picked up a carton of baking soda and put it down. There were canisters of household cleaners, some more deadly than others. There were even bags of sugar.

"Stepping on it," McCarter concluded. "Refining the quality product even more for their rich customers…and lacing the junk with all manner of filler for the poor ones. The rough-processed heroin is shipped here, and then split into different grades of product. Probably distributed accordingly."

"There's…a lot here," James whistled softly. He was right; the sheer volume of heroin here was staggering.

"I've got a trapdoor here," Manning announced. He had found a wooden door in the floor near the center of the factory area.

"All right," McCarter said. "T.J., guard the prisoners. Gary, you're with me. Calvin, Rafe, watch our backs up here." He motioned to the door. Manning drew his .357 Magnum Desert Eagle, setting his Kalashnikov on the floor by the door. McCarter covered the door with his own rifle as Manning reached out with his free hand to yank it open.

"Don't shoot!" someone screamed. "Don't shoot! Don't shoot! I have no weapon!"

Manning reached down with his free hand and yanked the man bodily from the small room dug out beneath the factory floor. McCarter could see several computers arrayed on a folding table inside. The fumes from the generator running somewhere below were very strong.

"Bloody hell," McCarter said, waving one hand in front of his face to dispel the exhaust cloud. "It's a wonder he's even breathing."

Manning put his Desert Eagle to the man's forehead. McCarter looked him over. He was small and balding, with a pot belly. He had the dark features of an Indian and spoke with an Indian accent.

"Who are you?" McCarter demanded.

"Ranjit," the man said quickly. "I am Ranjit Khing.

Please, I am only the…the bookkeeper! Yes, that is what you would call me. I only keep the books."

"Books?" McCarter asked.

Ranjit gestured to the computers still running below. "Books," he said simply. "For the…the money. The shipments. Everything."

"Well, then," McCarter said. "We'll have lots to talk about, won't we?"

"Are you out of your minds?" Khing screamed. "Do you have any idea whom you attack when you attack this place? From whose house you steal gold? From whose mouth you steal bread? Oh, we are doomed! Doomed! All of us!"

"Gary," McCarter said, "I have a feeling we're going to have a present to e-mail Barb."

The big Canadian smiled.

CHAPTER SEVEN

The Southern Tier Expressway, New York

"How many hours are we going to have to sit here?" Lyons growled.

"Shouldn't be more than a couple," Schwarz said. "Barb said the NetScythe gave us a window of six to eight hours, max."

"Which means it might be six to eight hours."

"Well, sure." Schwarz grinned. "But doesn't it sound better when I say, 'a couple'?"

"There are days," Lyons said, sipping from a foam cup of fast-food coffee, "that I genuinely hate you."

"That's part of my charm." Schwarz smiled innocently.

Their Suburban was parked in a gravel-covered parking area off the side of New York State Route 17. The highway was the longest in the state, stretching nearly four hundred miles across eleven counties. Parts of it, Lyons had discovered firsthand, were also practically in Braille, as the truck bounded over bump after bump in a seemingly endless series of patched seams of asphalt.

"Any word from our friends up the road?" Blancanales asked from the seat behind Schwarz.

"Nothing yet." Schwarz shook his head. "Don't worry, they won't let us down. I think they think we're an elite counterterrorist unit on the lookout for religious extremists carrying a nuclear bomb. They're highly motivated."

"Gee," Lyons growled, "I wonder how they might have gotten that impression? Could it be that was the exact line of bullshit you fed them?"

"Uh, well," Schwarz said, "I mean, I might have had someone from Hal's office call to confirm…"

"I thought so." Lyons shook his head. The "friends up the road" were a contingent of state police, who had been drafted to serve as lookouts. It took only a call to the Farm and another from the Farm to the closest troopers' barracks to make the arrangements. Able Team had needed another set of eyes, but Lyons didn't want to split the trio in the face of what might be a fairly serious firefight, so they'd opted for a little local law-enforcement cooperation. As they couldn't simply tell the state police the details of their mission, Schwarz had felt free to invent a fanciful cover story that would get the cops' attention nonetheless.

"All right, let's go over it once more," Lyons said. "When we get the signal, the state cops will divert traffic so we don't have to worry about any civilians blundering into the way. Pol, that will be your cue. You'll drive the Suburban down and block the highway."

"I will, in turn," Schwarz said, almost singsong, "leave my position in the drainage ditch down there when they get here—" he pointed to the side of the highway, where there was a ditch large enough for him to fit into "—and neutralize the van in the rear, boxing in the van in the middle."

"Which leaves the middle van for me," Lyons said.

"Our objective is simply to stop these vehicles and neutralize anyone inside. We'll take prisoners if we can."

"If they let us," Schwarz put in.

"If they let us," Lyons reported. "We have the list of distribution points according to the map, and according to Barb, NetScythe is processing that data along with whatever else it's looking at from up there, so if there's better intel to be had, we'll have it. Assume, then, that the reason we're doing this is to damage the Triangle, and nothing more. Three vans' worth of heroin and meth amphetamine is no small thing—it will hurt them, and hurt them badly, to lose it."

"We should probably use the breathing masks," Blancanales said. "Three burning trucks' worth of drugs will put off a lot of fumes."

"Good idea," Lyons said. "When the signal comes, masks on. Then we rock and roll."

"That's what I've always liked about you, Ironman," Schwarz needled. "So many layers of subtlety and complexity."

"Eat me," Lyons shot back.

"You see?" Schwarz turned to Blancanales. "He makes my point for me."

The walkie-talkie sitting on the dashboard crackled to life. "Big Apple One to Deep Dark, come in."

"You gave them code names?" Lyons asked.

"It seemed like the thing to do," Schwarz said sheepishly.

"Big Apple One to Deep Dark, urgent," the voice came again.

"Uh, Deep Dark is you, Ironman," Schwarz said.

Lyons shot him a venomous look but picked up the radio. He sighed. "Deep Dark to Big Apple One, you're… five by five." He stopped to roll his eyes and shot Schwarz another look of pure evil. "Go ahead."

"Three identical panel vans just passed this location," the state trooper reported. "Traveling at a high rate of speed. There are a couple of passenger cars ahead of them, but not more than two, and those have a pretty good lead."

"Okay, Big Apple One," Lyons said. "Commence your roadblock. We will advise."

"Good luck, sir," the trooper radioed back. "And God bless you, sir."

"Thank you, trooper." He looked back at Schwarz, started to say something and stopped. Finally he looked to Blancanales and then back to Schwarz. "All right," he said. "Show's on."

Lyons grabbed his Daewoo USAS-12 shotgun, while Schwarz drew his 93-R and checked the 20-round magazine. Then Schwarz scurried down to get in position in the drainage ditch, while Lyons moved to crouch behind one of the large oil-drum trash barrels positioned at intervals around the parking area. It wasn't a perfect hiding spot, but he only had to stay out of sight long enough for the vans to stop.

Blancanales rolled the big Suburban down and into position after the last of the civilian cars went past. Lyons was grateful that there would be no complications with innocent motorists caught up in their impromptu roadblock. Things were about to get hot enough.

Blancanales took up a position behind the engine block of the Suburban. He held an M-4 assault rifle in his hands, part of the standard gear Able carried with them in the vehicle. "I'm ready," he said. His words were carried over the earbud transceiver link to the other two.

"Ready here," Schwarz said.

"Good to go," Lyons acknowledged. "Put your masks on."

They didn't have to wait long. The first of the three

panel vans, when it saw the Suburban parked across the road, screeched to a halt on abused brakes. The second vehicle very nearly rear-ended it, but the driver managed to avert the crash. The third van slowed and it looked as if the driver of that vehicle was considering turning around completely.

Schwarz sprang into action, jumping from his drainage ditch with his machine pistol blazing. The compact weapon belched flame as he triggered a series of 3-round bursts, blowing the tires front and back on the third van. The driver tried to floor it anyway, his rims gouging the pavement and sending a shower of sparks to the rear. Schwarz dumped several bursts through the van's grille, emptying his 20-round magazine. Something critical finally gave. The engine belched smoke and the van stopped moving.

Lyons was up and moving, too, his automatic shotgun blasting the tires of the middle van. Blancanales had already done as much for the lead vehicle.

"Federal agents!" Lyons bellowed at the top of his lungs. "You will all step out of the vehicles with your hands held high! Make no sudden moves!"

The answering automatic gunfire from inside the vans was all the confirmation the men of Able Team required. Lyons kept running, throwing himself up against the side of the panel van that was his target. The gunner made the mistake of leaning out his open window to try to get a shot. Lyons leveled the Daewoo and hosed the man off the side of the van, dropping him out the window onto the pavement.

Blancanales's M-4 was stuttering now, its unmistakable sound bringing to Lyons's mind memories of battles past. A pair of shooters was attempting to make a run around the tail of the lead van, but Blancanales was on them. He plugged one with a neat head shot and raked the second with a short burst to the chest as that man brought up an Uzi. The old Israeli submachine gun stuttered and fired a blast harmlessly into the pavement. Lyons was grateful the stream of rounds had not gone into the air. Bullets fired into the air had to come down again, and he didn't relish the idea of peppering the countryside with stray shots, even those whose energy had largely been expended.

Blancanales ripped open the passenger door of his target van and disappeared inside. There was a series of shots as holes were punched through the van's metal skin from the inside out. A man screamed. Finally the rear doors of the van were kicked open and Blancanales fell out amid an avalanche of plastic-wrapped kilos of heroin. A few of these burst when they hit the ground, leaving clouds of white powder to linger in the still New York air. As Lyons watched, Blancanales turned and emptied the magazine of his M-4, obviously finishing whomever he'd been fighting inside.

Schwarz, meanwhile, was busy firing his way through another 20-round magazine in his machine pistol. Lyons checked to make sure both he and Blancanales had their targets well in hand. Then he reached out and, holding the mighty automatic shotgun with one hand, wrenched open the side door of the van.

There was a man inside, pressed against the kilos of heroin packed inside. He had been hit by a stray shot, perhaps even one fired by the dead man in the passenger seat of the van. With his left hand, he struggled to bring up a stainless-steel Browning Hi-Power.

"Save it," Lyons growled. He reached out and simply snatched the gun away. Dropping the hammer and snapping on the safety, he crouched on one knee while keeping the wounded man covered with the USAS-12. He set the shotgun on the ground, grabbed the man inside the van, and yanked him out much as he had yanked away the pistol.

The prisoner was a tattooed-biker type, probably one of whoever was left of the group they'd hit. Lyons threw him to the ground. "Now that we've got the introductions out of the way," he said, "let's see just how much information you might be able to give me."

The ratcheting noise was what saved his life. As he heard the distinct metal click-click-click of the mechanism, Lyons took a step back. That was when the wounded man on the ground lunged up and toward him, a very large Spanish *navaja* fighting knife held in his hand. He hit Lyons with all the force he could muster, driving the air out of the big cop's chest and throwing him to the ground.

The ground is deadly. The thought echoed through Lyons's head as he realized he was flat on his back with a knife-wielding attacker on top of him. He could expect, at any moment, to feel the sewing-machine stabs of repeated thrusts to his gut as the biker, most likely a convict with more than a little experience in prison shankings, left him dead or, if he was lucky, maimed and wearing a colostomy bag for the rest of his life.

Even as he hit the pavement, he was rolling, letting the Daewoo go and wrenching his attacker off him, rolling him over. The knife came at his face, but Lyons grabbed it with one hand and began twisting it to the side. The knifer grunted and looked up at him, his craggy features twisted with hate. Lyons got a knee on his wounded arm and, while holding the knife arm, reached under his jacket and pulled out the Colt Python.

"I," he said, pistol-whipping the man with the butt of the gun, "have had…about enough…of knives this time out!" He punctuated each part of his sentence with another blow of the weapon, finally managing to knock the biker into unconsciousness. The knife fell to the pavement.

Lyons sat, breathing heavily, the Python still in his fist. "Clear," he said.

"Clear," Schwarz returned.

"Clear—" Blancanales started to say.

That was when the Suburban roared to life.

Somebody they'd missed was now behind the wheel of the big SUV that was Able Team's transportation. The truck nearly mowed down Blancanales. He managed to dive to the side, rolling and bringing up his M-4, raking the driver's side of the truck with a single short burst. The truck slowed, the big engine's growl dying back as whatever pressure had been on the accelerator was suddenly released. The Suburban rolled to a stop nose to nose with the first, crippled van.

"Ironman, you aren't having a good day, are you?" Schwarz offered a hand, standing over Lyons. Lyons took it and almost pulled his partner to the ground. He holstered his Python.

"Very funny," he said. He looked around at the damage done. "Pol?" he asked.

"Here," Blancanales said. He was busy at the Suburban but his voice was crystal-clear in Lyons's transceiver. "I'm okay."

Lyons bent, picked up the *navaja* and examined it.

"Nice knife," Schwarz said. "You seem to be attracting them these days."

"Well, maybe it will make a decent good-luck charm, then," Lyons said. He folded the knife and slipped it into his pocket.

The two men checked each van as they went. Some of the heroin had been shot up badly; there was white powder all over the road. The gunmen who had driven and ridden shotgun in the vehicles all appeared to be bikers or at least had the look and the body ink to fit the part. More important, they were jockeying panel vans full of a staggering amount of illegal narcotics and carrying illegal weapons, which they had fired at men who identified themselves as federal agents.

"Pretty open-and-shut case, huh?" Gadgets asked.

"I was just thinking that." Lyons nodded.

They found Blancanales pulling the dead man out of the Suburban.

"Well," Schwarz said, "there goes our deposit fee." The rounds from Blancanales's M-4 had taken the would-be car thief in the head. The damage from 5.56 mm rounds inside the cab was minimal, but driver-side and passenger-side windows were broken out and there was blood all over the cab. Lyons could see, as he stuck his head through the opening where the driver-side window had been, that the steering-wheel column collar had been knocked off.

"Hot-wired it," he said. "Bastard."

"Our automotive karma catching up with us," Schwarz ventured.

"Yeah, whatever," he said. "Get on the horn with the Farm and make arrangements for a new vehicle. Pol, contact the state troopers and spin them a convincing yarn."

"I could do that," Schwarz offered.

"I said convincing," Lyons said.

"Ouch." Schwarz grabbed his chest as if pained.

Lyons ignored that. "Make sure they know we've got a righteous shoot here, but that it's a mess. We're going to need wreckers in here to move the vans, get the highway open again. And we need to go through channels to secure these drugs."

"Damn, that's a lot," Schwarz said. "It's going to be awfully tempting."

"Tempting?" Lyons said.

"I believe," Blancanales said, "he means it's very likely a quantity like that might not find its way, in its entirety, to law-enforcement evidence lockers."

"Are you saying the cops are corrupt?" Lyons, ex-LAPD himself, bristled at that.

"No," Schwarz said, "but think about it, Ironman. How many millions of dollars are we looking at? That's a pretty amazing amount. It's going to be awfully hard to keep everybody honest in the chain of custody."

"That's a good point," Lyons said. He had moved his breathing mask down. Now he pulled it back over his face. "Keep your masks on," he said.

"Uh-oh," Blancanales said.

"What 'uh-oh'?" Schwarz asked. "Don't tell me he's going to—"

"He's going to," Blancanales said firmly.

Lyons went to the rear of the Suburban. From the gear locker in the back he removed a canvas messenger bag.

"Uh…" Schwarz said.

"Yeah," Blancanales said.

"Uh, Ironman? That's the bag of grenades. Carl? Carl, I know you can hear me."

Lyons ignored his partners. He rummaged around in the bag until he found what he was looking for: a half-dozen AN-M14 TH3 incendiary grenades. He walked calmly from van to van, pulling the pins on three of the grenades at a time and tossing them into the vehicles.

"Holy—"

The three men hit the ground, Lyons last and almost reluctantly. When the incendiary charges blew, each van became a miniature hellscape, a furnace on flat tires that burned like a hundred suns. The Stony Man commandos were immediately plunged into a cloud of toxic gases from the burning drugs. Lyons took a deep breath in his mask; he was well protected.

"As I was saying," he said calmly. "We're going to need wreckers in here to move the vans, get the highway open again."

"We should warn them that the vans are on fire," Blancanales said.

"Nah," Schwarz said. "Probably be puddles of liquid metal by the time they get here."

"Then arrange for mops," Lyons said. "But we need to get this cleaned up. A replacement vehicle is top priority. I don't want to ride in that one."

Schwarz made a disgusted noise. "Yeah, Pol," he said. "Thanks a lot, man."

Blancanales chuckled. "You would rather I let him steal it?"

"Couldn't you have, I don't know, karate-chopped him through the open window or something? Dragged him out without killing him while riding on the still-moving vehicle in spectacular fashion?"

"Who do I look like," Blancanales asked, "Carl?"

"Good point," Schwarz said.

"I hate you both," Lyons muttered.

CHAPTER EIGHT

Moscow, Russia

"Bear and his team are working on decoding the data you uploaded," Price told McCarter over his secure satellite phone. The Briton stood on a small side street from which he could just see Saint Basil's Cathedral. Around him, Moscow, the largest city in Europe and capital of the Russian Federation, pulsed with life in all its corrupt, decaying, decrepit glory. The Russian people did their best to go about their daily business in a country alive with, simultaneously, dynamic hope for the future and the unctuous odor of past political dread. There was no doubt about it; Moscow was unique, and uniquely fascinating. McCarter did not believe he would ever feel truly comfortable there.

"And Ranjit Khing?" McCarter asked.

"Secured by some cooperative CIA assets in Yangon," Price said. "They say his predictions have become more and more dire."

McCarter chuckled at that. After they had captured the expatriate Indian, who turned out to be an accountant and sometime-hacker with a history of wire fraud and embezzlement in his native India, Ranjit had repeatedly and elaborately, as Hawkins had put it, "freaked out." He had gone on at great length about the mighty and unnamed individual whom they were "stealing from" in hitting the heroin plant in Burma, and had said that all their lives, including his own and those of his family, would be forfeit for this disgrace. The man had been on the verge of hysteria by the time they'd finally left him with Peng, who had reappeared as mysteriously as he had disappeared, once the fighting was over. The man would offer no explanation for his behavior and McCarter did not press the issue. He sensed something was going on here that was larger than it at first seemed.

"Bear says that Khing was good, but not exceptional," Price sent on. "He says Akira will have it sorted out reasonably soon, but wouldn't say how many hours he thought that meant." Uploading the data in the computers Ranjit Khing had been running was a simple enough matter, but the encrypted data would have to be carefully interpreted by Kurtzman's team to ensure it would not be destroyed as they attempted to access it.

"Fair enough," McCarter said, nodding even though she could not see him. He was hidden in the shadows of the alleyway, with the rest of Phoenix Force waiting in an old imported Land Rover they had rented at the airport. McCarter had spotted the old girl on the lot and insisted they have it; he had been secretly terrified they would end up traveling Moscow in an old Trabant.

As usual, the Farm's formidable political power, funding and computer expertise had resulted in a set of forged travel documents and diplomatic waivers for Phoenix Force and their equipment. Grimaldi was once again camped out at the airport, probably seeing if he could lay his mitts on an old Hind gunship or some other

Cold War military relic. It wasn't likely, despite the fact that so much old Soviet-era hardware had found its way to the international arms market. Here in Moscow, the climate was a curious mixture of the corrupt and the controlled, with Russian *mafiya* crime bosses in control of most of the country's urban centers. As the often cash-strapped Russian government struggled to fund its aging military, however, the supply of arms and matériel was drying up from secondhand and black market sources. The Russians were having trouble keeping their own fighter jets in the air, while their submarines and destroyers rusted away dockside.

These problems might explain why elements of the Russian military were guarding the Triangle drug plant in Burma. In the mop-up of the raid on the plant, Phoenix Force had transmitted digital pictures of the dead to the Farm. While many of the men could not be positively identified, a few profiles had come back. The men were active in the Russian military, not even black-bag operatives whose deaths had been faked. There was no plausible deniability here. Some element within the Russian military was actively working with the Triangle.

"What we *can* tell you, before Akira goes deeper into the data," Price said, "is that a lot of it details and confirms transfers of funds from Burma and financial entities with ties to Thailand."

"Transfers to whom? Can we verify that it's Katzev? Prove it?"

"Not yet," Price said. "We'll have to hack our way into that. But we do know that many of the transfers terminate with a set of accounts centralized in a single bank in Russia. That, as you know, is your initial target."

"Right," McCarter said. "Barb, you know this is likely to get…sticky."

"I know," Price said. "Do what you have to do. Just be aware that there are limits to what we can do to extract you if it goes really wrong."

"Meaning that if the Russians get their hooks on us and we've made too much of a mess, we're on our own."

"Essentially," Price said.

"Understood," McCarter said. "Let me know if you learn anything from the data. I'll be in touch."

"One more thing, David," Price said. "We intercepted an Interpol message not long ago. It seems operative Peng has gone missing."

"Our Peng?" McCarter asked.

"Yes," Price said. "One of our contacts in the Central Intelligence Agency verified for me that Peng is, at least part of the time, on the Interpol payroll. But just after he helped you he failed to report in. Nobody's seen him since."

"He was alive when we last saw him," McCarter said. "We left Khing with him, and we know Khing got where he was going, so those CIA chaps must have seen him, too."

"They did," Price said, "but not long thereafter, Peng dropped off the world."

"He did that during the mission, following some agenda of his own," McCarter said. "Or maybe just keeping his head down. I'd wager he'll turn up on his own."

"Possibly," Price said, "but he's never failed to check in before, from what I'm told. His superiors are concerned. I thought you'd want to know."

"Well, it's bloody unlikely we'll run across him here in Russia," McCarter said, "but he was a solid chap and I hope he comes out of it okay. Let me know if you hear one way or another."

"I will. Good hunting, David."

"Right-o," McCarter said, and hung up. He made his way back into the Land Rover and closed the door. It rattled.

"Careful on that side," Hawkins said from the driver's seat. 'I think that mirror's fixin' to come off."

"She'll hold together," McCarter said. "You hear me, old girl?" he muttered.

"What did Barb have to say?" Encizo asked.

"They're working on getting the dirt on Katzev, if he's in fact involved directly," McCarter said. "In the meantime, we're to proceed to the first target, identified by computer analysis of the data as the clearinghouse for most of the transfers. It's a privately owned bank here in Moscow." He rattled off the address, though of course the other team members had received the same briefing and were as aware of it as he was.

"Let's do it, then," James said.

"Onward, gentlemen," McCarter said.

The bank, which was not labeled and not open to the public, sat in the middle of a crowded block of old buildings with impressive stone architecture, not far from the Moskva River. There were two men in black, double-breasted suits and sunglasses, standing outside the double doors leading in.

"Well, that's subtle," James said.

"Might as well be the First Bank of Mafiya," Encizo said, nodding.

"We'll have to get inside and confirm," McCarter said. "The computer data points here, but we don't know for certain everyone inside is dirty."

"Sure looks that way," Encizo said.

"And I will be surprised very much if it's not that way," McCarter said. "But we will confirm nonetheless."

"Roger," Encizo said. The other team members sounded off in the affirmative.

"All right, here's what we'll do," McCarter said. "Gary, take the front. Introduce yourself, make friends and get past them. T.J., take the Rover 'round the opposite side of this block—see if you can find a rear entrance. Take Rafe with you. We'll motor down the end of the street, and Calvin and I will get out, then walk back up the block to follow Gary after he's made his introductions."

"Weapons?" James asked. Their rifles and other heavy weaponry were stowed in duffel bags in the back of the Land Rover.

"No way we can walk around with the rifles on the streets of Moscow," McCarter said. "It'll have to be handguns. Watch your backsides, lads."

"I'll go now," Manning said.

"Good luck, Gary," Encizo said.

GARY MANNING STEPPED out of the Land Rover and watched it drive away. The two men in front of the covert bank were probably watching him. They did not turn their heads and he could not see their eyes behind their sunglasses, but were he in their position, he'd watch anyone approaching on foot as Manning was doing now.

Sighing inwardly, he steeled himself for what he would have to do. There was no other way. He had to admit that sometimes McCarter's plans were a little less methodical than he would like, but they got results, and that was what mattered. That was what they had signed on to do, after all. Phoenix Force existed to take the fight to the enemy, an enemy that targeted the helpless and the innocent. The men of Phoenix Force, and of Stony Man Farm, took risks that others could not, and they did so willingly.

Now it was his turn.

Manning walked up to the two men, taking the steps two at a time. One them said something in Russian, most likely a warning. Manning gave the man his most innocent smile. He took a step closer; now he was within arm's reach.

One of the men reached into his jacket.

Manning lunged. He grabbed fistfuls of both men's shirts and neckties, flexing his big arms and slamming the two men together. Then he rammed them backward into the doors, knocking their skulls against the wood. One of them was still moving, dazed, so he pushed that one against the doors a third time. Then he released both men and let them collapse to the steps.

He tried the door. It was locked. He bent and searched first one guard, then the other, but found only walkie-talkies, handguns and a few personal items. Shrugging, he tossed the captured guns into one of the two planters framing the door. Then he drew his Desert Eagle, stepped back, targeted the lock and fired.

He followed the shot with a heavy kick that slammed the door inward. Then he was in and moving forward, the Desert Eagle in a two-handed grip, moving in a combat crouch that kept him stable, balanced and mobile while reducing his target profile.

The foyer was a lavish affair in marble, with two staircases leading up to right and left. Several men, shouting in Russian, were running down those steps with submachine guns in their hands.

Manning felt he just might be outgunned.

Breaking right and heading for the stairs, Manning emptied the magazine of his Desert Eagle toward the opposition, trying to keep their heads down. The enemy were doing their best to gun him down. Automatic gunfire ripped into the marble steps as he raced up them, reloading and triggering blast after blast. He made the top of the stairs and, confronted by two more men, did the only thing he could. He threw himself at them.

He hit them and rolled, taking their legs out from under them. As the three men struggled to right themselves, he grabbed a cut-down AK-74 from one of them as he threw a brutal hammer-fist blow into the face of the other. Then he slammed the wooden foregrip of the AK-74 across the temple of the other, knocking him cold.

He heard a woman scream in pain.

The shout had come from down the hallway. Shoving his Desert Eagle in his belt and cradling the captured AK-74, he scooped up a canvas bag of spare magazines that one of the downed men had been carrying. There was another scream. "I am encountering heavy resistance," he reported, trusting his earbud transceiver to carry his words to the rest of Phoenix Force. "Going to need backup."

"We're at the entrance," McCarter's voice came back to him. "We're coming in."

He found the door at the end of the corridor on that level. The woman on the other side of the door screamed again. Manning slammed his foot against the door once, twice, and a third time, feeling the wood give each time. Finally he managed to break it open.

The room was some kind of courtesy suite, decorated in lush, expensive furniture. A half-naked woman was lying on the bed, her lip bloody. Standing over her was a man in trousers and socks, stripped to the waist. He looked up at Manning as if seeing him for the first time. So intent had he been on beating the woman, apparently, that he'd taken little notice of the door being broken in. The man said something in Russian and lunged for the nightstand. Manning saw the Makarov pistol there before the man could reach it. He stepped in and clubbed the man with the AK-74, folding him over.

"Don't move," he told the woman on the bed. This scene

was a little too familiar for his tastes; he didn't want to risk a repeat of the incident with McCarter in Thailand.

"English," the woman said with a heavy accent. "I speak…I speak English. Please, I am only…only working, here. I am not *mafiya*. I want no part, any mafiya business."

Footsteps sounded in the corridor outside. "Don't shoot," McCarter's voice came in his ear and echoed outside. "It's us. The team has converged on your location, Gary."

"The men in this place," Manning said. "They're Russian *mafiya?* Criminals?"

"*Da.*" The woman nodded. She began swearing in Russian, unleashing a tirade that, could he understand it, Manning was certain would have made him blush. "Stinking pigs," she said in English. "They do not pay, and when I insist, they tell me, I pay instead." She spit on the unconscious Russian who had been beating her. "Give me his gun and I will shoot him with it."

"I don't think I had better do that," Manning said. He secured the Makarov and tucked it behind his belt. "Stay here," he told the hooker. "Don't leave this room until the shooting stops and stays stopped for a while. Then go home."

The woman was already bent over the unconscious man, riffling through his pockets. She found and emptied his wallet.

"Don't worry," she said. "I stay here. When he comes around again, I hit him with lamp." She indicated the very heavy lamp on the night table. Manning imagined that would probably kill him. Looking at her swollen, bleeding face and the bruises that were still livid on the rest of her body, he couldn't say he blamed her. She caught him looking at her and almost looked self-conscious for a moment.

"I'm sorry," Manning said. He opened the door, which was now sitting crooked on its hinges. "Get out of here when it's over," he repeated. "Don't stop to look. Don't come back. I was never here."

"*Da, da,*" the woman said, nodding. "You help me, I help you. Go, man who was not here. I say nothing."

Manning backed out of the room and shut the door behind him as best he could.

"I've got confirmation of *mafiya* presence in the building," he said, probably unnecessarily if the rest of the team was listening to his conversation.

"Copy that," McCarter said. Manning could hear gunfire from somewhere in the building. It sounded faint.

"Hawkins here," T.J. said. "I'm on a lower level, accessed through a door behind the left staircase. We've got a computer room down here. There's a couple of shooters holed up on this level, too. Calvin's taken a round."

"I'm fine," James said quickly. "Grazed my forearm. Nothing serious."

"Copy," McCarter said. "Gary, form up on T.J.'s position. I'll join you. Rafe, cover the lobby, watch our backs."

"No problem," Encizo said.

Manning stepped over the bodies of the men he'd knocked out. There were a couple of corpses in the foyer now. Manning recognized one of them as one of the guards from outside. Apparently he'd come dashing in and tried to kill one of the Phoenix Force team members, who'd stopped him. Something about that bothered Manning. He'd had it within his power to take both men out entirely earlier…but of course that was not how Phoenix Force did things. They were not assassins. They did not simply kill everyone and let God sort them out. They would no more kill two men guarding a building like this than they would kill two people at random walking down the street outside. Without confirmation of criminal activity, without a real threat to a team member, there simply was no justification for murder.

Manning shook his head. They played by rules. They followed a moral code. And while they were pragmatists, particularly in the realm of combat, there were principles they followed and things they would not do. That was what set them apart from the enemy, no matter how ruthless Phoenix Force was forced to be in pursuit of that enemy.

The chatter of gunfire broke him from his thoughts. He approached with caution. Calvin James had ripped off part of the hem of his shirt and wrapped it around his left forearm. If the lack of blood was any indication, the wound truly was not bad. James, Hawkins and McCarter were crouched against the wall, occasionally trading fire through an open corridor that led to the computer facility beyond. There were two gunners hiding behind a metal desk and occasionally firing from it. On this side of the wall, the Phoenix Force members were sharing the space available with a large metal filing cabinet.

"Dug in well, they are," McCarter said, firing a few times with his Browning Hi-Power before ducking back behind the cover of the wall.

"They can't last forever," Hawkins said.

"Neither can we," McCarter pointed out. "We've already touched off a small war in downtown Moscow. We need to get out of here before the Moscow police show up."

"Right, that," James said. "International incident. Plausible deniability. Us being boned. All that stuff."

Manning nodded. "Then I will push them out."

The big Canadian grabbed the filing cabinet, lifted it

and moved toward the doorway. He waited for a lull in the sporadic shooting and then hurled the entire cabinet through the corridor opening. He jumped in after it with his Desert Eagle in his fist.

The terrific crash of the file cabinet against the desk beyond was followed by the mighty booming of the Desert Eagle. The weapon thundered twice, then a third time and then a fourth and fifth. Finally, Manning's voice sounded in his team members' ears.

"It's clear. Come ahead."

Several of the computers had taken gunfire. A few were operational. James sat behind one of these, removed a USB cable from his pocket and connected his secure satellite phone to the computers. He dialed the Farm and presumably waited through a series of cutouts while the connection was established.

"I'll see if Bear and company can get in, and then see what they can do while they're poking around." James nodded to the computers.

"Search them," McCarter said, pointing to the two dead men on the floor.

"I'll do it," Manning said. *If I'm going to shoot them,* he thought, *I had better be able to look at them.* Even given as much death and combat as he had seen, he did not wish to take it for granted. He had no desire to lose his soul as part of the battle Phoenix Force waged. He'd long since come to understand that if he did lose some part of himself, it would be his fault and not that of his teammates. He could not blame the missions they chose to take, and certainly not the rules of engagement under which they fought.

He found a Personal Data Assistant on one of the dead men. Picking it up and switching it on, he waited while it displayed a welcome screen. Then he thumbed through the text messages and e-mails on the PDA. His Russian was not exactly stellar; they would need a translator to see if anything in the device was more than just dating games and diary entries.

Scrolling through the calendar datebook entries, however, Manning found something he could understand.

"David," he said. "Look at this."

McCarter took the PDA and scanned it. "That," he said, "looks like a reference to Katzev, doesn't it?"

"This man had an appointment with Katzev today?"

"Or Katzev's people." McCarter nodded. "Come on, lads, there's no time to waste."

"Why?" Manning asked. "What are we going to do?"

"We're going to keep that appointment," McCarter said.

CHAPTER NINE

Buffalo, New York

The trip to Buffalo had put Carl Lyons in a foul mood, as far as Herman Schwarz was concerned. The electronics expert and veteran warrior could understand that; Lyons owed Thawan for a crack in the face, and the Able Team Leader was not one to forget debts like that. It didn't help that the first half of the trip had been made in their damaged Suburban, before they could arrange to replace it with another rental SUV.

"I see Buffalo hasn't exactly thrived since our last visit," Schwarz offered, staring out the window.

"How would we know?" Lyons shot back. "All we ever see are the seediest parts of every city we visit."

"Why, Carl, are you saying you'd like more time to see the sights?" Schwarz teased. "Maybe we could take a special trip over to Niagara Falls. I hear it's popular with honeymooners."

"Can the chatter, Gadgets," Lyons said. "What's the rundown on the latest tourism jewel we visit?"

"Pretty standard, really," Schwarz said, becoming

serious, sensing he would not be able to break Lyons out of his foul humor. "I've been looking through the intelligence data the Farm sent to our phones. The distribution point corresponds to an address cross-checked and confirmed by NetScythe's analysis. Thermal imaging shows a huge concentration of human activity there."

"Not normal activity?"

"Not at all," Schwarz said. "It's an industrial address, yet another warehouse in what must be the endless chain of warehouses we spend our days shooting apart."

Lyons snorted at that. Schwarz was glad; perhaps he was getting through, after all.

"If it's a distribution point, a link in the chain that was to receive some of the shipment brought along that route, then they'll be divvying it up, maybe stepping on it or refining it further. There'll be personnel to do the sorting, maybe a chemist or two if they're altering the drugs," Blancanales said. "There'll be guards to watch those people, because the Triangle won't trust their workers."

"And if what we've seen so far holds to type," Lyons said, "they'll be running some other kind of operation, too, to cover the drug distribution. Piggybacking some sort of bootleg retail on the deal, to cover the drug traffic."

"We could be dealing with a lot of innocents, then," Schwarz said. "Bad for us."

"Bad for us." Lyons nodded. "So we'll have to be careful."

"You want to do the usual thing?" Schwarz asked. "Burst in, bust the place up?"

"No," Lyons said. "I think it might be time for a little finesse."

"He must mean you," Schwarz said to Blancanales.

They found the warehouse was surrounded by several other prefabricated steel structures just like it, in a neighborhood just as seedy as Lyons had described. Lyons parked the new Suburban rental across the street and down the block a bit, where they would have a good vantage point to observe Blancanales's run.

"Copacetic?" Lyons asked Blancanales.

"Of course," the Politician said, making sure his Beretta 92-F was secure in his waistband under his jacket. "I'll just go in there and sweet-talk them all."

"We don't even know who 'them' is, necessarily," Lyons said.

"No," Blancanales said, "but I can guess. If they're using a lot of labor, they'll be using a lot of illegal labor. And even this far north, there are plenty of Hispanics who don't have papers."

"Papers…" Lyons said. "Pol, are you talking about green cards?"

Blancanales grinned at him.

"Who are you today?" Schwarz asked.

"INS." Blancanales grinned again, wider this time, showing white, even teeth.

"Oh, this is going to be good." Schwarz smiled.

Blancanales made his way across the street. There wasn't much traffic. He walked right up to the main door of the warehouse—or rather, the only door that wasn't a loading dock or overhead slider—and rapped on it. He knocked again when it took a while to get an answer. His earbud transceiver transmitted his voice and the sounds around him to Lyons and Schwarz.

"What do you want?" someone asked from the other side of the door. The speaker had a Spanish accent.

"I need you to let me in, man," Blancanales said conspiratorially. Schwarz could hear that he'd emphasized his own Hispanic accent to establish an instant psychological rapport with the man. "I'm INS. Immigration, man. But listen, I don't want to roust anybody. I just want to help out." Blancanales would be flashing the Justice Department credentials with which Brognola had supplied Able Team's members. To the average nervous illegal alien, one federal badge and ID would look much like any other. At least, that was the theory under which Blancanales was operating. Schwarz hoped it proved successful.

Right now the doorman would be getting nervous. He'd understand the dangers of an INS raid, but he'd also know quite rightly that any government agent walking into that warehouse was going to see something illegal going on. Whether it was the workers, the cover merchandise or the drugs themselves, the poor guard working the door was having one hell of a dilemma forced on him.

"Listen, man," Blancanales said soothingly, "I know the score. My department, they want me to make a show of rousting the business down here, right? I figure… I figure we can help each other." His words held just the right note. Schwarz thought it funny that the same principle the Triangle used to hide its operations was being used, in this small way, right here and now. No one would believe an INS agent who appeared from nowhere and claimed only to wish to help the poor, mistreated workers inside the warehouse. If that same INS agent appeared out of nowhere and appeared to be fishing for a bribe while covering up for a job he didn't intend to do, well…people believed something like that far more readily.

"Tragic, what humanity has come to on a societal level," Schwarz commented out loud.

"Cram it, Gadgets," Lyons growled.

Schwarz sighed. It was going to be a long mission, at this rate.

"What is it you want?" the door guard was asking Blancanales.

"Just let me in, man," Blancanales said. "My boss could be watching me. He spot-checks me all the time. You know how it is."

"Uh…yes," the guard said. Clearly he didn't, but Blancanales would pretend he didn't notice that.

"Just let me come in, rap with you folks a while, and then leave. I'll claim I saw everybody's paperwork in order. I won't look too closely at whatever you are doing in there, and everybody'll be happy. Maybe you could, I don't know, make a donation to my widows-and-orphans fund."

"Your…what?"

"You know, man," Blancanales said. "Maybe you… make it worth my while, you know? I ain't greedy."

"Wait here." There was a long pause.

"Either he's blown," Lyons said, "or they're doing something. Maybe hiding all the guns. Trying to make the place look a little more reputable."

Finally the door guard said, "Come inside." Through the earbud transceiver link, Lyons and Schwarz could hear the door being shut and locked behind Blancanales.

"Okay, he's in," Lyons said.

"Now it gets good." Schwarz nodded.

"Just take me on the nickel tour, man," Blancanales was saying. "I won't make any trouble. Maybe if there's somebody around here who handles petty cash, that kind of thing…"

Schwarz couldn't help but chuckle at Blancanales's wheedling. "He'll walk out of there and make a profit to boot," he said.

"We don't call him 'Politician' for nothing," Lyons noted.

They listened as Blancanales was ushered quickly in and out of whatever the main area of the place might be. There was a lot of ambient noise.

"Is that…sewing machines?" Schwarz asked.

"I think it might be," Lyons said.

"Sewing machines," Blancanales said, hearing their questions through the transceiver concealed in his ear. "What are you running, some sort of clothing factory here? Good business, clothing."

"Smart aleck," Lyons muttered.

"Hey, check it out," Blancanales said. "Gucci? Man, that's some fine stuff. And these are…well, I'm not expert on jeans, but these look expensive. And I know these jackets cost a bundle. Pretty diverse bunch of brand names you handle here. Good stuff."

"It's a damned counterfeit-label sweatshop," Lyons said. "Handbags and goddamned polo shirts with alligators on them."

"Had to be something." Schwarz shrugged.

"Well," Blancanales said, "I've seen enough. Say, what's through this door?"

"Nothing. There is nothing through that door. Do not open it."

"Well, honestly, I can't see that there would be any reason not to—"

They heard the creak of the door opening. Then came the sudden burst of static they had come to recognize as their transceivers cutting out the sound of gunfire.

ROSARIO BLANCANALES KNEW, when he opened the door, that he was opening up a can of worms. The smart thing to do would probably have been to back out, find a relatively safe spot, signal Lyons and Schwarz, and then hit the place with gusto, but there were just too many workers in and around the sweatshop. He'd seen a few boxes that were probably heroin, hastily covered with this or that; there were probably more in other rooms he hadn't seen.

The workers all looked terrified. They'd watched him closely, no doubt hoping he wouldn't see anything that caused him to call in reinforcements. Only the fact that the loss of a field agent would bring down heat on the facility—the very heat they were hoping to avoid by letting him quickly tour the place—was keeping him alive. Blancanales had no doubt that the Triangle's thugs would just as soon kill him and dump him, had they the option.

When he didn't see any guns and didn't see any gunmen slouching about conspicuously, he had a hunch he knew why they'd kept him waiting for so long before letting him in. The door guard had obviously told the Triangle's henchmen what was happening, and they'd tried to bluff it out by hiding themselves in this small room off the sweatshop proper. It wasn't a bad plan, really. It just couldn't withstand Blancanales blundering into the entire room of them and asking awkward questions. If he really was the INS agent he claimed to be, opening that door would probably be the last thing he ever did in life.

As it was, Blancanales knew the score, and he was going to take this advantage. They would not get a better setup, all or most of the distribution point's thugs were contained in a single small room, with no cover and nowhere to go. Blancanales wasn't normally the charge-in-with-guns-blazing type, but this was one of those rare instances when he had to ask himself what Ironman would do.

As the door opened and the Kalashnikov-toting gunmen inside sprang to their feet, Blancanales was already drawing the 92-F from his waistband. Not knowing just how strapped or hostile the door guard might be, Blancanales paused to throw an elbow into his erstwhile guide's head, dropping him to the floor. Completing the arc of his movement, Blancanales brought up the 92-F. He began cycling through the 17-round magazine, bringing up his support hand to fire two-handed, double-tapping each of the guards as they scrambled to return fire in the fatal funnel that was their impromptu holding cell.

It was, almost literally, like shooting fish in a barrel. Blancanales dropped each gunner, ducking to the side as one of the faster among them managed to rip off a burst from his AK. Blancanales put a round between his eyes and kept shooting until all the Triangle gunmen were down.

"Going to need backup fast," Blancanales said. "I have engaged and neutralized multiple hostiles, but I cannot confirm how many more might be active in the building."

"We're on our way to you," Lyons said over the link.

"Securing the entrance," Schwarz called out.

"I'm coming to you," Lyons said.

Blancanales relayed his approximate position. He then checked to make sure his guide was still out. Searching the man, he came up with only a pair of keys. The man had no weapons and no identification. It was possible he was the equivalent of a trustee—a worker the guards trusted with more authority, but hardly one of the Triangle's goons.

Lyons showed up and helped him drag the guide back to the sweatshop floor. There was a stir among the workers, but Blancanales assured them that the man was just knocked out and had not been badly injured. Then he had them all get down on the floor, cross their ankles and lace their fingers behind their heads. Lyons went from person to person with a fistful of plastic zip-tie cuffs, making sure none of them had weapons as he strapped their wrists together.

"You will not be harmed," Blancanales said. "Federal authorities will be summoned to this location. It is vitally important that you tell us if there are any more men with guns hiding in this place."

One of the workers spoke up. "There is one." It was the door guard, the man who had guided Blancanales. He had a nasty welt puffing up part of his face, but otherwise he seemed unharmed.

"Cooperation will go a long way toward helping you here," Blancanales said. "What is your name?"

"Manuel," the door guard said. "There is one who is sometimes here. He was here today. He was not in the room. I do not know where he has gone."

"Can you describe him?"

"Small. Dark skin. He speaks well. He is a petty, miserable man. He beats the workers. Rapes them, sometimes. Or his men do…did."

"Do you have any idea where he might have gone?"

"There is a basement," Manuel said. He pointed. "Take that hall. To the end, then right. There is stairway down."

"On it," Lyons said. He hefted his shotgun and marched off.

"Why do you work here?" Blancanales asked.

"What choice do I have?" Manuel shook his head. "There are no jobs. I need money. I have a family. It was this, or it was nothing."

"Did you know what they were doing here?"

"The drugs? Of course," Manuel said. "I am not stupid. And I am not a coward. I did not like what they did. But I have to feed my family."

Blancanales couldn't fault the man for that.

THE BASEMENT WAS DIMLY lit. Carl Lyons removed the tactical flashlight from his pocket and clipped it to the barrel of the Daewoo, using a special mount Cowboy Kissinger had cobbled together for him. Using the mount, he could activate the light's tailcap switch with his support hand. He brought the big automatic shotgun to his shoulder and started to sweep his way through the dark, cramped cellar, brushing against the damp cinder-block walls.

He was careful to illuminate his surroundings only in short bursts, then move with each burst, trying hard not to make himself an easy target. There was no way not to give away his position momentarily to anyone who might be observing. It simply could not be helped, so he used appropriate tactics to compensate.

"Carl?" Schwarz called to him over the transceiver link. "Have you got anything?"

"Nothing but spiders," Lyons said. "I hate spiders. Anything up there?"

"Area's secured," Schwarz said. "We've notified the Farm and they're arranging for federal support here, to get the workers situated and debriefed and to clear the warehouse."

"Good," Lyons said. "We can get gone and move on to the next target, then."

"You about done down there?"

"Yeah," Lyons said. "I don't see—"

The flashlight beam caught the blade of the knife as it flashed toward his face.

"You," Lyons said, backing off a pace and bringing the big shotgun on target.

"Me," Thawan said. "But it looks like this time it is I who brought the wrong weapon."

"Looks like," Lyons said. "Now get on your belly."

"I do not think so," Thawan taunted. He held up his left hand. It gripped a device of some kind, a spring-loaded clapper switch.

"What is that?" Lyons asked, already dreading the answer.

"This," Thawan said, "is a dead man's switch. The entire building is wired to explode."

"Don't do it," Lyons said.

"I do not intend to die," Thawan said. "But you will have to guarantee my safe passage out of here."

"You're not taking any hostages with you," Lyons said.

"I do not have to." Thawan smiled. "Merely let me leave and, once I am out of range of the explosion, I will also be out of range of the bomb's receiver. Your problem, and mine, will be solved."

"Not the way I see it."

"I speak of immediate problems." Thawan grinned at him.

"Tell me something," Lyons said, his fingers aching on the stock of the USAS-12, eager to pull the trigger and end Thawan's miserable life. "You don't sound stupid. You sound like an educated man."

"I was, in fact, given a fine classical education. In Burma, if you care."

"I don't," Lyons said. "But I want to know how someone like you becomes a glorified pirate."

"Do not let the clothes fool you," Thawan said. "I do quite well for myself, American."

"I'm sure you do," Lyons said. "But I think losing as much as we've cost you is going to cut into your lifestyle a little bit."

Thawan's arrogant mask faltered then, and Lyons knew he'd hit the man somewhere painful at last. Thawan replied angrily, "That is none of your concern. Now stand aside, or I will blow this place apart and everyone in it. You may not care about your life. I do care about mine. But I will die before I will rot in one of your prisons."

"Then surrender," Lyons said. "We can work something out."

"Yes, I am quite certain you would like that," Thawan said. "I should have killed you when I had the opportunity."

"Why didn't you?"

"I was in a hurry," Thawan admitted.

"Running for your life?" Lyons chuckled. "Yeah, I can see that."

"I could still kill you." Thawan gestured with the dead man's switch.

"You could," Lyons said. "But you won't. You like yourself too much. I know the type."

"Maybe you do, American," Thawan said. "Maybe you do. But I will make you pay for what you have done."

"And I will kill you," Lyons said. "That's not a threat, little man. That's a promise."

Thawan made a disgusted noise and scuttled off.

"Heads up," Lyons said. "Thawan is here. Repeat, Thawan is here. He's got some kind of failsafe switch gripped in his hand, and he says he's got the building wired with explosives."

"What do you want us to do, Ironman?" Schwarz asked.

It burned Lyons to say it, but he did so. "Let him go," he said. "He's one man and we've taken several Triangle soldiers as well as the facility. It's not worth risking the lives of everyone in the place. But get them the hell out! I don't trust him not to blow it up once he's clear."

"Already doing it," Blancanales called back. "I'm hustling everyone to the parking lot now."

"Make sure they're far enough away," Lyons said. "I wouldn't put it past the little ghoul to have enough plastic explosives or something else to blow the entire block to cinders."

The big ex-LAPD cop made his way out of the building, each step reminding him that he'd failed to get his hands on Thawan yet again. He knew he should hurry, lest Thawan detonate his explosives, but he was just angry enough not to give a good damn. When he finally made the parking lot and saw his partners standing guard over the knot of workers, he walked slowly towards them. They were gathered in the farthest corner of the lot, where they would see cars coming from down the street when the federal assistance finally arrived.

Lyons was about to say something to the other two Able Team members when an object in the parking lot caught his eye.

He bent and picked it up. It was Thawan's dead man's switch.

"Son of a bitch," Lyons said.

CHAPTER TEN

Burma

The old stone temple was located in the most desolate, most isolated area of Upper Burma, squatting like a finger of rock pointing to the sky. Ancient as it was, the temple had long since ceased to be a place of any spiritual peace. Its current residents had no religion save that of their master, and even whether it had once been Buddhist was a fact long since lost to the soulless wretches who walked its halls.

In the main chamber of that temple, now a throne room, on a carved teakwood chair replete with relief scenes depicting ancient warriors at battle, sat the warlord known only as Than.

Torches set along the stone walls provided the only illumination. Their flickering orange-yellow light danced across his heavily lidded eyes and created forests of shadows in which he could lose himself for hours at a time. At his order, the throne room was now empty, but should he clap his hands, he would be surrounded by hangers-on, bodyguards, women and workers. His was the life of a medieval king, as much by his stylized tastes and dictates as by necessity. For Than, form followed function, and function dictated form…but always, his tastes were paramount.

He had been born on the streets of Rangoon to a drug addict mother, the product of a rape. This last, his mother had almost delighted in telling him, for as long as she was with him in those earliest days. Than, she had said, was born so scrawny and so wanting that he was not believed capable of surviving the night. When he lived out the week, it was considered a miracle. When he lived a month, it was considered a true sign from the gods. Than, of course, had always suspected himself born under an auspicious sign and, despite his mother's prattling about how pathetic he had been as a baby, he knew he was destined for greatness the moment his lungs first sucked in air.

Had his mother not managed to die of an overdose when he had but six years, he would have killed her himself. Even at that age, he had become skilled with a blade, taking what he wished from even older children as he roamed the streets, his belly always aching, ever empty. He lived with the knowledge of his eventual greatness gnawing at him much as that ever-present hunger chewed at his guts. It would have driven a lesser man insane, to know that he had such potential but to be forced to live so limited an existence.

From the age of five he carried a knife. At first this was half of an old pair of scissors he found in a garbage pit in an alley in Rangoon. He sharpened the scissors obsessively on an old round stone he had found, quite literally, in the gutter. With that crude weapon he took his first life at the age of six.

At eight years, he had murdered several other children, both boys and girls. At twelve, he had lost count of the number of the dead, and he was running a ring of pick-pockets and other thieves, most of them children, in the worst neighborhoods of Rangoon.

At the age of sixteen, he was running underage prostitutes. He had, by then, committed his first rape and decided he quite liked it. Also by then, he had tasted opium, heroin, hashish and cocaine, finding all to his liking in limited quantities. While obsessive, Than was also smart; he knew that to indulge in the poisons of the mind or of the flesh was to tempt fate, and he had no desire to relinquish the birthright of greatness under whose star he had been born. So he was careful when it came to drugs, and even to women, after a fashion.

From these humble beginnings, and learning early on just how much could be accomplished through brutal, thorough and quickly unleashed violence, Than built a small criminal empire that made him the most wanted young man in Rangoon. Eventually he branched out to other cities. Attaining the maturity of experience, sometimes earned through hard mistakes, Than even managed to hang on to his empire from behind bars, while serving several stints in prison. The convictions were minor, revolving around his drug and prostitution activities. The sentences were, comparatively and for the time, harsh. He managed, however. In prison, in fact, he became more terrible and more powerful than ever before. He had money and contacts on the outside, and he ran an organization from his cell, sending messages to his people through the women who visited him. He spent his money like water whenever he had it, bribing the guards lavishly, currying favor with those in prison who could help him. He was introduced to Burma's organized crime network, earned their favor, entered into treaties with them and promptly broke those treaties when he was released.

The ensuing crime wars established Than as the predominant force in Burmese drug trafficking, prostitution and a host of other organized crimes. When the country of his birth proved too small to satisfy his lust for power and money, for influence and, yes, even for challenge, he expanded beyond its borders. He discovered, to his delight, that demand for the drugs he could produce was insatiable and infinite. It was everywhere, from the most decadent Western nations to the most repressed Eastern ones, and in every country in between. The drugs, and the desire for them, became for Than a kind of religion itself, and in this echo chamber he began to develop the megalomania that had characterized him from middle age. He became, in word, deed and affectation, the warlord Than, and he ruled from his appropriated stone temple in Upper Burma. He was the terrifying old man in the mountain, the reincarnation of those ancient hash-taking assassins who so terrified the ancient world. At least, this was how he saw himself, and he saw no reason others should not share this vision. The legend of the Triangle grew, and as the legend grew, so did fear of the Triangle and what it could do.

It was in early middle age that Than had fathered a bastard child. He was quite certain this was not the first, nor would it be the last, but the mother had sought him out. She had, years after the boy's birth, made the arduous trek through the hills and found him in his stone temple, demanding that the boy Than had fathered be cared for, be raised as the warlord's own. Than admired her courage, and while she was not as comely as he remembered, he afforded her the honor of a quick, clean death. He thought that very magnanimous of him; he could easily have had her tortured. No one came before Warlord Than making impudent demands. He would not stomach such behavior.

The boy he did raise as his own; something of the child

reminded Than of his own childhood, of his own struggle for survival as a scrawny, sickly child only moments away from death. For years he had eked out an existence, feeding on garbage and murdering other children simply to survive, let alone thrive. As his servants brought the child before him, still splattered with his mother's blood, Than holstered the Webley revolver he had used to shoot her in the head and held out his bejeweled hands to receive the child he would raise as his heir.

Now, squatting on his throne, a corpulent study in self-indulgent excess, haughty vanity and arrogant isolation, the mountain of a man who was the Burmese warlord Than held an Iridium satellite phone to his ear and cursed in every language known to him, squeezing the phone as if he would choke the life from it.

"You are certain?" he demanded.

"Yes, father," Mok Thawan said from somewhere in the hated, decadent United States. "I have made certain of it. The entire shipment, all three vehicles, was captured and destroyed, as was the distribution center in Buffalo."

Than cursed again, long, low and loud. "How did you come to escape again?"

"Trickery, father," Mok Thawan said.

Than allowed himself a smile. Truly, Thawan was a worthy heir. It was very unlike him to fail in the manner he was describing now. It was obvious to Than, who had always viewed the West as weak and the Americans weakest of all, that something new was happening. He quickly apprised his son of the destruction of the old shoe plant outside of Yangon.

"But, Father, this should not have been possible." Thawan sounded shocked. "I…accept the possibility of American raids here. Their law enforcement has always been inconsistent, but sometimes inspired. I am gravely sorry for the deep losses we have so far experienced. I have killed, and killed, and fought to protect your property."

"Yes, yes," Than said, cutting off Thawan's histrionics before they could go further. Were he allowed to do so, Thawan would engage in such effusive apologies for hours at a time. Normally, Than enjoyed the gestures, but there was no time for that now.

"A thousand pardons, Father," Thawan said, perhaps realizing his father was in no mood. "But, as I was saying… the shoe factory was wired with surveillance cameras. It should have been impossible for an attacking force to approach it with stealth, even if they managed to get past the mines hidden on the road to the factory. We should have had ample warning to stop them."

"Well, that is another matter," Than said. He reached out and grabbed a bell from the floor next to his throne. This he rang, once, then again, then three times. A pair of burly guards appeared, dragging a much smaller man between them. They brought him forward, threw him on the stone floor before the throne and then stood over him, their Chinese-made AK-47 rifles held at the ready.

"It would seem," Than said into the phone, "that we have not been as rigorous with our employees as we might have been."

"Father?" Thawan asked, confused.

"The man hired to run the surveillance equipment whose installation you oversaw," Than said. "He was very good at what he did. He deactivated all of the cameras in the facility…except for the camera monitoring him. I have seen the tape."

"The tape was recovered," Thawan said hopefully. "Then the factory…"

"A total loss," Than said. "But pay attention, my son. This is most important. It seems the man in our employ owed a blood debt to another man. The first man is Sheng. The second man is Peng."

Peng looked up at the warlord from the floor. He had been badly beaten. His face was bloody and swollen, and he held one arm as if it had been broken.

"I remember Sheng," Thawan said. "I do not know this Peng."

"A Chinaman," Than said. "And once a resident of a village not far from my temple, a village whose people did not all pay the obeisance I require. I remember the day, in fact, years ago. An informant from the village brought to my ears tales of the disloyalty of his fellows. He wished money for this information. He was given money, and I, in turn, had the families of those who would dare oppose me put to a slow and…careful…death, as an example."

"You are wise, Father."

"Indeed I am," Than said. "It seems this Peng, grieved over the loss of his family, has been working against me for some time. According to his conversation with Sheng, he works with many governments. And now he has helped a special team of Westerners who have come to my shore to hurt my business and perhaps even to kill me."

"Westerners…soldiers, such as have attacked us here in America?"

"Possibly," Than said. "Certainly it is too great a coincidence not to be related. Peng came to Sheng, his long-ago village mate, who apparently has never stopped being an informant for Peng or whomever else would pay him." Than's distaste was evident in his voice. "It was time to call in the old blood debt, according to Peng. Sheng, whose careless greed had resulted in the deaths of Peng's family at my hand, agreed to switch off the surveillance machines at Peng's direction. Apparently, Peng has tracked this Sheng for some while, using him whenever possible to gain information about our Triangle and about me. Guiding his Western killers into our lands, he stole away from them to find Sheng, whom he knew to be employed as the keeper of the camera machines at the factory. And thus did he have Sheng stab me in the back while he sought to stab me in the eye himself."

"A brave man," Thawan said. "A clever man."

"Indeed," Than said. "And not an enemy I will suffer to live, for long." He snapped his fingers and the guards grabbed Peng by either arm. "Take him to his cell," he ordered. "Beat him. That arm, the one that is broken. Choose a finger from that hand and remove it. Make him watch. He has helped my enemies to do me grievous damage, and he will pay for it, slowly, before he begs for death."

Peng stared at him, stone-faced, as he was dragged off.

"What of this Sheng?" Thawan asked.

"I have had him killed already, and his body thrown to wild dogs," Than said, almost offhand. "I shall have his family rounded up and publicly killed, too, and slowly, so that all know the price of betraying me. My son, they have hurt us badly. The loss of the factory is a significant one. Coupled with the complete destruction of the poppy field in Thailand, about which you already know, it deals us a nearly fatal blow. You must secure the resources still under our control in the United States."

"We can weather this, Father," Thawan said. "The new markets we will open in Russia, with Katzev's coopera-tion—"

"Are already under attack," Than said. "There is more, my son. Our contacts within the Russian criminal groups have verified an attack on the banking house there, the one we have used to transfer millions of dollars to Katzev. The banking house has been attacked. The data…ransacked.

The style of it reeks of these same, bold Westerners. They have followed the trail, somehow, using some magic I do not understand. They have made the connections as if they can see the future… I do not pretend to understand it. But it means they now seek to attack the only market that can save us in the face of these losses. We cannot afford to let them inflict more destruction on our holdings."

"What will you do, Father?"

"I have sent hired assassins to Russia," Than said. "My contacts among the *mafiya* will guide them to the Westerners. They will make these men, these men who have dared to oppose me, pay and pay dearly. They will root out the Westerners who have followed our interests into Russia, and they will destroy them utterly."

"What will Katzev think of this?"

"He will be vexed, surely," Than admitted. "He will not like that we have sent men of violence into his nation, men of violence whom he does not control. It will anger him. But he does not know the extent of the damage done to us. He knows only how much money we have sent him before. He knows how much we paid him to purchase his men to guard the factory."

"He will become aware of their deaths."

"Perhaps," Than said. "Perhaps not. Word may reach him soon enough, but he will still think our coffers endless. He will want more money, and we will promise him more. He will tolerate the interference of our assassins in return for these promises."

"I grow weary of keeping this man placated," Thawan said.

The edge of menace in Than's voice was dripping with imminent violence even through the satellite phone link. "You forget yourself, my son."

"A thousand pardons, Father," Thawan said quickly. "I

meant only that he is not worthy of you, and his demands grow repetitive."

"That is true," said Than, somewhat mollified. "And, in truth, I share your disdain for this man. We will finance him, and continue using him, until his power is assured and our markets have been established. When we have our fingers firmly intertwined with the *mafiya* and with all local crime here, we will not need him anymore. Then we can sponsor his replacement and see to his removal."

"I would welcome the chance to put him to hot irons myself, Father."

"I do not doubt that you would," Than said. "Tell me, where are you now?"

"I am at the distribution center in Albany, Father. I am, as you have instructed, attempting to secure and consolidate our interests. I am gravely worried that somehow the Western commandos will find me again. I have ordered the men to high alert, but there is only so much here I can do."

"Is it perhaps time to withdraw to Boston?"

"I do not think so, Father," Thawan said. "There is yet more I can do. I do not wish to hide myself. I wish to fight for you."

"That is good," Than said. "That is very good. Now, tell me what you know of these men who have attacked us, these men you have personally faced and escaped."

"Were our own pressures not so great, I would relish so worthy a foe," Thawan said. "I have faced down the leader of the men who stalk us here. He is a very big man. Yellow hair. Features like granite. Hollow eyes that show nothing but death. I have not seen his like before."

"Do you think it is the American government?"

"I do not know who else it could be," Thawan said. "But this man, he is not like the other government agents and police I have faced. The tactics he and his men use, they are not those of the government here. These men strike hard and fast, using powerful weapons. They are not afraid to kill. They are not afraid of overwhelming odds. They seem to dare death to come take them, and in the daring, they succeed against all probability."

"You sound as if you admire them."

"Perhaps I do, somewhat, Father, for they are truly warriors of a type I have not encountered before. I regret that in my haste to escape to secure your interests I failed to take the opportunity to kill one of them. I faced him again, in Buffalo, and escaped again. He made me know true fear, I will admit. But I would gladly have fought him had I been able to do so without capture."

"Do not lose your head, my son," Than said. "There will always be enemies to fight, and in due course. Do not force a battle when it may be avoided. There are battles enough. In all things, do what makes profit for us."

"Of course, Father," Thawan said. "I seek only that which is in your best interests."

"My interests are your interests," Than said.

"Your interests are my interests," Thawan repeated.

"Promise me," Than said after a pause, "that you will retreat to Boston if you must."

"The option has always been mine, Father," Thawan said.

"But I know you, my son," Than said. "You are proud. Your men see you as a fighter, and thus you do what you think they expect. I have seen it. I have watched it. I know you."

"You do, Father. But I will not put my personal desires before your business affairs. On this, you may always rely."

"You are the only one I can trust," Than said in a rare moment of complete candor. "Without you, there is no one who can run my operations whom I would trust not to steal from me. There is no one to whom I may leave it at my death. Without an heir, even the mightiest of kings is forgotten."

"You will not be forgotten, Father," Thawan said. "Nor will your reign be a short one. I face a mighty foe, an enemy unlike any we have previously seen, but I will prevail. You taught me well. I will not give up."

"No," Than said. "No, you won't. I know that. We will triumph. Our killers, the most black-hearted, deadliest men in my employ, have already been dispatched to Russia. They could be arriving even now. They will destroy these Western commandos, these *cowboys,* and you will fight them in America. On two fronts, we will be victorious, and our empire will expand once more to my eternal glory."

"To your glory, Father."

"Very well," Than said. "Go and do what you must. Keep me informed."

"I shall, Father," Thawan said. The connection was closed and Than was left staring at his phone, thinking of what his life could have been…and what it still would be.

He felt anxious and unsettled. For all of his confident talk to his son and heir, he was deeply troubled. It was unlike Mok Thawan to fail in battle. While it was good that he had survived, the fact that he had not beaten the enemy decisively was disturbing. The Triangle had always been the fastest with the blade or the bullet, always the most overwhelmingly violent. To be met and matched on those terms was unthinkable. It challenged the very fabric of what they had built.

Still, he had faith in his son. Mok Thawan would not disappoint him.

If he did, Mok Thawan would have to die, and that would sadden Than greatly.

He sat on his throne for hours, staring into the torchlight, wondering if perhaps, for the first time in his life, he had met an enemy with greater will than his.

CHAPTER ELEVEN

Washington, D.C.

Hal Brognola walked up the steps of the Lincoln Memorial. It was a pleasant day in Washington. The weather was bright and cool. Plenty of tourists were out sightseeing, as was usually the case, and the city had the aura of bright promise it always had when the sun hit it just right. Brognola, always involved in the most delicate of covert and counterterrorist operations, rarely let himself get away from the office for more than a few minutes. Price had told him many times that she worried he was working himself too hard. He didn't know what else he could do. The secrets of Stony Man Farm and its missions were entrusted to him. He did what he could with the staff that he had and delegated when it was possible. There were times, though, that he wished for the simpler but much more dangerous existence of the Stony Man commandos themselves. They dealt in tactical realities; they dealt in firm solutions when Brognola gave them tasks and they implemented them within defined mission parameters.

Defined mission parameters. That was what he lacked

in Wonderland. He felt as if his life was split between two worlds. The first was the Farm, where missions had defined goals and the enemy had a face. The second was the world of government, where the goals were ever-shifting, the targets were ever-moving and the closest friends could become the harshest enemies in the time it took to stick a metaphorical knife between your shoulder blades.

Of course, he had seen his share of real knives, too, and guns. Brognola walked up to the Lincoln Memorial with a .45-caliber Glock pistol in an inside-the-waistband holster under his jacket. There had been a time, once in his life, when he would have thought it absurd to walk around toting quite that much firepower. Now he wondered if it would be enough, should he encounter some of the monsters he'd seen in the course of his travels between the world of court operations and the world of government.

"Hello, Hal," a man farther down the steps said.

Ah, Brognola thought to himself. My first fare of the day.

"Hello, Daniel," Brognola said. "I trust you're well?"

Senator Daniel Harris made a noncommittal gesture, which was typical of a senator bearing potentially bad news. "As well as can be expected," Harris said. "Shall we walk?"

"Let's take a look at Lincoln," Brognola said. "I don't see him often enough."

"All right," Harris said.

They made small talk for a few minutes. They'd known each other for years. The appropriations committee on which Harris sat had direct bearing on the Sensitive Operation Group's ongoing budget. Unlike many whom Brognola dealt with, Harris had a security clearance high enough, and knowledge deep enough, to have at least an inkling of what Brognola dealt with on a day-to-day basis. While the details of the Farm itself were highly classified, Harris knew that Brognola was involved in black ops and that many of the bills in Harris's appropriation committee eventually found their way to Brognola, or through him.

"Well, let's have the bad news, Daniel," Brognola said. "We've been dancing around it long enough."

"You always make this so easy, Hal," Harris said.

"It's never easy," he sighed. "But if it's any consolation, I do understand."

"I know," Harris said. "You've never taken it personally, and for that I'm grateful. I wish we had more like you."

"If you *needed* more like me," Brognola said, "we'd all be in big trouble."

"Well, see, that's just it," Harris said. "You know I deal a lot with reconciliation in Congress, making sure bills on one side eventually reach signable compromise with bills on the other."

"I do."

"I hear a lot, Hal," Harris said. "I've got my ear to the ground. I know which way the winds are blowing."

"Do you have some more metaphors you'd like to use?" Brognola asked.

They both laughed at that. "Seriously, Hal," Harris said. "They say nothing succeeds so much as success…"

"What are you trying to say, Daniel?"

"Well, the budget has come up for review," Harris said. "And there are a lot of people raising questions about the black-bag slush fund."

"You don't call it that?" Brognola looked alarmed.

"Of course not, Hal." Harris shook his head. "But these are veteran congressmen we're talking about. Senators who've been around the block more than once. They're not stupid, much as it would be tempting to brand some of them as such. And they know that there are certain appropriations that go to less…publicized branches of government, where certain very quiet things are done with them for the accomplishment of some very major goals."

"That's a very roundabout way to put it," Brognola said. "But I take your meaning."

"I'm sorry, Hal," Harris said. " I'm too used to the way things are done up here. You and I both know that *they* know we're dealing in security budgets here."

"Yes."

"Well, the thing is, and I'm sure you're tired of hearing about this, but…there just hasn't been a major—"

Brognola cut him off. "I know what you're going to say," he said, nodding. "And, yes, we've been relatively secure domestically, as least insofar as is publicly known, since that darkest day of terrorism on our soil. But you don't honestly think that was the end of it, do you?"

"No," Harris said. "But it's hard to sell Congress on spending money to stop things that just don't seem to be happening."

"Y2K," Brognola said. "The millennium bug."

"I remember it," Harris said. "But I don't understand where you're going."

"The millennium bug was, to hear some people tell it, going to wipe out civilization as we knew it. When thousands of computers across the country reached the year two thousand, their outdated software, which had only two numbers allocated for the year, was supposed to click over to the year 1900. Computer failures were predicted across the nation. When those failures occurred, they were supposed to cripple modern society. Everything from toasters to personal computers to cellular phones to the Internet was supposed to stop working. Our planes would fall out of the sky. Our cars would stop dead. We would all revert to the Stone Age, and only a handful of Y2K survivalists with the wherewithal and the foresight to store water and canned food in their homes were going to come out alive."

"Yes," Harris said. "I remember."

"Well, as you recall," Brognola went on, "we spent millions of dollars as a nation preparing for the millennium bug. Code in machines across the nation was retrofitted to prevent this impending disaster."

"Right."

"When the year two thousand finally rolled around," Brognola said, "nothing happened. Skeptics claimed that nothing happened because nothing was ever going to happen. The problem, they said, had been overblown from the beginning, and an entire industry had grown up that was nothing but profiteering on people's irrational fears about the turn of the century."

"Yes," Harris agreed.

"Believers, on the other hand," Brognola said, "claimed that it was precisely because we had spent all that time and money preparing for the millennium bug that we never experienced it. If we hadn't done all that, the believers claimed, we would have gone through that very disaster, we'd all be running around in bearskins carrying stone knives about now."

"What's your point, Hal?" Harris finally asked.

"My point is," Brognola said, "can you tell me who was right?"

"Well…" Harris thought about that. "No," he said. "I suppose I can't."

"And why is that?"

"There's no way to know," Harris said. "If we hadn't prepared, we'd have had to go through the disaster, and that would have destroyed us, supposedly. So we worked to prevent in order to survive."

"And so, either our preparations never meant anything and were a big waste of time and money," Brognola said, "or they did *everything* and preserved society in the face of impending disaster. But because we did prepare, by definition, we can never know whether preparing was necessary."

Harris looked at him. His jaw worked, but nothing came out.

"You see?" Brognola asked him. "That is the world in which I live every day, Daniel. It's a world of uncertainty in which I never know, necessarily, which preparations will be necessary and which preparations will not be necessary. Either we can spend the money preparing this country to deal with terrorism, and equipping our warriors to go out and do just that, or we can trust to providence. I've never been a big believer in providence, Daniel. I believe in prudent preparation."

"But, Hal," Harris said, "you can see the position this puts me in. Everything you do is so secret, so hush-hush. There's only so much I can do telling people, 'Well, we need the money, and it's really important, but I can't tell you what it's for, because it's so classified even I don't really know.' Then they ask me how I know it's important if I don't know what it's for, and what can I tell them? That my friend Hal Brognola said it was, and I trust him? You know that's good enough for me, Hal, but for the average congressman? It's never going to be enough. They survive on hot air. They live and breathe information. If somebody has it, they want it. If they don't have it, they want to get it. If they think they're being left out of the loop, they get petty and start looking to exact retribution. Next thing you know, you've got a senator who could help you get the appropriations you need, but he won't do it unless you clue him into the exact nature of those appropriations, even though you couldn't if you wanted to because you don't have the information to start with!"

"I understand that it's frustrating, Daniel," Brognola said. "I'm just explaining the whole picture. Only a small percentage of what we do, of what we fund, is preparation for something that never comes."

"What are you telling me, Hal?"

"What I've always told you," Brognola said. "In my job, I live with the knowledge every day of just how many ways everything can go off the rails. Do you have any idea how many threats I've dealt with in the past six months that concerned weapons of mass destruction alone—weapons that very much existed and that posed a real threat to the security of the United States and other nations?"

"The cynical answer," Harris said, "is that, no, of course I don't, because you can't tell me."

"No, I can't," Brognola said. "But I can tell you that, yes, there were such incidents. I can tell you that there were more such incidents than you can possibly imagine—and of course, when dealing with something like this, even one threat is one too many. There's no margin for error when dealing with poisonous plagues, suitcase nukes, satellite weaponry and intercontinental ballistic missiles."

"I never said there was, Hal. I don't doubt that you and your people deal with terrifying crap every day. I'm just saying that if I'm going to keep funneling appropriations to you and your groups, sight unseen, with no knowledge of the purpose or outcome…well, that puts me in a very awkward position, doesn't it?"

"I'm sure it does," Brognola said. "But that's the other part of security work, Daniel—national security work, issues that affect the entire nation and the world beyond our borders in profound ways that stretch from the possible deaths of hundreds to the possible deaths of millions."

"Listen, Hal," Harris said. "I've got a coalition of congressmen on the hill who are positively gunning for you. Not you specifically, mind, but all the black-bag slush-fund stuff. In this economy everyone's looking for a scapegoat. Everyone wants to be able to report back to their constituents how much they cut. They want to look good. If they don't know what's something's for, they can't put a value on it. Hell, some of them probably wouldn't assign a value to it even if they did know. They're just that shortsighted. But they're in power, and they're holding the purse strings, and they're ready, willing and able to cut your budget."

"All right," Brognola said. "Let's say that it's my budget, and let's say I could own up to any part of it. What would you have me do?"

"Well, see, that's where it gets significantly easier," Harris said. "All I need is for you to, you know, bend the rules a little."

Brognola looked at him. "What do you mean?"

"Just bend them, don't break them," Harris said. "Give me a little something to go on, completely off the record."

"Daniel," Brognola began, "let's walk some more." They moved away from the Lincoln Memorial, down the steps. Washington in all its white-marble glory stretched before them. "Why don't you come with me back to my office," Brognola suggested.

"Now you're talking." Harris nodded. "Trust me, Hal, it's really not as hard to play ball as you might think."

"Play ball?" Brognola asked.

"We both know that what you do is top secret," Harris said. "Top, top secret. The only reason I know it's top secret is because I've got to apportion funds, and over time you get the feel for these things. You've never had to admit anything to me because either I already knew it or you told me you wouldn't say."

"Uh, yes."

"Well, see, Hal, that's what's got to change. But it doesn't have to be all that painful. It can even be mutually beneficial."

"Mutually beneficial in what way?"

"You know as well as I do, Hal, that in Washington, information is power, and power is money, and money is the lifeblood on which we operate."

"I thought we were talking about appropriations."

"We are," Harris said. "That's just it." They entered Brognola's office building, where he had a small office overlooking the Potomac. The big Fed ushered Harris upstairs. When they were finally seated in his office, Brognola behind his desk and Harris in his chair, Brognola spread his hands.

"I'm listening," he said.

"Look, it's simple," Harris said. "I know, you've never heard me talk quite like this." Harris looked down at his hands, then back at Brognola. "But to be honest, until now I was worried you wouldn't be receptive and, well, you know."

"Yeah, I know." Hal offered him a half smile.

"Well, see, now I'm glad we had this talk," Harris said.

"How long have we known each other?" Brognola asked.

"Come on, Hal." Harris grinned. "You know it isn't that simple."

"I suppose not."

"Hal, you do a difficult job," Harris went on. "I know that. I can see that. I'm in your corner. Lots of folks would be in your corner, too. Once the word is out that you're playing ball, a lot of people will fall in line. Maybe even people who've never been able to see it that way before."

"I'm not sure I'm following you," Brognola said. "Maybe you should spell it out in terms of the *exact* benefit to me."

"Oh, one of those, eh?" Harris chuckled. "All right, Hal. Because it's you. Let's say you've got an appropriation you need for, oh, let's call it ten million dollars. Well, any idiot knows that's an overestimation. You don't just ask for ten million dollars when you need ten million dollars. You ask for more. So, going on the assumption that there's room left over in that ten million dollars, we cut an agreement before the bill gets to the committee, and then we make sure those earmarks are widely known among the folks who do the cutting up of the bill. They're, you know, playing ball, too, so it all works out."

"How do you mean?" Brognola asked.

"Well, see, your ten million, you get, say, five of it for your project, whatever that hush-hush project might be. You get another two million for, well, you. The rest gets spread around among the other folks involved in the process, to make sure everyone's happy. It also covers everyone's back. See, if everyone's taking some of the funds, then nobody can go rat someone else out because, well, we're all equally guilty. Make sense?"

"I suppose it does," Brognola said. "What do I have to do to earn my two million in that case? It can't simply be for nothing. We both know that in Wonderland, nothing's ever for nothing."

"True," Harris said. "Well, that's where the whole information-equals-power-equals-money equation comes into play. The information you have, that's the value. And it's that information that the appropriations personnel want."

"Meaning what?"

"Meaning we'd want you to, you know, talk about some of the ways in which the money is spent," Harris said. "I know, for example, that you've had a hand in that new satellite system, which is unspecified. I'd really love to know what's so expensive about a satellite, and what it does. I mean, is it a communications satellite? Is it something else? Is it a space-based weapon? And, God, if it's a space-based weapon, please tell me it is, because some of these congressmen positively drool at the prospect of reviving Star Wars and weaponizing space. I mean, that's the kind of thing that would instantly establish you as a player in these circles."

"You want to know about my satellite project," Brognola said.

'Yes, that or anything else you're spending money on," Harris confirmed. "Even if it seems mundane to you, it's like gold to the guys on the Hill. They're hungry for it, Hal. Each one of them is hungry to know what the other guy doesn't know, and one of them wants to know how he can get in the know faster, better and deeper than the other guy."

"What would be done with this information?"

"Oh, probably nothing," Harris said. "I mean, come on, Hal, it's practically its own currency, you know?"

"So sensitive security information is valuable simply for being sensitive security information, because a bunch of legislators feel more powerful when they know things, and they want to know more than their neighbors so they can feel more powerful than those neighbors."

"That's it exactly," Harris said. "I'm telling you, Hal, it's the easiest route to a financially stable retirement you'll ever take. And, come on, you and I both know that you work yourself practically to death. As long as I've known you, you've barely taken a vacation, if at all. You almost never get out of this office, unless you're flying off to wherever it is you go when you're not here, and you almost always come back. You've given your life to this job, and what has it gotten you? Heartburn, if not an outright ulcer. Probably a lot of suits that don't fit as good as they used to. An expensive house that would be ten times cheaper in a nicer, cleaner city that wasn't Washington, which is worth less now than it was when you bought it. Are you getting me here? Am I making sense?"

"Oh, yes," Brognola said. "You're making perfect sense."

"So, we can do business? Play ball?"

"I guess that depends," Brognola said. "Would I get my appropriations?"

"Well, of course," Harris said. "You'd get your appropriations, and more. You'd get a steady stream of income that would serve you well. You've earned it, Hal. Play this right, as much as you know? You could be a wealthy man."

"Wealthy," Brognola said. "I never really pictured myself wealthy."

"Well, not a lot of others have until now, either." Harris nodded.

"What do you mean?"

"Well, Hal," Harris said, smoothing his hair back. "There's no…delicate way to say this. You make a lot of people nervous."

"Nervous how?"

"In that way that nobody wants to sit next to a nun in church…or on the subway."

"I don't follow you."

"You're Mr. Untouchable, Hal," Harris said. "Nobody's approached you because they figured they'd be staring down the barrel of a gun if they tried. They figured even talking to you about this was a ticket straight to disgrace and jail. Hell, there are people who go so far as to call this kind of accounting some kind of treason, and that's ridiculous. We both know that there's treason, and there's just looking after your own interests. I don't see why anyone would confuse the two."

"Well, look at it from the outside, Daniel," Brognola said. "You've got sensitive government information floating around. You've got people who want it. You've got people willing to pay to get it, broker it, pass it. They're not just willing to pay for it, they're asking for it as a contingency to get government appropriations, classified appropriations, pushed through. To some people that would sound like treason salted with blackmail. 'Play ball with us, or you don't get your funding. Tell us what we want to know, and we'll not just get you your funding, we'll grease the wheels for you, too.'"

"When you put it like that," Harris said, "I suppose it does sound negative. But it doesn't have to be like that."

"Why not?" Brognola asked.

"What do you mean?"

"I mean, why doesn't it have to be like that?"

"Well, I mean, you just, you know, look at it in a more positive light."

"So it's not treason if I don't believe it to be treason."

"Jesus, Hal, you have a way of making everything sound bad. Trust me, this isn't any big deal."

"All right," Brognola said. "Give me an example."

"Okay," Harris said. "Remember the Supercannon Project?"

"Refresh my memory."

"The supercannon was supposed to be some new, super-long-range answer to artillery and intercontinental ballistic missiles," Harris explained. "The thing was enormous. I mean, it was so huge, they were talking about adapting it to shoot capsules into our space, to save on the costs of shuttling out of the atmosphere. Sort of a latter-day Jules Verne take on going to the moon, you know?"

"I'm aware of the idea."

"Well, see, the supercannon had some issues," Harris said. "For one thing, its cost overruns were huge, to look at the official documents. For another thing, well, it didn't really work as advertised. There were some reports floating around that were really critical of it. When the funding finally came before the committee, nobody wanted to attach his name to it. They didn't want to be the senator who funded that gigantic silly supersize cannon boondoggle come election day, and can you blame them? That's the story officially."

"Okay," Brognola said. "What's the story unofficially?"

"Unofficially," Harris said, "the supercannon was actually a pretty workable idea. It just needed some more funding to bring it up to snuff. There were some overruns, sure, but nothing as extreme as was eventually reported. See, the supercannon was fine, but let's look at this realistically. There are plenty of defense contractors manufacturing existing weapons systems, employing tens of thousands of people, who need that money more. The people responsible for securing that funding, well…they had no problem making sure it went through, as long as we were willing to play ball on the supercannon. So we sacrificed it. The project became a black pit of funding from which not even light could escape…officially. Unofficially, we all took a cut, and a lot of very good, very stable American defense contractors got their funding. They got exactly what they needed and everyone was happy, and the people who saw to it that they got what they needed repeated the rewards of doing the right thing."

"The right thing," Brognola said.

"Yeah, you know," Harris said. "Playing ball."

"Daniel," Brognola asked, "how long have you been involved in these types of financial deals and maneuvers?"

"Oh, the past six or seven years," Harris said. "I wasn't always hip to how things run. It took me a while. And, hell, Hal, you've been here how long? Don't feel bad. There's no shame in being the guy with the squeaky-clean image. Hell, if there ever were to be an audit down the road, that image would serve you well." He held up his hands quickly. "Not that you need to worry about being audited. We have people on the audit committee who look out for that kind of thing, and steer it away from the folks who know how to do the right thing."

"So this is extremely extensive," Brognola said.

"Oh, sure," Harris said. "It's everywhere."

"Would you say you're hip to a lot of these things, Daniel?"

"Most of them, actually," Harris said proudly. "A few years in and you get to know the ins and outs. It's not all that difficult."

"I see. So what would you want from me to get started? To establish my bona fides?"

"Hell, Hal," Harris said, then chuckled at his own alliteration, "that's easy. Your satellite project? Word is, it's going to be up for a revamp. I don't know all the details because of course they're classified, but the original was very, very expensive. I don't know where all that money went, but wouldn't it be better served looking after those folks who've already proven they have a product we can buy and use, or those people looking out for those people?"

"You're losing me." Brognola shook his head.

"Sorry, I get excited," Harris said. "My point is that your satellite project, one of the few that I can actually attach to you by name, cost a bundle when it started, and now it's up for another bundle because they want to retool it. They won't tell us what it will do—they just say they want to redo what it does and, no, please don't ask about it. Well, see, that is exactly the sort of attitude that the folks on the Hill don't like. It's uncooperative. It doesn't share information. And the funds just disappear into a black bag and are never seen again, when in fact, if played right, we could do something really great with the money."

"I see." Brognola nodded. "So, what happens to the satellite?"

"Well, I'm assuming the thing truly is nearly as expensive as the sum that was appropriated first time out." Harris smiled. "Which means the thing is an absolute hog. That's great—hogs we can use. We get the appropriation, and the overrun. We apportion it to the types of folks I've been telling you about. I mean, we divert the funds to those contractors—defense contractors, if you like, because I know how you feel about security—that we can trust, whom we know deserve the money and have an established track record with us. Then we dump your satellite and say it didn't work, it never really worked. Maybe a few heads roll at the company where it was designed, maybe they don't—depends on connections."

"Well," Brognola said. "All right, Daniel. I have to say you've really taken me by surprise with all this."

"Well, like I said, Hal," Harris continued, "you're practically regarded as Eliot Ness around here. Mr. Untouchable. But as long as we've been friends, I knew you'd understand."

"I didn't understand before," Brognola said. "But I understand perfectly now. Daniel, I'm sorry."

"Sorry? For what, Hal?"

"I've misled you all this time. I thought we really were

friends. Clearly we weren't. That's a very significant lapse of judgment on my part, and one that I will have to spend some time thinking about. It's possible I could have foreseen the error. I don't know. I probably should have."

"Hal?" Harris backed up in his chair a little bit. "You're, uh, scaring me, buddy."

"Well, if you were scared before," Brognola said, removing a digital recorder from his desk, "you're really going to be scared now."

"What's that?"

"That," Brognola said, "is high-definition audio. I've been recording you since you stepped in here."

"Whoa, whoa, Hal," Harris said. "This is me we're talking about. This is Daniel. I'm not trying to set you up. I wouldn't do that."

"I didn't think you were."

"Hey, look, if you're worried about covering your own ass on this, you don't have to be. Like I told you, it's all mutually assured. None of the folks involved can get into you, for blackmail or anything else, without getting themselves hanged in the process. It's the perfect system."

Brognola glared at the senator.

"Did you…" Harris feigned a laugh. "Did you think I came here to blackmail you with this? Hal, buddy, I wouldn't do that. Look, man, we're completely cool."

"No, 'buddy,'" Brognola said, "we most certainly aren't completely cool. You're a traitor, Harris. And let me tell you something. You were right about one thing." He reached into his jacket and pulled the Glock. The .45-caliber barrel probably looked impossibly huge pointed at Harris's face, and Brognola was glad of it. "You don't know how hard it is for me not to just wipe you off the face of the planet right here and now," Brognola said. "As it is, it's going to take me a very long time to get the sour taste of your filth out of my mind. Now get out of my chair before you stain it."

He marched Harris to the door. "Hal, wait. This is serious. You can't do this."

"I can," Brognola said, "and I most certainly will. Did you see the sign on the door when you came in here?"

"What are you talking about?"

Brognola spun him around, pushing him up against the wall, the Glock pointed at his face. "The sign on the door! The sign that everyone sees who comes to this office! The sign that I have seen every morning of every day of the week for more years than I care to count! That sign means something, you son of a bitch."

The sign on the door read simply, Hal Brognola: Justice.

CHAPTER TWELVE

Syracuse, New York

"Maybe we could catch a basketball game while we're in town," Schwarz suggested.

"No," Lyons shot back.

"Just like that?" Schwarz asked, pretending to be crestfallen.

"Yes," Lyons said.

"So we can go?" Schwarz said hopefully.

"No," Lyons said.

Blancanales could hear the two banter back in the Suburban, which was parked in one of the two parking lots attached to Onondaga Lake Park. The park was busy with people; it was a beautiful day, and there were many people walking, biking or in-line skating along the asphalt walking and cycling trails that paralleled the lake.

"I don't like this at all," Blancanales said. "Too many civilians wandering around. Too much potential for collateral damage."

"Good thing the target's not in the park," Lyons said. He conferred with Schwarz and the three men looked over the satellite imagery and tactical maps the Farm had transmitted to their phones. As confirmed by NetScythe's analysis and based on the primitive scribbling on the route map they'd recovered, the target, the next distribution point in the Triangle's drug network, was a house adjacent to Onondaga Lake Parkway on First Street. The sleepy central New York city, known for its harsh winters and not much else, at first might seem an unlikely spot for such a distribution point—until one looked at a map. The city of Syracuse sat in the geographic center of New York State, making it an ideal hub for activity centered around that state. Thus far, the Triangle's network within the United States ran roughly north-south, west-east, linking New Jersey to New York, covering most of the state of New York and running on into New England, based on the map and the data the Farm had processed. Left to its own devices, there was no telling how far the Triangle's cancer would spread.

That was why they were going to cut it out.

"All right," Lyons said. "This is a residential neighborhood and I don't want a major firefight here. Gadgets, you have your suppressor for the 93-R?"

Schwarz nodded. His machine pistol had come to him equipped with one of John Cowboy Kissinger's excellent silencers, which reduced the blast of the fully automatic handgun to the sound of hands clapping.

"Use the GPS units in your phones," Lyons said. "We have the exact coordinates of the target house. The two of you, take a little walk in the park. From what we've seen, the properties fronting the lake have rear yards that butt into the park. You'll take a little stroll until you're opposite the target, then take the back. I'll drive up to the front, just one man, no real threat."

"That'll be the day," Schwarz said.

Lyons ignored him. "Gadgets, it will be your job to neutralize anyone inside. I'll try to keep it quiet. We need to stop at a convenience store before we start our run."

"Got it," Blancanales said.

They drove to the nearest gas station and convenience store. Lyons bought a two-liter bottle of cola and a roll of electrical tape. Then they were headed back to the park.

"You want any?" Lyons gestured with the soda.

"I'm good," Schwarz said.

"No, thank you." Blancanales shook his head.

"Suit yourselves," Lyons said. He uncapped the bottle and took a long drink. Then he upended it, chugging the bottle, sucking the air out until the bottle started to fold in on itself. When he was finally done, the two-liter bottle was almost gone. He opened the window of the rented Suburban and dumped out what little was left.

"That was…awesome, Ironman," Schwarz said.

Lyons burped at him, very loudly.

"This is what I enjoy about working with this outfit," Blancanales said dryly. "The incredible class and professionalism of my teammates."

Lyons ignored that. He withdrew his Colt Python and shoved the empty soda bottle down over the barrel, sealing it with electrical tape.

"You're honestly going to try that?" Blancanales asked.

"I saw it in a movie once," Lyons said, nodding.

Blancanales and Schwarz, with their handguns under their jackets, got out of the truck. Lyons leaned out the open driver's-side window and wagged a finger at them. "No sightseeing."

"But I wanted to see the Salt Museum," Schwarz said, looking around the parking lot.

"Check in when you're in position," Lyons instructed. He drove away.

"Well," Blancanales said, "let's look like we belong."

"That will be easier to do without Carl," Gadgets said.

"He'd tell you to shut up."

"I know."

"Shut up, Gadgets," Lyons said over the earbud transceiver link.

"Touché," Schwarz said.

They fell into step behind the crowds walking the parkway. It was a sunny day, and foot traffic was heavy.

"Gadgets," Blancanales said.

"Yeah?" Schwarz ducked aside as a man on bicycle sped past. Several inline skaters followed.

"We're on the wrong trail," Blancanales announced.

"This one is closest to the yards opposite First Street," Schwarz said.

"That may be true—" Blancanales stepped aside as two more cyclists went past "—but we're still on the wrong trail."

"I can't see that it makes much difference," Schwarz said.

"Not until the park rangers show up," Blancanales offered.

"Well, it doesn't matter," Schwarz said. "We're here." He held up his phone, which had the GPS application running.

Blancanales nodded. They stepped off the trail onto the grass. Beyond a drainage pipe and ditch that formed a small moat between the paved park trail and the yards of the houses on First Street, they saw a small chain-link fence around the perimeter of the rear of the target house's property.

The house itself was a dull yellow in color, an older Cape Cod style with a rear porch and, presumably, a front porch. It was crammed very close to the houses on either side of it, lake-adjacent property being at a premium in any city. Even here in Syracuse, where the lake was among the most polluted in the United States, people paid extra to live by the water, and as many property owners as possible crammed in around the limited lakeshore space.

Today, in the sunlight, the lake looked beautifully blue. A faint smell of dead fish wafted from it, but the people visiting the park didn't seem to mind. There were sailboats and motorboats out on the lake, and several people were even fishing from a dock.

"Come on," Blancanales said. "Stop gawking and let's go. Be casual."

They walked up to the fence as if they owned the place. Blancanales even stopped to look around as if checking out the foot traffic—which, in fact, he was, but not for the reasons a casual observer might think. Satisfied that they weren't being watched too closely, the two men walked across the lawn.

"We're in position," Schwarz said.

"I'm out front," Lyons said. "I'm knocking now."

They heard the sound of Lyons knocking, and then heard him ring the bell. There was movement from inside the house. At least two, maybe three people were moving around inside.

Schwarz looked left, then right, making sure nobody was scrutinizing them. He drew the 93-R with its suppressor fitted, holding the weapon between the house and his body. He and Blancanales stood at either side of the door.

Schwarz motioned for the doorknob. They could hear Lyons at the front door, chatting up whoever had finally answered.

"Hello," Lyons said cheerfully, in an entirely unconvincing manner. Blancanales winced.

"What do you want?" The voice that answered had no accent.

"Say!" Lyons said, painfully chipper. Again, Blancanales winced to hear it. "Is that your Harley outside? I've always wanted to join a club. Are you three in a club? The three of you look like you might be in a club."

That was Lyons cluing in his teammates as to what they faced.

"I said, what do you want?" The voice became more hostile.

"I'm sorry, gentlemen," Lyons said. "I didn't mean to waste your time. But I have a very important question. If you died today, do you know if you would go to Heaven?"

"Get the hell out of here, fruitloop," the man at the door said. "Or I'll put a bullet in your—"

"No," Lyons said, his voice returning to its normal low growl. "It's a serious question. Are you sure? Because if not, I'm going to help you find out."

"The cops!" someone inside yelled. "Take 'em out!"

"Go!" Blancanales said to Schwarz.

CARL LYONS WOULD NEVER be the covert operative that Blancanales was; that much was certain. It was all he could do to keep the fake smile plastered to his face when the door to the target house opened. If he'd had any doubts about the location, they were canceled by the look of the hardcases who answered the door. The lead man was stripped to the waist and covered in tattoos, the biggest of these a large flaming skull that arched up across his chest. His head was shaved. He wore several earrings in the shape of inverted crosses.

Lyons held his arm behind his back. The Python, with the impromptu silencer strapped to its barrel, was hidden behind his leg. He only hoped that nobody passing by on the relatively quiet street noticed him and called the cops.

The conversation went about as well as Lyons had

assumed it would. When the big man filling the door frame threatened to shoot him, he was already dragging a revolver from his waistband at the small of his back. Lyons dropped the unwieldy Python-and-soda-bottle creation and struck like a cobra. He put the web of his hand into the man's throat while grabbing, twisting and redirecting the revolver in the man's other hand. Plucking the weapon from the hardcase's fingers, he reversed it and jammed the muzzle against the bald head.

"No," he said, shaking his head. "It's a serious question. Are you sure? Because if not, I'm going to help you find out."

"The cops!" yelled the man behind Lyons's prisoner. "Take 'em out!"

Lyons didn't wait for a bullet to find him. Deepening the painful wristlock in which he held the bald man's gun hand, he yanked the man toward him and smashed the revolver into his temple, dazing him. The staggering, tattooed bald man became a human shield.

Lyons's teammates burst in through the back. Schwarz had his 93-R up and seeking targets. The loudmouth who was quick to shoot cops ducked and grabbed a pump-action shotgun from behind a nearby sofa. Blancanales, acting quickly, picked up a heavy ceramic ashtray sitting on a card table next to the door and hurled it. The projectile struck the man with the shotgun right between the eyes. His eyes actually rolled back into his head as he fell.

A third man, still mobile, was running for the kitchen. Schwarz pursued. The suppressed Beretta clapped once. The man in the kitchen screamed and something heavy crashed into the wall out there, knocking over what sounded like a kitchen table.

"One down," Schwarz said. "Still alive. Clear here."

"Clear here," Blancanales said. He looked at Lyons,

who was wrestling his prisoner to the ground in a painful armlock.

"Clear…here," Lyons grunted.

The three men—one with a field dressing wrapped around his thigh—were dumped on the sagging couch in the living room, their hands and feet secured with plastic zip-tie cuffs.

"Gadgets," Blancanales said, "you're going soft. You aimed low."

"Seemed like the thing to do," Schwarz explained. "At least now we just have to arrange for a prisoner transfer and not a cleanup crew. Saves time and hassle."

"There is that," Lyons said. He was pulling the electrical tape from the barrel of his revolver.

"I'm kind of glad you didn't try to use that cockamamie thing," Blancanales said.

"'Cockamamie'?" Schwarz chimed in. "Who says 'cockamamie'?"

"It would have worked," Lyons huffed. He tossed the empty soda bottle into a pile of empty, crushed beer cans and pizza boxes piled in the corner of the living room.

"Not exactly big on housekeeping, are they?" Schwarz asked.

"You can bet they don't live here," Lyons said. "Not looking like that, in this neighborhood. They're not exactly the suburban type."

One of the men looked as if he wanted to say something, but a glare from Lyons silenced him.

"I'll check the basement," Blancanales said.

"And I'll look upstairs," Schwarz said.

"Guess that leaves us together," Lyons said. He found a folding metal chair and reversed it, placing it in front of the couch so he could straddle it and lean on the backrest. He kept the Cold Python handy. He'd seen too many "secure" prisoners suddenly attack after working their way through their bonds.

"So," Lyons said to the sullen trio, "you're part of this Grubs club?"

"Yeah," one of them said.

"Working for the Triangle?"

The three men exchanged glances, obviously trying to decide if they were going to cooperate.

"Look, we're federal agents," Lyons said. "I have a few friends in high places. Work with me and we cut you a deal, maybe. Refuse to help and, well, it makes no difference to me. We just drop you in a hole and keep going."

"What's a Triangle, man?" one of them asked. It was the biker Blancanales had cracked in the face with the ashtray.

"You don't know?" Lyons asked.

"Look, man," said the man Lyons had subdued, "we just run stuff for the club. They say hold stuff here, we hold it. They say pack it up and move it out, we do that. We aren't in charge. We just run with the Grubs, man."

"Do you realize," Schwarz said, returning from his check of the upper floor, "that you're accessories to a multimillion-dollar drug and bootlegging ring?"

"Offhand I would say they do," Blancanales said, emerging from the basement. He held out a small, silver plastic rectangle. Headphones dangled from it.

"What's that thing?" Lyons said.

"That," Gadgets said, taking the device from Blancanales, "is a fairly decent copy of a very popular MP3 player."

"Empty what?" Lyons asked.

"MP3," Schwarz repeated slowly. "It's a digital music format, Carl."

"I still own a cassette deck," Lyons said. "Explain it to me like I don't know what you're talking about."

"Look," Schwarz said, "if Pol had found a basement full of old illegal copied vinyl albums, we'd be dealing with a piracy ring you could recognize."

Blancanales chuckled at that. "He's right. The basement's full of boxes of these things. They're not real. For one thing, the company logo is silk-screened backward on most of them."

"I don't get it," Lyons said.

"Don't get what?"

"Why bother with these things?" He pointed at the MP3 player.

"Because these are popular," Pol said. "Very high in demand. A high theft item, too."

"What's the point in stealing a music player like that?"

"Well, come on, Carl," Schwarz said. "Nobody bootlegs the actual music anymore. Everything is available on the Internet, though the copy protection varies from case to case. Manufacturing and selling the device that plays the music is as close as you're going to get to piracy for profit. People won't pay for music anymore, but they'll pay for the players."

"Freaking weird." Lyons shook his head.

"Find any drugs?" Schwarz asked Blancanales. "There was nothing upstairs."

"A few plastic bags with residue in them," Blancanales said. "And a lot of boxes and packing tape. Unless I miss my guess, I'd say most of the inventory here was packed and shipped out, and recently."

Lyons turned to the prisoners again. "Well?" he said.

"Yeah," the man with the ashtray welt said reluctantly. "We boxed everything up and moved it all out of here, last night and this morning. Orders."

"Orders from whom?" Lyons asked.

"Our contacts, the ones who usually drop off the stuff."

"I'm listening," Lyons said.

The biker explained that their contacts with the rest of the trafficking ring were largely anonymous. Trucks showed up, a driver spoke a code phrase and the merchandise was shipped out.

"What's the code phrase?" Lyons asked.

"Janis," the man said.

"Janis?" Schwarz asked.

"You know," the biker said and shook his head. "Janis Joplin."

"Ah." Blancanales nodded. "As in high all the time. Makes sense."

"Whatever, man."

"What's the next link in your distribution chain?" Lyons asked.

"No idea," the biker said. "We do everything through here. We don't take the stuff anywhere."

"Where does it go when you receive a shipment, then?" Schwarz asked.

"Somebody from the club usually picks it up. I ain't in charge, man."

"So you've said." Schwarz frowned.

"All right," Lyons said. He motioned for Schwarz to follow him to the next room, out of earshot of the prisoners. "Gadgets, get with Barb again. Let her know we've taken down another spoke in the wheel, but that we've come up bust here. It looks like the bad guys are starting to pull up stakes, possibly because of all the heat they're getting. Have them put their Frankenstein crystal ball to work finding for us where Thawan might be. We could keep nickel-and-diming these drug houses, and find a bunch more that have closed up shop, or we could go straight for the source, use that satellite the way it was meant to be used. I want to get out in front of this."

"And you owe Thawan a pretty righteous ass-kicking," Schwarz said.

"And I owe Thawan a pretty righteous ass-kicking," Lyons confirmed.

"Well, who am I to stand in the way of that?" Schwarz went to make the call, farther away so there was no chance of the prisoners overhearing.

Blancanales had been watching the prisoners and occasionally taking a glance out the living room's dirty bay window, which was covered with an old sheet in lieu of an actual curtain. Lyons kicked aside a pile of old Chinese takeout cartons and moved to join him. The filth in which the bikers had lived was pretty typical of such fringe-living criminal types. The carpet had been worn bare. Trash was strewed everywhere. Holes had been kicked or punched into the walls. The place reeked of stale beer, cigarettes and urine.

"This place smells like the bottom of my gym bag," Lyons said.

"Then I don't want to know what you do for a workout," Blancanales said.

"Any activity out there?"

"No," Blancanales said. "I checked the front and the back. Looks like we're clean for now."

"Good." Lyons nodded. "Fewer calls for Hal and Barb to make. We'll get them," he said, jerking his chin toward the prisoners, "packaged up and shipped off somewhere, and then see what the Farm can tell us. I want him, Pol. I want him bad. I want to stop him."

"We will," Blancanales said.

"Hey!" one of the bikers shouted. "What about our deal?"

"I said maybe," Lyons shot back. "Now shut up."

The biker swore a blue streak. Lyons ignored him.

"I think you may be mellowing in your old age, Carl," Blancanales said.

"Don't you start, too," Lyons said.

CHAPTER THIRTEEN

Sportivnaya Station, the Moscow metro

The men of Phoenix Force, spread out among the crowd in the Moscow metro station, moved among the white marble pylons beneath the impressive embossed, asbestos-cement tiles that made up the ceiling of the station. T. J. Hawkins, as the youngest of the group, had drawn the duty with the surveillance equipment provided by the Farm. Designed to look like a fairly typical digital camera, the device was actually a very sensitive multidirectional-focused microphone. Once tracking an audio source, while the camera lens would see only what it was aimed at, the audio pickup would rotate on microswivels within the device to keep contact with the first audio surveillance source until the link was deliberately separated. It was really a rather brilliant piece of equipment, David McCarter had to admit.

The audio feed would be fed through their transceivers. The device's little audio processor included a real-time speech-recognition program that would render a slightly delayed synthetic translation, too. Once their quarry was identified, they would be as good as sitting in on the meeting.

The recovered PDA's information had been transmitted to the Farm and quickly analyzed by Kurtzman and his crew. Unfortunately, they'd learned little more than they already knew—that a meeting between the *mafiya,* of whom the former owner of the PDA was a known member with a long criminal record—and unknown representatives of Katzev was to take place at this time and in this place. That left them trawling the Metro station, looking for suspicious knots of people, while trying very hard not to look like that was what they were doing.

It was Calvin James who finally spotted them. "I've got something over here," he said. "Looks like two groups of suits. Based on the cut of the coats and the price of the shoes, not to mention the black-on-black fashion sense, one of the groups is definitely *mafiya.* The other could be businessmen, or something else. I see suits, I see briefcases and I see sunglasses everywhere."

"Watch those cases, lads," McCarter said. All the men of Phoenix Force were only too familiar with the types of automatic weaponry that could be hidden easily inside such a case—not to mention fired from within it. For that matter, dressed as they were, the Russians could have a small arsenal of hardware under their coats and suit jackets.

Hawkins moved into position, taking a photograph of the ceiling of the metro station, a common enough act for a tourist. His youth worked for him. He looked like a foreign traveler on holiday, trying to record the sights of this exotic locale.

They heard a burst of static over the transceiver link. Then the voices of the men, now clustering around a group of low benches, were transmitted at very low volume through the link. A moment later, the English translation came. While the translation wasn't perfect, it was easy enough to imagine the exact dialogue of the meeting, give or take.

"Generals Karpov, Ryenko," one of the *mafiya* thugs was saying. "I believe you know Ivan."

One of the *mafiya* men spoke up. "Ivan Dubinin."

"We do, we do," Karpov said.

"Generals," Encizo said. "Dressed as civilians." That might or might not be significant, and each team member knew it.

"I am Brusilov," said the man who had made the introductions. "Shall we sit?"

The two *mafiya* men, who were probably lieutenants, sat on the benches across from the two generals. Their entourages spread out, taking up defensive positions while trying and failing to look casual. Several of the *mafiya* types looked particularly agitated, scanning the crowd repeatedly. Chances were good they were wondering why the owner of that PDA had missed the meeting. Either they did not know the man was among those taken down at the mob banking house, or word of the hit had not reached them.

The latter case was not unthinkable. Except for Manning's dramatic entrance, they'd managed to keep things fairly quiet; the old building had muffled the sound of the gunfire from anyone on the street, and they'd managed to mop up after themselves quickly before extracting. Sooner or later, however, someone was going to find the bodies in the basement, or the men they'd left tied up were going to get free and go for help. They would not call the authorities, necessarily—the *mafiya* would look after their own—but as corrupt as things were here in Moscow, the dividing line between organized crime and public law enforcement could be very blurry.

"So," Brusilov said. "What is it that we, mere local businessmen, can do for you, the claws and teeth of the Russian bear?"

"Save your flattery, for one thing," General Karpov said.

"Now, now, my friend," General Ryenko chided. "There is value in social pleasantries. Forgive my comrade. He has been in a sour mood for years now."

"Bah," Karpov muttered.

"We have a…proposition for community-minded leaders such as yourselves," Ryenko said. "I… Comrade, what is it that vexes your men so?"

"Eh?" Brusilov turned and followed Ryenko's gaze. The general had apparently noticed the nervous behavior of the *mafiya* soldiers guarding the meeting. Brusilov conferred with Dubinin briefly. The exchange was far enough from the line of the focused transmission that it was not picked up or translated. "It is nothing," Brusilov said finally. "One of my people, whom you may remember as one of your contacts with Dubinin here, when you first requested this meeting, has failed to show up. My apologies for this. I am sure he means no disrespect."

"Is there a problem?"

"No, no," Brusilov said quickly. "None. Think no more of it. My men are simply overanxious. Being in the presence of such esteemed military greatness plays on their nerves."

Karpov snorted.

"Now then," Ryenko went on, smoothing the front of his suit. He appeared uncomfortable in it, as if he had been born and quite intended to die in uniform and not civilian clothing.

"You had a proposal," Brusilov prompted.

"Yes." Ryenko nodded. "As you know, the military has

found a good friend in President Katzev. We believe it is in his best interests to continue for another term."

"We, too, have found a strong ally in our president," Brusilov agreed. "But then, you know that."

"We do." Ryenko nodded. "President Katzev's time in office has seen record funding for the military, at a time when the Russian Federation needs strength most. The president should be heralded for his vision in securing the funds needed for this expansion."

"Indeed he should." Brusilov smiled. "We, too, have benefited from the president's unconventional approach to appropriation of funds. We would like to continue benefiting."

"We would like that, too," Ryenko said. "As you know, because you have assisted with certain banking matters relative to the venture, President Katzev, with the support of the military, has embarked on certain enterprises abroad. We believe those enterprises can be further expanded domestically, to the benefit of all."

"You speak of Thai and Burmese imports," Brusilov said. "Funding from these sources has proven most beneficial to our investment banking activities."

"Indeed it has," Ryenko affirmed. "If Katzev retains power, you can see, I trust, the ways in which we would all stand to benefit, as Russians. And you in particular, as businessmen, would benefit should these business partners be invited to open markets here in Russia. It is precisely the sort of economic activity Russia needs to thrive."

"I do not disagree," Brusilov said. "Some of my compatriots have a certain amount of hesitation when it comes to the presence of these…fellow businessmen, should they be given free rein to operate domestically. There is the matter of inviting…competition?"

"Katzev has planned for that," Ryenko said. "We, the

military, are prepared to place you and your fellow communitarians in direct control of various business ventures domestically for which you are so well suited."

"We would have direct and positive control?"

"Yes, working in partnership, but always with seniority, side by side with these new partners in commerce."

"That does sound most profitable."

"Let us cut the shit," Karpov broke in angrily. "I grow tired of these metaphors." He looked directly at Brusilov, then to Dubinin, as if daring them to protest. "We both know that Katzev is using the military to provide material assistance to Burmese drug traffickers. He promises them open markets here in Russia in return for their continued financial support. You, the *mafiya,* the proud Russian Federation's unspoken shadow government, you will be given significant control of organized crime in return for your cooperation with these Burmese drug traffickers. And holding hands like one happy family we will all walk forward into a new age."

"I sense you disapprove," Dubinin offered.

"Disapprove? *Disapprove?*" Karpov spat. "Am I the only man here who remembers our nation when it was a nation run by a strong government and not by criminals? When it was truly a superpower? When the West feared us?"

"I remember long lines for toilet paper," Ryenko said.

"Bah," Karpov scoffed. "You may enjoy being Katzev's errand boy, carrying messages to criminals. I remember a better time. I remember a more honorable time."

"Why do you do this, then," Brusilov said mildly, "if you find such dishonor in doing business with us? President Katzev and the *mafiya,* to use the Americanism, have enjoyed a long and profitable partnership. This is not new to you."

"It…it is the only way," Karpov admitted. "Katzev says he will restore our national pride. He says he will restore military might. That is why we serve him. That is why we allow our soldiers to die on foreign soil as little better than mercenaries. That is why Katzev uses us as his private security force. Because he promises. Always he promises."

"And he delivers," Ryenko pointed out. "Our funding has increased. New weapons, new resources…the strength to challenge the arrogant West. All of these are ours. No matter how you feel about the source."

"At what cost?" Karpov said. "Katzev plays a dangerous game. The West may appear weak, yes. It may be decadent. But its decadence is found in its indolence. Only when the West is at peace can we count on it to be asleep. Threaten it, and we wake the sleeping giant…again."

"And so?" Ryenko prodded.

"And so we must do this if we are to finance the military and preserve the strength of the Russian Federation," Karpov said finally.

"Good," Brusilov said after an extended pause. "In return for what you will bring to us, and what you give to us now, what do you want?"

Ryenko smoothed the front of his jacket again. "You are not stupid, gentlemen," he said, "and as my friend General Karpov has seen fit to dispense with the metaphors and flowery talk, I will speak frankly, as well." His tone became a bit more businesslike, a bit less ingratiating. "There is a certain…political rival," he said. "Andulov, of course. Very popular with the people. Good-looking, experienced, but yet in his prime. He has much support. Yet he projects weakness. He does not understand the need for military expenditures as do we. Certainly he does not understand the role you gentlemen play in our great society."

"Andulov is no friend to us, no," Brusilov said, frowning. "He promises to be harsh on organized crime, if elected. Many believe his is the way to a better life."

"And so you see," General Ryenko interjected, "the problem, and the solution, in one neat package."

"Explain, please," Brusilov said.

"It is simple." Ryenko spread his hands. "Andulov is holding a rally tomorrow night. We wish him to be killed, violently and spectacularly so, by the *mafiya*."

"His death obviously profits Katzev," Brusilov said, "and he would be a thorn removed from our sides, as well. But why do you wish it done in such a manner?"

"Katzev wishes his rival removed and his next term for president secured," Ryenko said, "but he is not one to waste an opportunity. Andulov styles himself as the savior of Russia, the man who will fight organized crime. If he is killed by the criminals he says he will fight, he becomes a martyr…and of course no suspicion falls on President Katzev or those of us in the military who are loyal to him. President Katzev can then, in turn, take up the cause, vowing to fight these criminals who have flouted the will of the people and interfered in a diplomatic election."

"We are to become the scapegoats, then?" Brusilov asked, his eyes narrowing.

"In the popular media only," Ryenko said. "The prosecutions against your people will go nowhere. Your operations will continue unabated, though President Katzev will of course stage certain raids whose purpose is to demonstrate that his fight against organized crime progresses. A victory here, a victory there. Symbolism only, while you continue to operate with our protection."

"It is a good plan," Dubinin said.

"And the populists will fall into line as Katzev uses the military on all fronts to fight for the will of the people." Ryenko smiled again.

"I have certain parties I must consult," Brusilov said, "but these issues have been discussed among our… community…and we are in general agreement. I believe it can be arranged, as you request."

"Tomorrow night, then?" Ryenko asked. "During his rally?"

"Yes," Brusilov said. "The president will not be disappointed."

"To a new term, then," Ryenko said.

Karpov scoffed again. The general rose to go, his body language that of a man disgusted with what he had just done. Then he froze.

He was looking straight at Hawkins.

"That man," Karpov said. "He has been photographing the same parts of the metro station over and over again, the entire time we have been talking."

From his vantage point among the crowd in the station, McCarter resisted the urge to put his finger to the earbud transceiver he wore. "We're blown, lads," he said quietly. "Let's see which way they break."

"We are leaving," Ryenko said, standing quickly. "I suggest you do the same."

"It could be nothing," Brusilov said. "Tourists."

"Or it could be Andulov's people conducting surveillance. I suggest that you do not let him or any with him continue to follow you."

"We are not children," Dubinin said. "We will deal with him if he is a spy."

"See that you do." Ryenko bowed. "Good day. We will be in touch."

"I can hardly wait," Brusilov muttered.

The *mafiya* lieutenants, surrounded by their guards, began hustling from the station.

"They're running for it," James said. "What do you want to do, David? Split up?"

"No," McCarter instructed. "We don't need to follow the generals. They'll head back to Katzev, or go wherever it is Russian generals spend their time when they're not doing whatever it is they do. Our priority is Andulov. Pursue the mobsters. They'll be heading for a vehicle. T.J., since they've already seen you, give them something to think about. Stay on their heels."

"Will do," Hawkins drawled.

McCarter watched his team move out and through the crowd.

The mobsters were moving faster now. McCarter shadowed them, and felt as much as saw the rest of Phoenix Force doing the same. Now was delicate; things were very close to the boiling point in a very public place, and the Briton was keenly aware of the potential for an international incident should Phoenix Force and Russian nationals engage in a firefight out here in the open, despite the fact that those nationals were most likely wanted criminals with lengthy records.

Once outside, Hawkins continued to shadow the mobsters. The other members of Phoenix Force made their way outside the station and down the street to where the Land Rover was parked. "Rafe, take the wheel," McCarter said. "Stay alert, chaps."

Hawkins's voice came to them from his position farther down the street. "They're getting into an old ZIL limousine. They know I'm following them, all right."

"What are they doing?" McCarter asked.

"Just moving out. Nothing hostile."

"We're coming to you." McCarter directed Encizo to

move out. The Cuban-born guerilla fighter stepped on the gas and the Land Rover moved away from the curb.

They picked up Hawkins while still on the move; T.J. simply ran alongside the truck, jumped on the running board and let himself in. He slammed the door shut behind him as they maneuvered into the dense Moscow traffic.

"Stay on them," McCarter said.

"No problem," Encizo said.

"Can I assume," McCarter asked, "that we have that entire conversation, including the automatically generated translation, digitally recorded?"

Hawkins examined the display screen on the rear of the small camera-size device. He pressed a few buttons and called up a menu. After making a few other adjustments, he pressed Play on the small screen.

"In the popular media only." The voice of General Ryenko was clear as the translation echoed it. "The prosecutions against your people will go nowhere. Your operations will continue unabated, though President Katzev will of course stage certain raids…"

"Damning." McCarter smiled. "Hawkins, get on your satellite phone. Establish an uplink to the Farm and make sure they get copies of everything."

"Doing it now."

"We've got them by the throat, lads," McCarter said. "Bloody hell, but we got them. Now we just have to do the hard part."

"What's that?" James asked.

"Keep Andulov alive."

The ZIL was moving in and out of traffic. The big armored limousine started to speed up, then move more aggressively.

"They've spotted us," Encizo said.

"Or they're just nervous on principle," McCarter

nodded. "I would be, too. Keep it up, Rafe. Right now they're our best link to stopping the hit on Andulov. We put our hands on them, we can cut off the hit attempt before it begins."

"Katzev's people could just contact some other branch of the mob," Manning said from the back of the Land Rover.

"They could, at that," McCarter said. "But we'll burn that bridge when we get to it, lads."

Encizo looked over at McCarter and started to say something, then thought better of it.

"What's the plan, David?" Encizo asked.

"We put a stop to these blokes and end the direct threat to Andulov, or delay it," McCarter said. "Once we've done that, we can consult with the Farm, see about the most effective way to take this public. We can see to it that Andulov wins the election simply by exposing Katzev for what he is."

"You sure we want to go that far, David?" Encizo asked.

"No." McCarter shook his head. "Bloody hell, I'm not. We need to talk to Barb, and to Hal, before we start nation building."

The Land Rover began to slow.

"Rafe?" McCarter asked. "What are you doing? We'll lose them at this rate, mate."

"We have a problem," Encizo said, checking the rearview mirror. "There are two Volkswagens moving up on our tail, fast compacts. They've been following us since we left the metro station."

"Bloody hell," McCarter said.

CHAPTER FOURTEEN

Albany, New York

The basement of the house in the Albany suburbs was crammed full with cardboard boxes. Half of these were full of drugs, almost haphazardly thrown into the cartons. The haste with which their dwindling resources were thrown together and shipped here was evident in the lack of order. Mok Thawan uttered a disgusted sigh.

His father had been almost kind in speaking with him on the phone, and that worried him. The warlord Than was known for many things, but kindness was not one of them. He had little mercy in his soul, and still less pity. While he did value his heir, and Mok Thawan had always known he was being groomed eventually to take over the Triangle's many operations, Than was not the sort of man who would tolerate repeated failure. If Thawan did not start to show real results in the fight against these mysterious, brutal Western fighters, he would eventually displease Than to the point that the warlord saw fit to remove and replace him. No doubt the loss of time and effort invested in Thawan would grieve the warlord, but Thawan was not so arrogant as to believe that Than would shed many tears over him were it to come to that.

If his attitude was already almost welcoming, it might mean that Than was slowly resigning himself to the eventuality of replacing Thawan. He could be allowing himself to feel…nostalgic—that was the word. He could be remembering Thawan's rise to power within the Triangle, and regretting what might have been, all while arranging to have his failed heir thrown to dogs.

It was the way the warlord operated.

Withdrawing to this safehouse was not the last option available to him. There was yet a refuge to which he could turn. If he relocated to Boston, however, he would be admitting that the distribution network had collapsed. It would be tantamount to admitting failure…and of course that brought him back to the possibility that Than's patience with him was not infinite.

The men of his entourage were stationed in vehicles around the house, guarding it from the street. It was not the most inconspicuous of methods, but it was necessary; Thawan was nervous, and he needed to know that his people were stationed on the perimeter. He took the walkie-talkie from his belt and keyed it.

"Report," he said simply.

"Nothing," came one voice.

"It is quiet," said a second.

"Nothing here," added a third.

He listened as the rest of the guards reported. He had been checking every hour. He did not wish to project any sort of weakness to his men, and these frequent status reports might, he knew, make them wonder what it was he feared could be coming. But he could not help himself. He needed to know that the commandos were not even now closing in on him.

He leaned against a stack of boxes and wiped his face with his hand, sighing deeply.

The other half of the goods stacked in the basement consisted of counterfeit high-definition DVD players. These were manufactured at a small Triangle-run plant in Thailand, smuggled into the United States past bribed Customs agents and used in the domestic distribution operations. Each unit had much empty space inside its chassis, and these spaces were packed with drugs when the units were shipped to their final destinations. These were most often small electronics sellers run by illegal immigrants who were part of the Triangle's operations within the United States. Many were simply plucked from the streets or from migrant farm and work gangs, lured by the temptation of easy money as they struggled for their part of the American dream.

American dream. What a joke, Thawan thought to himself.

He had been in the country for some years now, occasionally traveling back and forth to Burma and Thailand under the cover of false identities or via private planes. He had come to hate the place. While he loved the money that could be made, the markets that could be exploited, the fools who would pay everything they owned and more to obtain the poisons the Triangle offered them, he despised everything about the people from whom he took these things. They were fat, lazy, decadent and arrogant. They lived in the richest nation in the world and did not appreciate what they had. They presumed to tell the rest of the world how to live, and yet their government forces were no match for the Triangle.

At least until now.

Thawan had started to dream of the big American whom he had faced more than once now. They were more than dreams; they were nightmares, and each one ended with the big blond man choking the life from him. Thawan had tried to sleep, tried to get a few hours of blessed rest, only an hour ago, and he was ripped from the embrace of sleep by the face of that American, by the feeling of the man's fingers wrapped around his throat.

He did not think he lacked courage. He had fought and killed many times in the name of Than and of the Triangle. The lives of those who opposed him meant nothing to him, but he was not a monster. He simply did not care about what happened to any man, woman or child who got in his way or defied the will of Than, who had been the means through which Thawan had earned everything he possessed in life. Money, power, the ability to live as he wished…these he owed to the warlord. Than had seen to it that Thawan was properly educated, trained, molded. He had, in part, built Thawan. The eventual promise of running the Triangle entire…well, this was almost an academic matter. Thawan arguably ran the Triangle now. But to be the warlord and to live in decadence, his every word law, his every whim met—women, power and access to the full wealth of the Triangle—that was a goal worth working toward. He flattered Than almost out of habit; his loyalty to Than was real, but not quite so slavish as he acted. Still, if ever he was tempted not to be loyal to Than, the very real possibility that he would one day replace Than was enough to keep him in line and working for the warlord's interests. For all practical purposes, after all, Than's interests were Thawan's interests, at least in the long-term.

To reach the long-term, however, he would have to face these men who had appeared from nowhere and attacked the Triangle and Than's holdings.

He walked up the stairs from the basement. The living

room of the suburban home had been emptied of furniture, save for half a dozen computer desks. Four of the computers were being operated by Thawan's handpicked men. While none of his criminal thugs were exactly geniuses when it came to computers, many of them were technologically savvy enough to use them. Right now, those men were listing the DVD players for sale on various online retail sites. Each listing contained a code known to members of the organization. They would respond in turn with a different code when buying the devices.

The payment received from such customers would, of course, be far more than the price listed for them. The units received by the customers would be those packed with drugs. It was a good system; it allowed customers from all over the country to buy the product, while providing a cover and a means of laundering funds under the guise of a legitimate—or semilegitimate, Thawan sometimes laughed to himself—business. If some foolish American paid for an overpriced, counterfeit DVD player without the code, he was shipped one of the units—without the drugs, of course. Most of these customers, what few of them there were, expressed their displeasure with the inferior product by leaving negative feedback on the retail sites where the machines were posted. Thawan did not care. The negative ratings helped discourage purchases by more American fools, while leaving his people free to conduct the trade and ship the drugs.

The other two computers were being used by Russian military men. These were soldiers provided by Aleksis Katzev as part of his ongoing effort to court Than's favor. Thawan did not know if these soldiers were aware of the deaths of their comrades in Burma, and he doubted they would be overly worried about it if they did. He kept a close eye on the men nonetheless.

They had their uses. They were well-trained and competent professionals, unlike the thugs Thawan normally employed. He had them searching online now, through both public databases and private resources known to the Russian military, in an attempt to find some information on the killers tracking the Triangle in the States.

He stood behind the two soldiers, looking over their shoulders. They had both said more than once that this annoyed them; Thawan did it purposefully thereafter. It was important that the men under him understand that he was in charge and was not to be defied even in small things. The Russians did not intimidate easily, unlike many of his own people.

Among the men operating the other computers was Gig Tranh, one of his commanders. Thawan was not overly fond of him. While he was indeed competent and even popular among the other men in Thawan's employ, Thawan found the unctuous little fellow a bit much, best tolerated in measured doses. He was simply…annoying. He was good with the computers but hard to keep on task. When Thawan moved to look over Tranh's shoulder, he found the man looking at pornography.

"Gig Tranh!" Thawan smacked the man in the back of the head. "Back to work! There is time enough for this nonsense later. We need funds! Get back to work!"

Gig Tranh swore under his breath, but closed the window and went back to making listings for the DVD players.

Thawan turned back to the Russians. "Have you anything?"

"Nothing," the more talkative of the two Russians said in accented English. "But perhaps there is a connection."

Thawan's eyes narrowed. "Explain."

"I was Spetsnaz," the Russian said. "Special forces. There were rumors."

"Rumors of what?"

"There was talk of special commando teams," the Russian said. "Men working outside the American government. Well trained, well funded. Ruthless. Capable of hitting even the most protected of targets, disappearing like ghosts, killing like the plague."

"Old women's tales," Thawan scoffed. "The sort of thing told to children to make them fear."

"Perhaps." The Russian shrugged. "I only know what I heard."

"Such men," Thawan said, "if they exist at all, are only men. They are no more deadly than anyone else. Certainly they are not more deadly than me."

The Russian shrugged. Clearly he was not convinced.

Thawan suddenly felt very tired. "I am going upstairs," he said. "Continue your work. Report to me if you learn anything I can actually use. No more stories."

The Russian turned back to the computer screen without a word.

Fools, Thawan thought to himself. *I am surrounded by fools and frightened old women.*

Even as he thought the words *frightened old women,* he chided himself for his hypocrisy. He entered one of the upstairs rooms, which were largely devoid of furniture. The bomb he had rigged squatted in the center of the room, crushing the carpet fibers beneath it. It was a simple, even crude affair, wired to an RF transmitter that was identical to the dead man's switch he'd used to bluff his way past the big American the last time. This time, the switch was very much live. He removed the switch from his pocket, made sure it was not yet armed and returned it, patting the bomb almost for good luck.

There was enough Semtex plastic explosive packed

inside the street-mailbox-size bomb to level the house. The debris would likely damage the adjacent buildings, but these were vacant. Well, they were vacant now. It had only taken his people a few months of constant harassment and threats, when this distribution point was first established, to persuade the neighbors to accept a sales offer and move away. The money paid was the price necessary to remove those neighbors without inviting police attention, for killing them would certainly have brought the very scrutiny the Triangle wished to avoid. Forcing the neighbors to abandon the properties would have caused just as many problems; what was a few hundred thousand dollars in inflated housing costs if it bought him security? At the time, they had had more than enough money. It was only the cruel, sadistic sense of humor possessed by the unfeeling gods above that the housing market had since collapsed, driving down the values of all of the properties in this suburban development.

Satisfied that the bomb was there and ready, his last line of defense and security, Thawan tried to calm his mind. As he lay down on the mattress thrown in a corner, his thoughts returned again and again to the threats looming over him. Thus tortured, he tossed and turned, wondering if sleep would ever find him.

"SO YOU'RE JUST GOING to walk up to the front door again?" Schwarz asked.

"Why not?" Lyons asked. He was loading double-aught buck rounds into a 20-round drum magazine for his Daewoo USAS-12 shotgun.

"Every time you knock on the front door, there's a firefight."

"That's not fair," Lyons said, still loading the drum magazine. "Those last guys lived."

"Not my point." Schwarz shook his head with mock outrage. "Not my point at all."

"Regardless," Lyons said, "I'm done screwing around. "You and Pol will take the back. I'll take the front. Pretty basic."

"It doesn't get any more basic," Schwarz needled. "You're regressing, Ironman."

"Simple works," Lyons said. "So shut up."

"Well, at least we got that out of the way," the Able Team electronics whiz muttered.

They were sitting in their rented Suburban parked down the block from the target location. NetScythe had verified that, from among the distribution points labeled on the map they'd recovered earlier, there was a very high probability that Albany was the most prominent among them. Its higher probability ranking made it the more likely location for Mok Thawan to be found, based on the previous pattern he had established.

"That thing," Lyons had said when the NetScythe data was transmitted from the Farm to Able Team's phones, "is freaking amazing."

"I don't completely understand how it does its analysis of the imagery," Schwarz said, "but it's definitely ground-breaking stuff. The field test we're giving it proves that it can work under real field conditions."

"Yeah, well, don't go getting too excited," Lyons said. "Remember, without some hardheaded lugs to bang on doors on the ground, none of that satellite imagery is worth a good damn."

"Well, you're certainly the hardheaded lug for the job," Schwarz retorted.

Now, as they prepared for yet another assault on a Triangle distribution point, Blancanales was using a pair of field glasses to examine the surrounding houses. The neighborhood was strangely quiet. There was no foot traffic.

"I know this isn't exactly the New York area," Blancanales said as he scanned back and forth, "but this is the capital of the state. There should be a few more people around."

"You've gotten too used to big-city life, Pol," Schwarz said. "Trust me, there are plenty of places in upstate New York where you'd swear they roll up the sidewalks at night. But I agree with you. This is strangely empty. Something's not quite right about it."

"I'm looking in the windows here," Blancanales said.

"Pervert," Schwarz cracked.

"Shut up," Lyons said absently.

"I'm not seeing anything," Blancanales concluded.

"No activity?" Lyons asked.

"No, no, nothing," Blancanales replied. "There is no furniture in the houses on either side or across the street, at least not that I can see through the windows, which have no curtains, either. Those houses are vacant, but there are no signs."

"It's a tough housing market," Schwarz mused. "They might be on the market but not being actively promoted."

"More likely," Blancanales said, "our boys managed to arrange somehow to have the place to themselves."

"Good point," Lyons said. "Blackmail, simple buyout, whatever. They make sure there's nobody around to wonder what they're up to, and basically establish a safe-house in the middle of town."

"Exactly," Blancanales said.

Lyons's secure satellite phone began to vibrate. He snapped it open. "Yeah," he said.

"Ironman, it's Barbara," Price said. "Have you made your raid yet?"

"We were about to," Lyons said. "Why?" He put Price on speaker, so the others could listen.

"We've just received an urgent communication from Interpol. It was routed through Justice but of course it was flagged in our computers as soon as it came in. Interpol has heard from their long-lost agent, the one deep-cover operative assigned to infiltrate the Triangle who hasn't yet turned up dead. I'm sending you his dossier now."

"And this is relevant because…?" Lyons asked.

"Because he's inside that house," Price said.

"Holy crap," Schwarz said.

Lyons shot him a sour look. "How'd that happen?"

"He's been part of Thawan's outfit for some time," Price said, "but Interpol lost contact with him half a year ago. His latest duty for the Triangle, however, is using a computer as part of their retail bootlegging operation. He's sent a series of e-mails to his superiors, verifying the address as the one you're about to breach."

Lyons peered at the phone's color display screen. The file had downloaded; he opened it.

"Sahk Nguyen, thirty-two," he read out loud. Nguyen's picture was displayed in full color, from the front and in profile, above the text. "Mixed Vietnamese and Thai parentage. Emigrated to London at eighteen. Studied abroad, got a criminal justice degree, eventually made his way into law enforcement, and then to Interpol. Impressive. I'm glad he's still alive. Any explanation for his long silence? I don't want to walk into a trap."

"He says he was watched closely for a long time," Price reported, "but eventually his education and his experience with computers prompted Thawan to give him this assignment. He's been able to communicate freely with his bosses at Interpol for the past two days."

"We're just hearing about this now?"

"The wheels of justice move slowly," Schwarz intoned.

Lyons glared at him. "Any direct intel from inside?"

"Yes," Price said. "He says you've got Thawan, two Triangle goons and two Russian soldiers."

"Russian soldiers?"

"We're processing significant intelligence data gleaned by Phoenix Force in Russia," Price told him. "We've verified that President Katzev is receiving funds from the Triangle and provided them with significant support in return, including the use of his military forces."

"He's pimping the Russian army like mercenaries," Lyons said. "Beautiful."

"The good news is that Nguyen says that's the limit of the forces there," Price went on.

"Can you let him know we'll be visiting? See if he can back us up in any way?"

"We've sent him a message," Price said, "and he's responded. He's apparently in front of his computer right now. Keep that in mind when you're choosing which heads to shoot and which ones to avoid."

"Understood, Barb," Lyons said. "Ironman out."

"Now?" Schwarz asked hopefully.

"Now," Lyons said. He climbed out of the truck with the shotgun in his fists.

Blancanales and Schwarz got out and worked their way around either side of the house. The curtains—this house had them—were drawn. They did their best to stay low and avoid the windows.

Lyons marched up to the front door, stood to one side and rapped on it. There was no answer, so he knocked again, harder this time.

"What do you want?" came a muffled voice from inside. The accent was Russian.

"The code word is 'Janis,'" Lyons said.

"What? Get out of here." The voice was dismissive.

"Well, it was worth a try," Lyons muttered. He took a step back, braced himself, leveled the USAS-12 and blew the locking mechanism of the door to fragments.

Schwarz and Blancanales kicked in the rear door of the house at the sound of Lyons's shotgun. All three men burst in, weapons before them, shouting for the residents of the house to get down.

Lyons spotted Nguyen, who wisely dived for cover under his computer desk. The other men started to reach for weapons—handguns on their persons, or, in one case, a shotgun leaning against the wall. Lyons put a blast of double-aught pellets between the would-be shotgunner's shoulder blades. Schwarz dropped one hardman with his 93-R, while Blancanales put precise shots from his 92-F through the head and chest of one more.

"Do not shoot!" the last of the gunmen shouted, throwing down the Tokarev pistol in his hands. He was a squat, scarred, misshapen fellow.

"Where's Thawan?" Lyons demanded.

"I am here," Thawan said. He stood at the foot of the stairs. "There is no need to torture Gig Tranh for the information."

Lyons turned. "Well, well," he said.

"You," Thawan growled. "I knew it would be you."

Blancanales kept the scarred gunmen covered, while Schwarz backed up Lyons. "I've got him, Carl," he said, leveling the 93-R machine pistol at Mok Thawan.

"Your weapons are quite useless," Thawan said calmly. He held out the dead man's switch in his hand.

"We've danced that dance before," Lyons said. "Not falling for it this time."

"Good," Thawan said. He hurled the switch at Lyons

and dived out the living room's bay window. It began beeping furiously.

"Run!" Lyons roared.

The members of Phoenix Force managed to just make it out the back door. Blancanales had the presence of mind to grab Nguyen as they fled; the Interpol agent landed on the ground under Schwarz and beside Blancanales as the heat from the incredible explosion hammered them into the ground like the fist of an angry god.

Lyons rolled over. Pieces of the burning house were falling all around him; he held his arms over his face and deflected a flaming chunk of two-by-four and then a piece of drywall. The ringing in his ears was the only sound he could hear at first, but he became aware of something else.

Horrible screaming.

The man who staggered out of the burning wreckage was on fire. He wailed in agony, a human torch entirely consumed by the hellish explosion. From the stature, the walking, burning corpse was the man Thawan had called Gig Tranh.

Schwarz raised the 93-R and put a mercy round through the burning man's head. The burning body fell to the lawn.

"Madre de Dios," Blancanales breathed.

"You can say that again," Lyons said softly.

CHAPTER FIFTEEN

The Streets of Moscow

"They are slowing," Sul said over his wireless headset for the benefit of Ven and Zun in the rear car. In the passenger seat, Ren smiled, sensing action was imminent. He cocked the micro-Uzi submachine gun in his lap.

"They are ours now," Ren said, flashing an evil little smile full of sharp teeth and wide gaps.

"So they are," Sul said. "So they are."

All four were Indonesian, born and raised on the streets of Jakarta. At early ages they had become intimately familiar with crime and violence; a life on the streets of any such city will do that to any human being, man or woman. Sul, with a gaunt, angular face, had first thought to ply their trades as assassins. He had gathered his then teenage friends. There was the obedient, stolid, blood-thirsty Ren, his second in command. There was the sinister-looking and quiet Ven, with his hooded eyes and shaved head. And there was Zun, smallest of them, fast like a monkey and absolutely fearless. They could, he had told them, make a good living eliminating those whom others would pay to see dead. There was relatively little work involved, too; they merely had to do something distasteful, once in a while, to enjoy a life of leisure the rest of the time.

Their first job had been a simple knifing. Sul had used Ren, Ven and Zun—street nicknames that had grown to become their true identities, eventually eclipsing their forgotten, given names—to herd the target into an alleyway. There he had plunged a blade into the man's chest again and again. Then, breathless and more than a little exhilarated, he had first riffled through the corpse's pockets before he and his friends fled the scene.

It got easier after that. As they became better financed, they added better weaponry to their equipment. Their first guns had been crude, worn and unreliable, practically antiques, but all they could get. In time they had the best of weapons, and enough money to travel for specialized training with various paramilitary and civilian contractors. It had at first surprised Sul to learn such training was even available to civilians. He had come to enjoy the knowledge and the feeling that he was a skilled professional.

From humble beginnings, Sul and his team had become one of the most feared groups of assassins operating in this part of the globe. As their reputations grew, so, too, did the law-enforcement scrutiny falling on them. More than once they had been forced to kill government agents and other police operatives who had tried to apprehend them. He had started to lose count, but he believed it was at least five dead in four countries. The exact figures were unimportant. So far, no one had come for Sul and his men who was a match for the four of them.

For five years, Sul and his team had been in the exclusive employment of the Burmese drug warlord Than. That arrangement had suited Sul well enough. Than paid a large retainer at the beginning of each year, which was more than enough to keep Sul and his men well fed and happy even if there was no work. There was plenty of work, however; Than was easily offended, and fond of exacting brutal, bloody revenge on any who dared oppose him. At least six times a year, if not more, he called on Sul, Ren, Ven and Zun to destroy someone he wished removed from the Earth. Usually he had specific instructions for the explicit, miserable fate the victim was to suffer. Other times he simply wished the party or parties dead, without fail, no matter how it was done.

This was one of those times. Than had many enemies abroad, he had explained on the phone. The connection was not good; Than was calling from a satellite phone in remote Burma, while Sul was on a conventional wireless, speaking from a safehouse in Greece where he and the others often stayed between jobs. The warlord had made himself clear immediately: he wished the four assassins on a plane to Moscow without delay.

Than explained that enemies who sought to do him harm—specifically, a team of armed men with very specialized combat training, from all appearances—had tracked his financial interests through the Russian mob in Moscow. These were men known to Than, men with whom he did considerable business, though he hoped to do a great deal more in the future. The warlord suggested that, once in Moscow, Sul and his people should follow a man named Ivan Dubinin, one of the men of higher rank within the *mafiya* in Moscow. He was one of the men with whom Than did business, and he was directly linked to the financial records that Than's enemies had tracked to Moscow. Those men would likely seek to do harm to Dubinin, or at the very least put him under surveillance; maybe capture and interrogate him or one of his men to get more information on Than. The best chance of finding Than's enemies was, therefore, to keep watch on Dubinin and any high-ranking Russian mobsters operating in Moscow, to see who else might be following these men. Once they had found such interested parties, they would have found the men who had so enraged and offended Than. It was a simple, workable plan.

Work it did. Sul and his men had acquired Dubinin at his home that morning, and spent the hours thereafter following him from location to location. Early in the day he met with another man, and the two of them had gone to various government and private businesses in downtown Moscow, presumably conducting the day-to-day mechanics of the *mafiya*'s affairs.

When the two had gone to the metro station in the company of several guards, Sul had feared he might lose them in the crowd. Instead, the mobsters had stayed relatively stationary, conducting a meeting with other Russians. This allowed Sul and his people to walk the crowd, looking for any who might also have an interest in their quarry.

It had taken a while, but he had spotted them. By his count, there were five of them. They did not move like the typical Muscovite, nor did they appear to be tourists. No, these men walked with the gaits of predators. It was obvious enough to any man who knew to look. Thus, their efforts had borne fruit early, and Sul looked forward to concluding their business and returning to Greece.

Always in his mind was the possibility that, one day, he might meet death on such a mission. The thought did not trouble him overmuch. His own life, while it had been good, could end at any time, for all he cared; if it did not, he would continue to sell his services, and those of his friends, to those who would buy. He did not know what Ren, Ven or Zun thought of the matter; he had not asked them.

Only a fool would believe the warlord Than had only these four at his disposal. Sul did not know or care how many other assassins might already have been charged with this duty. He intended to be the one to take the lives of Than's enemies. Once a job was accepted, this became a matter of principle. If he did not shoot down these men with his gun, he would let their blood out with the blade of his *karambit,* an Indonesian fighting knife. From afar or close enough to feel a man's dying breath on his face, Sul did not care.

He cared only for the killing, and for the money.

"HERE IT COMES," Encizo said. "This traffic is making it very hard for me to evade them."

"It's slowing them down, too," McCarter said. "Just roll with it, Rafe. We'll adapt."

"Got it," Encizo said. He poured on all the speed he could, trying to get position on the two Volkswagens, but they were smaller, faster and more maneuverable than the Land Rover. The heavy Moscow traffic hemmed them in on all sides.

"Let's just hope we don't find ourselves in a traffic jam," Manning said.

"That's what I like about you, Gary," Encizo said, fighting the wheel. "Ever the optimist."

"Sorry," Manning said.

"We need to find a parking garage," McCarter said. "Look for something below ground."

"Got it," James said. He took out his phone and activated the GPS program. "I'll find us one."

"Hurry," Encizo said. "I can't keep this up for long."

They moved back and forth in the traffic. "We're going to lose the *mafiya*," Enzico verified. "I can't stay on them and evade these jokers at the same time."

"Don't worry about it," McCarter said. "One threat at a time. We'll reacquire them later. I'll think of something, lads."

"Come up on the left," Manning said. He took out his Desert Eagle and thumbed the hammer back. "I think I saw a weapon."

"Now it really does get fun," McCarter muttered.

"I've got something," James said. "Right, turn right ahead."

Enzico did as James directed. "How far?"

"A couple of blocks, then left," James said. "I'll tell you when."

"Heads down!" Manning ordered.

With the exception of Enzico, who crouched as best he could, the Stony Man commandos ducked down as low as they could get. Bullets raked the driver's-side flank of the Land Rover as a submachinegunner in the lead Volkswagen fired out the passenger side. Horns honked. Someone, somewhere in the midst of all that traffic, screamed as the gunfire continued. Enzico swerved left and right, varying his speed, trying to give the Volkswagen driver something to deal with.

"Left!" James called out. "Left now!"

"Turning," Enzico said. "Hang on!"

They whipped through the turn with all the speed Enzico could squeeze from the Land Rover. Despite the weight of the five of them in the vehicle, McCarter thought he could feel the wheels coming up on one side. He silently willed the Land Rover to come back down on all four wheels without rolling over.

"Good girl," he said quietly.

"What?" Encizo said.

"Nothing," McCarter said. "Gary! We need some room! We can't take that kind of pounding for long."

"Roger," Manning said. The glass of the passenger's-side rear window was already shattered. He knocked away some shards that would otherwise cut him, then reached out with one arm. The triangular snout of the Desert Eagle loomed.

"Carefully!" McCarter said. To James, he said, "We've got to get out of traffic. We can't have a firefight in the middle of Moscow traffic. Too many civilians, and too much attention drawn to us."

Owing to the heavy traffic and Encizo's own driving skills, they managed to gain some space between them and their pursuers. It would be eaten up quickly, McCarter knew. They did not have much time.

"There!" James said. "Up ahead, the third turn-in on the right! That's the entrance!"

Encizo didn't need to be told twice. Manning was still trying to line up a shot that did not endanger anyone else when the Land Rover heeled around and hit the speed bump fronting the entrance to the underground parking garage. The suspension scraped the concrete below, raising a shower of sparks. Encizo poured on the speed as they cleared the metal barriers to either side. He smashed through a wooden lift-gate, no doubt surprising the hell out of the man sitting in the booth to the side of it. Then they were inside the parking garage.

"Go down," McCarter said. "As deep as we can go. We need room to maneuver, but also cover."

"Right," Encizo said. The Land Rover rocked like a sailing ship as he took the descending spiral ramp, taking them down first one, then another level. Finally, on the fourth level, he hit the gas, taking them to the end of the lot. Cars were parked on either side, although not all the spaces were taken this far down. Stopping suddenly and shifting gears, Encizo whipped the Land Rover around and used it to form makeshift cover in the middle of the lot, nose and tail pointing at the lines of cars on either side.

They could hear the squealing tires of the two Volkswagens negotiating the turns of the parking garage.

"Spread out!" McCarter said. "Get to cover! We need to make short work of these blokes and get right the bloody hell out of here, before the Moscow police show up."

"Or the military," Encizo said.

"Or the *mafiya*," James put in.

"Them, too," McCarter said. The men of Phoenix Force grabbed their Kalashnikov rifles from the rear of the truck and took up positions.

The Volkswagens screeched to a halt at the terminus of the ramp, parking nose to nose and bumping each other as they did so. The men inside leaped out and began firing immediately. They had small submachine guns with high rates of fire. McCarter recognized them as micro-Uzis— deadly, reliable weapons that were also relatively difficult to control, especially at these distances.

"Take them!" he said. "Aimed fire! Use your rifles to your advantage!"

The men of Phoenix Force began firing. McCarter counted four men, two per car. The men were small and dark of complexion; he could not tell anything more from this distance.

The Kalashnikovs barked with that familiar, hollow metal sound the Phoenix Force fighters had heard so many times before. One of the killers walked into a beautiful head shot; McCarter could not tell who had made the touch. The dead man flopped forward over the hood of one of the Volkswagens.

The other three got a lot smarter, a lot faster. They took cover behind the concrete pillars to either side of the ramp, taking occasional shots to keep the Phoenix Force members pinned in their position. McCarter and the others, in turn, returned sporadic fire.

"Time is not on our side, lads," McCarter said, his words carried on the transceiver link to all of the team members. "We can't trade shots forever or we risk getting picked up by the police. We also can't reach them from here. They may run out of ammunition before we do, but don't know how much they have in reserve. And that, too, would take time. I'm open to suggestions, men."

"I think I know what to do," Calvin James said. There was a hint of mischief in his voice.

"Yes, Calvin?" McCarter said.

"Cover me, and follow my lead."

The Phoenix Force commandos began firing in earnest once more, pinning the gunners behind the pillars. James took advantage of this fusillade to break cover and head for one of the closer parked cars, which was oriented nose-out. He smashed the driver's-side window with the butt of his Kalashnikov, reached in and opened the door.

"Calvin, what are you doing in there?" McCarter said, between shots. The gunfire was not relayed over their transceivers, but it was very loud in the enclosed space of the parking garage, and even the amplified voices in their earbuds were difficult to hear when the weapons were chattering away.

"I haven't had a chance to hotwire a car in at least a couple of hours," James said.

"What?" McCarter asked.

The engine of the ramshackle sedan, which looked not too far removed from a Trabant for McCarter's tastes, suddenly roared to life. James did something while crouched in the driver's seat. The car lurched forward, and James oriented it toward the ramp.

"This ought to be good," Encizo said.

CALVIN JAMES FINISHED twisting the ignition wires together and was pleased as the engine plunked away. The hard part was getting the car positioned as he wanted it. He ignored the gunfire that buzzed above the roof of the car and to either side. A slug hit the hood and dug a deep furrow in the metal before ricocheting away with a high-pitched whine.

That was one sound he would never get used to.

James removed the fighting knife he'd been issued for the operation, examining it. It was stout enough. He put the rusted car into Park and used the knife to wedge the accelerator to the floor.

"Off you go," he said. He ripped the shifter into Drive and rolled clear.

The car pushed forward, through the gunfire, curving slightly but making a relatively straight run at the two Volkswagens. The men behind them scattered just as the car struck the two smaller vehicles, forcing them aside with a horrible screeching of bent metal and shattered plastic.

James ran after the car. There was no time to wait for the other members of Phoenix Force; he was closest, and he had to gain and keep the initiative. He yelled like a Comanche warrior and fired out the magazine of the AK-47, striking first one, then a second gunman, dropping them forever. He threw himself over the crumpled hood of one of the Volkswagens, and on the other side of the barrier, he confronted the last of the four shooters.

The man raised his micro-Uzi and pulled the trigger. It was empty. James's own weapon was empty, too. The smaller man threw himself at the lanky Stony Man commando. They wrestled to the ground and rolled over each other before separating. When they came up, steel glittered in the smaller man's hand as he snapped open a wickedly curved blade. James recognized it as a *karambit* as the man began spinning the Indonesian fighting knife by the ring attached to its grip.

Instinctively, an experienced knife fighter himself, James went for the knife on his belt—only to remember that he'd used it to wedge the accelerator of the car he'd hotwired.

"Sorry, man," James said. "Looks like we won't be playing today." The man with the knife crouched as if to spring, his blade ready in his fist. James went for the Beretta 92-F he carried. The man lunged, closing the distance and grabbing at James's gun hand as he fell on him. James struggled to get his support arm up, taking a nasty slash across the forearm as he did so. He managed to get his left hand on his opponent's knife-hand wrist, twisting and bending, applying a wristlock.

The man was on top of James, nose to nose, grabbing for the gun, which James held pressed against his body. He fired from retention, the muzzle-blasts burning his abdomen, pumping rounds into his attacker's gut.

Everything was suddenly quiet. In the distance, despite the ringing in his ears caused by the gunfire, James could hear police sirens approaching.

The *karambit*-wielding dead man collapsed onto the pavement. The knife clattered across the concrete.

Encizo appeared behind the wrecked Volkswagen barrier. "Come on, Calvin," he said. "Let's get the hell out of here. There's enough room to push the Rover past these cars."

"Be hell on the paint," James said absently. He took out his secure satellite phone and snapped a digital photograph of the dead man, after first rolling him over with the toe of his boot.

"Well, not every security deposit was meant to be returned," Encizo said. "Come on, let's get that arm bandaged up. It doesn't look too bad." He looked down at the man James had shot. "Nice knife," he said. "That just wasn't fair, man." He grinned.

"It never is," James said. "It never is."

CHAPTER SIXTEEN

Aleksis Katzev looked out the heavily armored window of his office in the Hotel Matryoshka. He folded his arms behind his back and allowed himself a deep sigh. The phone on his heavy oak desk was ringing, but he ignored it. He watched the nearly deadlocked Russian traffic on the streets below. The headlights and taillights stretched out in a seemingly endless string, disappearing among the city buildings in the maze of clogged roads.

The phone stopped ringing.

He checked his watch. It was time. He raised the Iridium satellite phone to his ear as he stood at the window, making sure the exterior antenna was plugged in. Damned nonsense, some of this technology. He shrugged that off. There were far more important things about which to be upset.

He dialed the number from memory. It rang and rang and rang, and Katzev was suddenly reminded of his own habit of ignoring the phone when it suited him. This meeting, if such it could be called, was prearranged…but the party to whom he would be speaking was nothing if not capricious, arrogant and full of his own importance. More significantly, he lived in a world in which his whims *were* more important than any reality. His arrogance was thus entirely justified, at least within the sphere of his influence. Not for the first time, Katzev wondered if it was wise to invite the nose of this particular camel into his tent. He needed money, however. If he was going to do what he hoped to do, if he was to accomplish what he needed to accomplish, he could not afford to be particular about where the money came from. Now more than ever, with world economies in flux and old alliances falling apart, Russia stood poised to recapture her greatness. Only bold, decisive action could deliver on the promise of that future, however, and bold, decisive action often cost a lot of money.

"Yes?" The voice on the other end of the phone sounded vaguely amused when the call was finally answered. Katzev wondered how long he had been forced to stand there waiting simply for Than's amusement.

"It is Katzev," he said simply. "I would speak with you, per our previous arrangement."

"Speak you may," the Burmese warlord said, managing to sound as if he was doing Katzev a remarkable favor. "I always have time for my esteemed allies."

"I require more funds," Katzev said without preamble.

There was a long pause. Than usually responded readily to such demands; he was a wealthy man with the desire to buy power and future wealth, and saw investments in Katzev's regime as a fast track to both. The pause worried the Russian president. He was not sure what it meant.

"Are you still there?" Katzev said finally.

"I am here, yes," Than said. "You have had several very large transfers in the past month," he said in measured tones. "I would know what it is you are doing, what you require the additional funds for."

"You are well aware of the many fronts on which I

attempt to help my people," Katzev said somewhat indignantly. "You know I must have many infusions of liquid cash to do this. The Russian Federation's credit rating is as bad abroad as that of the Americans right now. The Chinese have stopped lending—I cannot afford to put us deeper in debt, anyway, or I risk inflation even higher than what we deal with now. I require funds from outside the system. Your investments have helped me greatly to now."

"Yes," Than said. "I know they have. There are times, therefore, when I must assess my investment."

"We have been over this," Katzev said. "My men, just today, brokered a deal with the *mafiya* to secure their cooperation for your expanded markets in my territory."

"At what cost to me?" Than said. He was remarkably probing today, Katzev thought; normally the warlord was more concerned that he be seen as all-powerful. Today he seemed much more concerned with the bottom line.

"The local *mafiya* will coordinate and run organized crime in Russia," Katzev explained. "That is the offer we have made them. We cannot afford to have a drug war on our streets. If you cooperate with them, they will cooperate with your people. Your product will reach far across this land. Everyone will profit."

"Profit I like," Than said. "I have spent a great deal of money on the promise of future profit. I need guarantees that you will be able to deliver on this. Your own election is in doubt. If you are defeated I will have lost the money I have spent on you thus far."

"That," Katzev said, bristling, "is well under control. I have put in motion plans that will remove Andulov completely and set me up to overtake him on certain key issues. His death will not only pave the way for my reelection, but

I will use him as a propaganda tool to promote my next term of office."

"I like the sound of that," Than said. "How much money do you require?"

Katzev named a sum. There was again a very long pause. "I can transfer you half of that," Than said. "More, I am not willing to send."

Not willing, Katzev wondered, or not able?

"You will not reconsider?"

"No," Than said. "But it may be possible to send more if I see proof of your further success. The death of your rival, for example."

"Then I will see to it that it is done, and done quickly," Katzev said. The warlord was stalling for time. That much was obvious, and Than had never behaved that way before. Katzev found this curious, and troubling. Perhaps if he kept Than talking he might get some hint of what was wrong.

"Esteemed Lord Than," he said, using a title he knew the warlord liked, "I perhaps have not explained myself sufficiently. As you know, the times have been hard for Russia since the dissolution of the Soviet Union. We have lost territory. We have seen our economy fall apart. We have seen our people lose faith. We have become a people living off the crumbling remains of a once-great regime, a people lacking in both national pride and national spirit."

"So you have," Than said.

"I know that you, of all people, have the wisdom to see this." Katzev shamelessly flattered the arrogant Than. "I have worked hard to give my people what they need. I would restore Russia to its former glory. This begins with a very expensive campaign to upgrade our military forces. This is why I need so much money, or why I needed so much to start. Did you know we were forced to ground fully sixty percent of our fleet of fighter jets recently? This cannot be allowed to stand. I am now upgrading our armed forces, including our air force and our navy. I have also instructed the military to make prominent shows of force."

"Much as the Chinese have done."

"Yes," Katzev said. "Yes, that is it exactly. The Chinese, though not yet perhaps the equal of their rivals in the West, know that they have the power, the money, the resources, the might to be such a rival in earnest. They are working toward that goal but, more important, they understand the power of symbolism. They understand that to be great, they must appear great. To be respected, they must be feared. Only when the nations of the world, and particular of the West, understand that there are severe military consequences for interfering in the affairs of a sovereign nation, do they even begin to pause in their incessant attempts to bully the world."

"Is that not what you seek?" Than asked. "You wish to be the bully rather than the bullied."

"Well, of course," Katzev said. "But I seek to empower a nation that does not suffer from the decadence of the West."

"Your nation suffered from the decadence of the West so greatly that you lost the Cold War."

"It was not decadence," Katzev said defensively. "It was finances. The West outspent us. It is part of the reason the Soviet Union collapsed on itself. And the West is now paying the price for that arrogance, as we struggle to right ourselves in this bold new world."

"And so you want money for planes and ships."

"Yes!" Katzev said passionately. "New destroyers. Aircraft carriers to rival those of the United States, which uses them to intimidate other nations. The newest fighter jets, which rival the West's air-superiority fighters."

"You have not talked about the most important thing."

"Have I not?" Katzev said. He smiled, though Than could not see him so many miles away. "Perhaps I have not. You speak of the nuclear weapons."

"Your nuclear arsenal is aging," Than said. "Many of your weapons have found their way to the world market."

"So they have, some of the warheads," Katzev acknowledged. "And it will take much money to upgrade our nuclear arsenal to become once more competitive with the West. More important, the Chinese are slowly working toward a functional arsenal, and as they get better at what they do, it will become more and more important to stay level with their attempts."

"You speak of a new global arms race. This is what my money will finance? I wish to sell my drugs to as many people as possible. Nuclear war is not in my plans."

"It is not in mine, either," Katzev said. "The threat of the weapons is enough to make them equivalent to power. But an empty threat is no threat at all. We must have a new, functional, powerful arsenal, one in which we can invest our national pride again."

"You would militarize your entire society once more. You would bring on a new Cold War."

"It may be called that," Katzev said. "It may be called something else. But it will not matter. What will matter is that we will prosper again. Our society will have common goals, common enemies. Men like you will profit from selling our people the leisure they desire. Everyone… everyone profits. *Everyone.*"

"What you say makes sense," Than said. "I will see to it the funds are transferred. Not all at once. But you will have what I see fit to give you."

The connection was terminated without warning.

Katzev stared at the Iridium phone in confusion. He had

thought his words persuasive, though he knew not everyone was a true believer like himself. And of course what did Than care for the state of the Russian Federation? The man was motivated by profit, which was as it should be. It made him a predictable quantity. Men who wanted money always responded to the potential for it, even when the outright exchange of it was not possible.

He would have to check the account in a few hours. Than normally sent his wire transfers quickly after their conversations, but the man had been very unlike himself. If the Triangle was having financial difficulties, or even if it was experiencing a temporary lack of liquid funds, this was a problem. Whether this was more serious than Than simply losing faith in Katzev, the Russian president was not sure. He could, of course, always attempt to persuade a reluctant Than to send more money, but a Than who was willing but had no funds could not be persuaded to send what he did not have.

The phone started ringing once more, enraging Katzev. He turned and grabbed the offending instrument. "What? What do you want?"

"Aleks," said Mikhail Mogranov, his chief of security. "I have troubling news."

"What now?"

"The *mafiya* bank," Mogranov said. "I have just received word from Brusilov. He says the bank has been hit."

"Hit? What do you mean?"

"Attacked."

"Attacked? Attacked by whom?"

"We do not know," Mogranov said. "Brusilov reports that he was followed by parties unknown today, from Sportivnaya."

"There was some sort of incident near there today, was there not?"

"Yes," Mogranov said. "Some sort of accident that turned into a gunfight, in traffic and in one of the parking garages. We found four dead men. Indonesians, whom our intelligence service believes are hired killers."

"Hired killers? Whom did they try to kill?"

"Again, we do not know," Mogranov said. "We know only that their international criminal histories point to work as assassins. Each has been sought in connection with unsolved murders. They were dangerous, deadly men."

"There is more you are not telling me."

"Much more," Mogranov said. "I received word today from my forces in Burma. Have you talked to the warlord?"

"Yes, just now," Katzev said.

"He is hiding things from you," Mogranov said. "Several of his organization's holdings have been hit in the past forty-eight hours. He has been damaged greatly, across the globe. Some of my analysts believe the Americans have mobilized a death squad of some sort."

"A death squad? Do not be absurd. The Americans do not have the stomach for such a thing."

"Perhaps not officially," Mogranov said. "but we both know the reality is often different from the political affectation."

"Than was very reluctant to send more money," Katzev said. "Can it be that his operations have been damaged so thoroughly that he is running out of money?"

"It could very well be," Mogranov said. "But we must get our own affairs in order. We do not know to what extent we have been exposed by the breach of financial data. This was always the risk in dealing with such criminal elements."

"You say that as if we have not been in bed with the *mafiya* from the beginning," Katzev scoffed.

"I was not chiding you," Mogranov said. "Merely pointing out what we are dealing with."

"I know," Katzev said. "I know."

"Brusilov did have some better news."

"I could use better news now."

"The rally tomorrow night will be Andulov's last. The *mafiya* has agreed to do the job for us."

"Good," Katzev said. "He has been a pest for far too long. I should have had him poisoned before he got so popular. It would have been simpler."

"He has always been popular," Mogranov argued.

"True," Katzev said. "I do not understand it, truthfully. I am not a monster, much as I am portrayed as such. I wish only for Russia to achieve its former glory. I wish for its people to be well. I wish for what is our birthright. Nothing more."

"Nothing more," Mogranov echoed.

"I know, I know, I am, as the Americans say, preaching to the choir."

"Where did you hear that expression?" Mogranov asked.

"It was probably that idiot of an American ambassador, the last time I spoke with him. Or perhaps the secretary of state. I do not recall. They are all such bores."

"There is a security matter to which we must attend, until Andulov is dead."

"Yes?"

"I think you should remain there, where I and my security team can best protect you," Mogranov said. "I am at the Kremlin now. I will come directly and remain on site until the threat is passed."

"You believe there is a threat to me?"

"I believe Than, and in turn the *mafiya,* have led the wolves to our door," Mogranov explained. "You know that your activities are not popular on the world stage, and among those of the West. It is no secret to you."

"No," Katzev said.

"I think the Americans, or some other entity of the West, are taking action against Than and have tracked him to you. I think a connection has been made. That is the only reason the *mafiya* banking house would be hit."

"How is this related to the shooting you mentioned?" Katzev said. "I do not see a connection. Unless you believe these dead assassins were sent for me."

"Quite the opposite," Mogranov said. "Remember, Than was attacked first, and from what you tell me, these attacks have been substantial. His organization is suffering under the onslaught."

"Yes?"

"Well, it is obvious, is it not? Than knows that the connection between himself and the *mafiya* has been made, or would be made. The money leads from one to the other. If you were the hostile force interdicting him, would you not follow it?"

"So you believe Than hired the assassins. That they are here…for this death squad of yours?"

"Is it so outlandish?" Mogranov asked.

"I suppose not."

"You must give serious thought," Mogranov advised, "to what you will do once the election is secured. If Than can no longer be of use to us financially, he is a liability."

"His network may yet serve us."

"His network cannot serve us if it is smashed."

"True," Katzev said.

"I recommend, as I said, that you remain here until we are certain the threat is passed. You have no appearances scheduled. There is nothing you must do."

"Not until I hold a press conference to express my deep regret at the passing of that fool Andulov." Katzev laughed.

"Not until that." The somber Mogronov actually chuckled a little at that. "I am serious, Aleks. Do not leave the building for any reason. I have already placed my men in the building on high alert."

"You truly believe the West has sent killers? Perhaps the killers were those found in the garage."

"Even if they were," Mogranov said, "someone killed the killers. It was not the *mafiya*—Brusilov was as mystified by it as I. It was not my people. It was not the police who found the scene after it was over."

"So some force walks among us, and you believe it will target me."

"I believe it is inevitable."

"Very well," Katzev said. "I will do as you suggest."

"All right, Aleks," Mogranov said. "I will be in touch." He hung up.

Katzev, somewhat mollified but also more concerned, replaced the phone in its cradle. He looked out the window again.

It was the curse of great men, he thought, to be forever surrounded by those who did not understand who they were or why they did what they did. To be truly great, one had to be willing to make tough decisions and to undertake actions that would disgust lesser men. To be a strong leader, one had to be strong in mind and body. Part of mind and body was intent.

Katzev knew that he had the intent that Russia needed. It meant he would be hated by some. He would be reviled by others. He believed he would be, and should be, feared and respected by many more.

"It is better to be feared than loved," Machiavelli had written, "when one of the two must be lacking." Katzev thought of that often. The quote came to him when he did things that other men might find…objectionable. Certainly his fellow men did not understand why he was willing to cut deals with criminals, to accept funds from illegal sources, to take blood money built on others' suffering. None of that mattered to Katzev. He was a firm believer that money was money, and bloody money spent as well as any other currency. He was doing great things with the funds, at any rate. Surely that redeemed him? Surely the ends really did justify the means, regardless of the often vile nature of those means?

He went to the liquor cabinet and, from the refrigerated cupboard, removed a bottle of vodka. He poured himself a glass of it and took a long sip.

To the future, he thought. To the end justifying the means.

There were those who called it liquid courage. He had never found alcohol to be emboldening. It was anesthetic to him. His fear, he knew from long experience, was invulnerable to liquor.

He took a long swallow, trying instead to drown his doubt.

CHAPTER SEVENTEEN

Downtown Moscow

Trying their best to look casual, the members of Phoenix Force waited in the lobby of the nondescript office building that housed the campaign headquarters of Yuri Andulov. They had spent a less than comfortable night sleeping in the Land Rover, parked in an alley while taking rotating guard shifts. It was very possible that five foreigners, whose damaged vehicle certainly was witnessed during the gunfight in traffic, would be wanted for questioning in connection with the gunfights of the previous day; they could not risk showing their faces in hotels or other places where the police might choose to search.

The alley was itself a risky choice, but McCarter judged it an easily defensible location. They backed the Land Rover up against a large metal trash container, covered it with loose cardboard and other rubbish overflowing from the bins lined up next to the container and spent the night trying to get comfortable in the old Rover's seats. Grimaldi, meanwhile, kept his head down and slept in the plane at the airport. He was confident that enough bribe money had been spread around by the Farm prior to their insertion; those in charge at the airfield would forget he existed, at least for a couple of days.

The Indonesian hit team, whom the Farm had identified as hired assassins with a long working history, had dossiers with detailed incident data until a few years prior to their fateful appearance in Moscow. After that, it was as if they had dropped off the planet. Their last working data, however, put them in the vicinity of Burma. The connection was slim, but good enough for McCarter, especially since the four were dead. It stood to reason that the Triangle had put the killers on their tail. Try as he might, McCarter could not think of another entity who might have brought in outside hitters to take them on. He could only assume that they'd tracked Phoenix Force by tracking Phoenix Force's quarry, the *mafiya*. It was what he would do in their position. Unless and until more mysterious hitmen showed up gunning for Phoenix Force specifically, he was going to consider the matter closed. Besides, they had enough issues to deal with.

McCarter yawned and wished he had a can of Coke. He was working on less sleep than the others; he had spent the night calling back and forth to the Farm, talking to Price in hushed tones, trying to arrange to see Andulov. The problem was, Andulov didn't know them, didn't want to know them and wasn't interested in anything the Farm was trying to send him.

The Briton couldn't blame Andulov for being suspicious. He probably felt as if he had half the bloody world gunning for him, having made an enemy of Katzev. As bad as the Russian president's reputation was concerning treatment of his enemies, anyone on Katzev's bad side would be a fool not to consider the possibility that he was, at that moment, in the crosshairs of a scoped rifle.

Barbara Price had tried to speak to Andulov through channels, and been rebuffed. Hal Brognola had tried to speak to Andulov's people, who were considerably less polite. The President himself was incommunicado, in defense talks abroad, so Hal would be unable to reach him for some time; nothing short of intervention by the Man was likely to get Andulov's attention. It didn't help that, for the sake of plausible deniability, the inquiries had to be somewhat circumspect. Given enough attempts, however, it was possible even these would have the desired effect. The problem was, they didn't have that kind of time. The rally was tonight, and the *mafiya* were probably already planning Andulov's "spectacular" death. They had to get to the man before them, with time enough to take action before Katzev's mob henchmen took Andulov's life.

"David," Manning said quietly, standing next to McCarter, "we are dangerously exposed here."

"That we are," McCarter said. "Maybe you should join Calvin and Rafe on the sofa over there. Read the paper."

"My Russian's a little rusty."

"We're in the business district," McCarter said. "I'm sure there's an old *Wall Street Journal* around here somewhere."

"We're standing in enemy territory, sitting ducks, carrying illegal weaponry under our clothing, with more illegal weaponry in a shot-up Land Rover parked in an alley outside, where it could be discovered and called in at any time. That doesn't bother you?"

"Of course it bothers me," McCarter said. "I hate to see a good Land Rover abused."

"I'm serious, David."

"You're giving me the same grief you always do." McCarter sighed. "Bloody hell, do you think I'm not keenly aware of all of these things, Gary? The falsified passports and other credentials we're all carrying can only take us so far. The second the local authorities decide to take us into custody and start sweating us, they'll know something's not quite cricket, and that's before they find the guns and start adding two and two. We're every one of us in for it if they take us down. You heard Hal and Barb—we're on our own when that happens. Which means we've got to operate quickly and act decisively if we're going to bring this off."

"Yet we're standing here in broad daylight," Manning said.

"We won't be standing for long," McCarter said. "Barb told me last night that Andulov's people, before they clammed up completely, admitted he had an interview scheduled for this morning, to be run in advance of tonight's rally. Either he'll be going to them or they'll be coming to him. We just sit tight and wait until one or the other happens, and then we take a go at him."

"We won't know they're here to see Andulov," Manning pointed out.

"Ah, but we will," McCarter said. "Haven't you noticed? Press checks in at the front desk. I've been watching that desk since we got here this morning."

Manning sighed. "I still don't like it."

"Nor do I, my friend," McCarter said. "But we play the hand we're dealt. Part of the game."

Manning had no reply to that. He moved away, careful to look as if he was simply drifting aimlessly while waiting on some appointment or other. McCarter watched him go.

The Briton knew exactly how Manning felt, because Manning's thoughts and feelings were very much McCarter's. He was the leader of the team, however; he could not afford to show any doubt. It was one of the hardest lessons he'd learned about leadership, for he'd always been the hot-headed one, prone to speaking his mind and questioning his superiors when he thought they were wrong. It was times like these that he missed Yakov Katzenelenbogen, Phoenix Force's original team leader. Katz had been a good man and a good leader. He was solid in a way that few men were, and while he was its leader, he was Phoenix Force's soul. McCarter did not speak of it often, but each day he led the team, he tried very hard to live up to Katz's example. He also knew that, while Manning and sometimes the other members of Phoenix Force spoke their minds, they understood the position McCarter was in as their leader.

But he still liked getting the last word.

They waited for as long as McCarter felt was warranted, but when Andulov did not make an appearance and no one showed who asked to see him, McCarter decided to force the issue.

"Lads," he whispered, knowing his transceiver would carry his words to the others, "I'm going to see what I can shake loose. Follow my lead. Gary, you're with me. Cal, Rafe, T.J., cover the lobby. Be prepared for all hell to break loose if this doesn't work like I hope it will."

"Roger," James whispered.

"T.J., give Gary the little camera."

Manning gave him a mortified look, but McCarter just nodded toward the front desk. Hawkins walked past Manning's position, ostensibly headed to a small water fountain at one end of the lobby. He handed off the camera as he passed by.

McCarter sauntered up to the desk and made a slight bow. "'Ello, miss," he said in an exaggerated Cockney accent. "I'm Nigel Carruthers, with the UK *Sun Times Union Nightly.* Do you speak English, by chance, lass?"

The woman behind the counter looked at him. *"Da,"* she said. "Only…a little. You wish to see Yuri Andulov?"

"We've an appointment, my cameraman and I." McCarter waved to Manning, who gestured with the surveillance camera on cue. To anyone unaware of its special features, it would appear to be any of several commercially available digital cameras.

"I do not see you on this list."

"Lass, would I be here if I wasn't scheduled for an interview? All press is good press, isn't it? And good press is naught to be taken lightly, now, is it?"

The woman looked dubious.

"'Ow silly of me," McCarter said more quietly. "I've forgotten to give you me card, 'aven't I?" He slipped the woman three folded bills, a rather sizable sum in Euros. These were part of the funds with which Phoenix Force always traveled. They weren't local currency, but in a city like Moscow, that meant nothing.

"You may go up," she said.

McCarter thanked her and waved Manning to accompany him.

"It's worse than I thought," he said when they were out of earshot. "There's no security at all in this place, and Andulov's a sitting duck. They can take him out any time they choose to do so."

They took the elevator up to the campaign offices, which were clearly labeled both in the elevator and on the third floor. The signs were in Russian, of course, but Andulov's name was easy enough to spot.

The two men pushed open the glass doors leading into Andulov's bustling headquarters. Volunteers were manning a busy bank of phones, while others were printing or painting signs and placards. Andulov himself would have been easily recognizable from the dossiers and briefing the

Farm provided, but his picture was all over the office, many times life-size, on campaign posters bearing his name. The candidate for the presidency of the Russian Federation was standing in the middle of his own campaign headquarters, conferring with several staffers. He looked up as Manning and McCarter approached.

"Mr. Andulov," McCarter said. "We need to speak with you."

"Who are you?" Andulov asked in lightly accented English. He waved the staffers away. One of them threw several rapid-fire sentences at him in Russian, but he made an impatient, dismissive gesture.

"We would like to speak with you privately, sir," Manning said quietly. "Could we perhaps talk to you in your office?"

"This is a bit irregular," Andulov said.

"It's a matter of life and death, sir," Manning said.

Andulov considered that. "Very well," he said. He led them to his office and closed the door.

The office was small but orderly. More campaign posters covered the walls. Andulov had a desk with a laptop sitting on it. There was a bottle of water on the desk next to a half-eaten sandwich.

"As you can see—" Andulov spread his hands "—I am pressed for time often. The campaign, it is very demanding. What is it you wish to talk to me about?"

"Mr. Andulov," McCarter said, "several attempts have been made to contact you. There are those in the international community who wish a moment of your time."

"International community?" Andulov asked.

"Yes," McCarter said. "For the entire world has a stake in your country's elections."

"Who are you, exactly?" Andulov demanded.

"We can't tell you that," McCarter said.

"Then you will have to leave," Andulov said.

"Please, just listen to us," Manning said. "You're in very great danger, Mr. Andulov. The Russian *mafiya* has been contracted to kill you at your rally tonight."

"I am well aware of this nonsense," Andulov said. "Katzev successfully wields this power, this fear, because no one will stand up to him. He makes threats, and he takes credit for coincidences. He has built up, by his own hand, this myth that all who oppose him will suffer for it. Well, I do not believe it."

"You *should* believe it," McCarter said. "Katzev really is that dangerous."

"You spoke of the international community," Andulov said. "If you truly do represent those outside of Russia who have an interest in this country's politics, mark my words. Katzev is a danger, yes. But he is a danger on the global scale. His militaristic policies, which are designed to strengthen national pride while intimidating other nations, will only cause those other nations to build up their own defenses against us. A new Cold War will benefit no one, save perhaps for Katzev and those who profiteer from strained national relations."

"We're well aware of that," McCarter said. "We want you to take the presidency, Mr. Andulov. But you can't do that if you're dead."

"Is this some perverse means of threatening me?" Andulov demanded. "I have turned away letters, visitors and call after call, all of them sycophants devoted to Katzev. I will not be intimidated!"

Andulov lunged for a switch mounted on his desk. It activated a buzzer. McCarter and Manning turned to find themselves staring at four very large, very angry-looking Russians in double-breasted suits.

Bodyguards.

Manning acted first. He threw a brutal elbow into the face of the first man, then drove his shoulder up and in, throwing the guard over and down. The big man hit the carpeted floor with a thud. McCarter was already aiming a side kick that knocked the legs out from under the second man. He lashed out with a kick to the downed man's head that put him out cold. The other two were going for their guns, reaching into their jackets with death in their eyes.

Manning was faster. He pulled his .357 Magnum Desert Eagle from concealment and rapped the triangular barrel of the heavy weapon against the forehead of the closer bodyguard. That man fell, his eyes rolling back up into his head. Manning leveled his gun at the only bodyguard still standing. He froze, his gun half out of the shoulder holster he wore.

McCarter spun, his Browning Hi-Power in his fist. Andulov was reaching for the middle drawer of his desk.

"Please, Mr. Andulov," the Briton said. "I wouldn't do that."

Andulov looked up. His face was twisted with fury. "So, this is how it is to end," Andulov said. "Katzev is so threatened by me that he really would have me killed? Very well. But you will not make me beg. I know how your kind works. I know the twisted mind of the man you serve."

McCarter, impassive, pointed at the desk drawer. "Remove the gun slowly, by the trigger guard."

Andulov glared, but he obeyed. The gun in his desk drawer was a Makarov pistol. He reached out and handed it to McCarter.

McCarter checked the pistol, making sure it was loaded. He holstered his own Browning. Then he handed the Makarov, butt first, back to an astonished Andulov.

"Now, sir," McCarter said, "will you please listen to us?"

It took a few minutes to get the bodyguards sorted out, and then another few minutes for Andulov, in rapid Russian, to convince them not to attack immediately. They were none too happy when the would-be president ushered them out of the office. Finally, Andulov sighed, sat at his desk, and shook his head.

"I am… I have… That is…" He stopped, then started again. "I am grateful for what you are trying to do," he said. "But I do not understand." He picked up the Makarov, after first glancing at McCarter to make sure it would be all right. Then he replaced it in the drawer.

"I can't tell you whom we represent," McCarter said. "But you're not stupid, Mr. Andulov. We have resources and a support organization behind us. We're here specifically to stop Katzev."

"Katzev," Andulov said quietly. He stood and went to the window, looking down at the crowded, congested streets of Moscow below. "You know, he was probably a good man once."

"A good man who poisons his enemies? Threatens his neighbors?" McCarter asked.

"Every man," Andulov said, "does what he believes is necessary. I am no different." He turned back to McCarter and Manning. "You are Americans?"

"I thought it was obvious I'm British," McCarter said.

"I'm not an American," Manning said. He did not offer the fact that he was Canadian.

"You know what I mean," Andulov said. "You are what, CIA?"

"Not really," McCarter said.

"No matter." Andulov waved his hand. "I am glad the United States has seen fit to do something about the threat Katzev represents."

"Exactly what is it they're doing, sir?" Manning asked.

Andulov smiled. "Very well," he said. "We shall play that game. Gentlemen, whomever you represent, I thank you for coming here. You obviously did so at great risk to yourselves. I know that you have your own reasons. Obviously I wish open relations with the West—I want trade, normalized relations. Why, I would even consider joining NATO, were I sufficiently encouraged."

"I'm sure the American president would be pleased to hear that, sir," Manning said diplomatically.

"Yes," Andulov said. "I'm sure he would, at that." He reached into another desk drawer. McCarter tensed slightly. Andulov caught McCarter's movement and slowed his own. He removed, very methodically, a pack of cigarettes and a silver Zippo lighter from the drawer.

"Would you care for a smoke?" Andulov said. "They are Marlboros."

"No, thank you," McCarter said.

"I don't smoke," Manning said politely.

"Very well." Andulov nodded. He flicked the Zippo open, thumbed it to life and was soon blowing smoke rings toward the ceiling. "My one vice," he said. "Apart from vodka. But we drink that like water here, *da?*"

"Sir, as I started to tell you before," McCarter said, "the Russian *mafiya* intends to kill you at your own rally. We would like to put a stop to that."

"Thus preserving me," Andulov said, "so that I might prevail in the election, and bring peace and improved diplomacy to the world stage on behalf of the Russian Federation."

"Something like that." McCarter smiled.

"The problem as I see it," Andulov said, "is that I must be in the public view in order to win the election. I cannot go into hiding."

"You can't win the election if they kill you, sir," Manning said.

"No," Andulov said, taking a long drag from the cigarette. "But that brings us back to my statement, does it not? I am well aware of the rumors that swirl around Katzev. I tell you again that I think it is the rumors that have power, not the man."

"You would be wrong, sir," McCarter said. "Our organization has proof that Katzev is accepting funds from terrorists and drug traffickers. People who use violence to secure their interests. Further, while he is working with the *mafiya* for his own profit, Katzev is also receiving funds from foreign nationals and using Russian military personnel to pay for these investments. He is essentially hiring out your armed forces as private mercenaries."

"That is troubling," Andulov said. "But not a great surprise. The military has always been loyal to Katzev. They see his willingness to spend money, and vast sums of it, on shoring up our military might, replacing old equipment, hiring more soldiers, building new weapons. None of these are goals I find objectionable. I would do them, too, were I able to finance these improvements. The Russian people need more than weapons, however. They need—what is the word?—infrastructure. I would see to their needs sensibly, while Katzev would simply pander to them and serve his own interests."

"We can put a stop to this," McCarter said. "We can see to it that Katzev doesn't win a second term by killing you. We just need your cooperation, Mr. Andulov."

"What exactly is it you wish of me?"

"It's very simple, Mr. Andulov," Manning said.

"We want you to die," McCarter said.

CHAPTER EIGHTEEN

Salem, Massachusetts

"Now leaving Salem?" Lyons said. "Now *leaving* Salem? When did we get to it? There's nothing but mile after mile of sprawl between here and Boston!"

Schwarz simply sat in the passenger seat, his eyes closed, listening to Lyons bellow. The big former LAPD cop had done nothing but complain about the traffic, the traffic signs, the traffic patterns and the rest of Massachusetts since they had crossed the state border.

"And what is it with these damned traffic circles?" Lyons went on. "What, whenever two or more roads come together, we have to form a circle in order to guarantee that no one knows who's got the right of way?"

"I didn't realize you felt so strongly about these civic matters, Carl," Schwarz said.

"Cram it, Gadgets."

"I have to admit," Schwarz said, undeterred, "that only when I'm in Boston do I feel like it's possible to drive as fast as I'd like to go…and that's still not fast enough."

"Speed, I don't mind," Lyons grumbled. "But this is just…ridiculous."

"I got flipped off by an old woman in a Volvo flying past me at one hundred miles an hour in Cambridge once," Blancanales admitted.

Able team was in Massachusetts following the latest location leads generated by NetScythe. There were two possible sites to which Thawan was predicted to go. The thermal imagery, in real time and through time-lapse analysis, confirmed levels of activity that would be consistent with a Triangle facility. If NetScythe's further analysis was correct, the Triangle was rapidly running out of distribution points and safehouses in its New Jersey, New York, New England circuit.

Able Team was rapidly putting Mok Thawan and his people out of business.

Nestled amid the sprawl surrounding Salem was an auto yard that was designated as the target. Able Team parked their Suburban two blocks over, shouldered duffel bags bearing their weaponry, and moved out.

"Standard pattern," Lyons said. "Spread out. We'll come at them from three sides."

"Then you'll knock on the front door, start a firefight and shoot them all?" Schwarz asked hopefully.

"Cram it, Gadgets," Lyons barked.

"I'm just saying."

Lyons ignored him. When they got closer to the auto yard, the members of Able Team turned much more serious.

"Go, go," Lyons directed. "Now."

They spread out. The auto yard was surrounded by a chain-link fence. Inside the fenced perimeter, cars of all makes and models were parked haphazardly. A few were up on blocks. Some had body damage. Inside the auto yard, Lyons could hear heavy equipment running.

"I smell chop shop," Lyons said, trusting his transceiver to keep him in touch with his teammates. "What do you want to bet they're running hot auto parts out of this place, and under cover of that, heroin or meth?"

"No bet," Schwarz said. "Though I'm thinking meth, given the clientele."

"Possibly," Blancanales said.

"Move in," Lyons said. "If they fold, so much the better. But I don't think that's going to be our luck."

"No bet," Schwarz repeated.

"In position," Blancanales reported.

"In position," Schwarz echoed.

Lyons climbed over the chain-link fence, landing heavily on the other side. He moved to stand next to an access door, which was nearly rusted through. Reaching out and grasping the handle, he tested it very slowly. It began to move through its arc, meaning it was not locked.

"All right," Lyons said. "Three...two...one...*now.*"

At the signal, Lyons, his USAS-12 shotgun freed from the duffel bag and cradled in his hands, ripped the door open, practically pulling it from its squealing hinges. "Federal agents!" he bellowed. "This is a raid! Everyone on the ground...*now!*"

There was shouting in a language Lyons didn't recognize, and in Russian. The answering automatic gunfire drove him under cover behind an engine block hanging from a chain hoist near the door.

Just once, he thought as bullets raised sparks from the equipment around him, *I would like for that to work. Just once, I would like for somebody to surrender.*

There were at least a dozen men shooting from the work pits set in the floor, using the cars above them for cover. Judging from the equipment on the walls, the hoists, the hydraulic lifts and the cars in various states of disassembly in the auto shop, chances were very good this was indeed a chop shop.

Well, it used to be, Lyons thought.

He leveled the automatic shotgun and began spraying out the 20-round drum magazine. The double-aught buck pellets shredded anything they encountered that was not made of heavy metal. Several men screamed as they were tagged. From two other corners of the auto yard, Lyons could hear his teammates firing away, their weapons adding to the deafening waves of noise, heat and pressure that washed over Lyons as the gun battle raged.

Carl "Ironman" Lyons was, in other words, completely at home.

He fought his way across the floor of the auto shop and toward the first of the work pits. There was no way to get an angle on the men hiding in it; the firefight could go on forever and he'd still never reach them. When he reached the pit, he flattened himself out, shoved the snout of the USAS-12 over the edge and held the trigger back. The big weapon bucked on full auto. The pit turned into a charnel house as the men were flayed alive by the rending, ricocheting shotgun pellets.

Lyons rolled to the next pit, staying low. He allowed himself to topple into the pit completely, surprising the gunmen who were lying in wait below. Lyons slammed the butt of the shotgun into the nearest man, breaking his jaw; he brought the barrel of the weapon around and triggered a blast that knocked a second man sprawling. The USAS-12 was now empty, so he let it fall and drew his Colt Python. The last of the men in the work pit died before he could clear the leather holster in which he carried a revolver. The .357 Magnum round from Lyons's Colt dropped him where he stood.

Vaulting out of the pit as he retrieved his shotgun, Lyons

scanned the room for more targets. There were gunners to his left and his right; he rolled to avoid a stream of full-auto fire, diving flat on his face, and lost his shotgun in the process.

"Carl, stay down!" Schwarz commanded. Lyons stayed where he was, and Schwarz's machine pistol barked and the men who were targeting Lyons were mowed down.

"Clear!" Schwarz called.

"Clear!" Blancanales echoed.

Lyons groaned. "Somebody help me up."

"Just once," Schwarz said, "I'd like it if they gave up when we identified ourselves as government agents."

Lyons looked at him curiously.

"What?" Schwarz asked.

"Nothing," Lyons said.

Blancanales chuckled. "I was thinking the same thing," he said.

"Gadgets, give this place the once-over," Lyons said. "I want to know what's here, if anything."

"Got it," Schwarz said.

"Pol, call 9-1-1," Lyons said. "Let them know what we've found, what we've got, and use the Justice cover so we can keep the bullshit to a minimum. I'm going to see what's in that office over there." He pointed to a small office area made of plywood at the rear corner of the auto shop.

He moved across the auto shop area, found the door handle and wrenched open the door.

A giant man fell on him.

The crushing weight of the big man, easily three hundred pounds, was a lot even for a man of Carl Lyons's stature. He felt himself being taken to the ground. He tried calling for help, but the wind was knocked completely out of him. He couldn't breathe. He couldn't see Schwarz or

Blancanales; it was possible that Blancanales was outside placing the call while watching the property. Schwarz might not realize Lyons was in trouble.

"You think you have beaten us?" the big man spoke in heavily accented English. He was obviously Russian born. He was also incredibly strong. Lyons tried to move from underneath the big man, but his arms felt as if they were being wrenched out of their sockets as his ribs were being crushed.

"Do not struggle," the big Russian said, close enough to whisper near Lyons's ear. "You will only die in more pain. You cannot escape. I have you trapped. I was sambo champion, three years running."

Lyons tried the usual grappling counters, attempting to worm his way out of the hold. He tried for a reversal; the Russian just squeezed harder. Lyons could feel his lungs burn as his vision started to turn gray and blurry. The Russian was slowly killing him.

"I have fought many men," the Russian taunted. "All were powerless against me. Once I grapple with you, I have you." The big man did not notice the metallic, ratcheting noise. "No man is a match for what I can do. I am the strongest. I am the best. I am—" He suddenly became quiet, his voice trailing off.

"You are not invulnerable to the blade of a knife," Lyons supplied for him.

The shocked Russian turned wide eyes on Lyons, then looked down at his flank. Lyons, with only one arm capable of movement from the elbow down, had drawn and snapped open the *navaja* knife, plunging it deep into his enemy, past the ribs.

"I…" the Russian said.

Lyons heaved the Russian off of him, watching the man roll onto his back. He yanked the *navaja* free and paused to wipe the blade on the dead Russian's striped T-shirt.

Lyons sat up and folded the knife.

Schwarz ran up, machine pistol ready. "Carl!" he said. "Are you all right?"

"Yeah," Lyons said.

"Where did he come from? Hiding in the office?"

"Yeah," Lyons said. "Do me a favor and make sure there aren't any more of them."

Blancanales returned from phoning the police. He was surprised to see the dead Russian at Lyons's feet. "That's a big one," he said. "Hiding in the office?"

"Why am I the only one who did not stop to think that was a possibility?" Lyons muttered.

They searched the Russian but found nothing of interest. Schwarz and Blancanales took the usual pictures of the dead men, for analysis at the Farm. It was Lyons, however, who found the videotape in the office. He had noticed no security cameras in the auto yard.

"What do you make of this?" he asked Schwarz, ducking his head out of the office area. An ancient television-VCR combo lay under a stack of empty foam coffee cups; he grabbed it and pushed it onto the center of the desk crammed into the little office. He found an outlet and plugged it in.

The Able Team electronics genius stuck his head in and immediately gagged. "It smells like feet in there," he said.

"Quit whining and help me with this."

Schwarz examined the tape. "Nothing remarkable," he said. "Could be porn. Could be anything."

Lyons stuck the tape into the TV-VCR combo deck and pressed Play. The tape ejected. He looked at it again and realized that, of course, it was not rewound. He replaced it in the unit, hit Rewind and waited. When the tape finally reached the beginning, he started it again.

The picture was grainy, but he could make out an elaborate throne in a shadowy room with stone floors. Stone columns held up an unseen roof. The picture closed in on the man on the throne, who cut an imposing figure. He was dressed in flowing golden robes with red accents. A leather coat was draped over his shoulders like a cape.

"Welcome, my brother," the man said. "Welcome to your new life. I am Than, your warlord, mentor and guide. You will serve me, and, in serving me, you will serve your comrades."

"What the hell is that?" Schwarz asked.

"Looks like some religious nut," Lyons said. "Guess some of the boys here were holding revival meetings."

"That seems unlikely," Blancanales said, looking in over their shoulders.

"Whatever," Lyons said. He reached to pop the tape out of the machine.

"The Triangle is all," the man on the tape said. "The Triangle is life."

"What the frigging hell?" Lyons asked out loud.

"As your leader and master, I, Lord Than, will command you, and you will obey," the heavyset man on the tape intoned. "You are watching this because you have chosen to work for the Triangle, to dedicate yourself to it so that you might prosper, so that your family might prosper. This is good. This is well. This is acceptable."

"This is starting to hurt my brain," Schwarz complained.

"We need to talk to Barb about this," Lyons said.

Just then, the local police began to arrive. "Fun's over, for the time being," Lyons said. He took some digital video with his secure satellite phone, recording Lord Than so that he could transmit the footage to Price and the Farm. Then he popped out the tape and pocketed it.

"Nobody move!" the first of the cops entering the premises began to yell.

"Somebody quiet him down," Lyons said offhand. Blancanales went to the officer and showed his Justice Department credentials, which got the cop's attention in a hurry. Lyons, meanwhile, called the Farm.

IN THE STONY MAN FARM operations center, Barbara Price picked up the incoming call on the first ring.

"Price."

"Barb," Carl Lyons said. "I've just sent you some video. The quality won't be great, but I need to know who it is that's on that tape. He talks crazy, like one of those public-access religious nuts, but he mentioned the Triangle several times."

"Could be coincidence," Price said. "Triangle is a common enough symbol, used by religions across the country and around the world."

"No," Lyons said. "It wasn't that. I'd bet money on it."

"All right, Carl," Price said. She had learned to trust the intuition and instincts of the Farm's field agents. Those operatives were irreplaceable and, given the dangers they constantly faced in the field, it would be both a disservice and a dishonor to them not to take into account the reflexes and knowledge gleaned through the most difficult of service to the United States. The Farm and its people were not untouchable. Stony Man Farm's personnel were entirely too mortal. The Farm itself had known hostile action, long past, and more than a few Stony Man warriors had made the ultimate sacrifice in service to the United States. Kurtzman was in a wheelchair for that very reason. Other men and women previously for Stony Man had not been so lucky, if being shot and permanently injured could be considered luck.

"Give me some time to process this, Carl," Price said.

"Will do," Lyons said. "The cops are here at the target

site. We've got multiple hostiles down. No sign of drugs, but I just killed a Russian mercenary, and the guys running this chop shop were all carrying illegal automatic weaponry. Looks like this first of two was a bust, but in the ballpark."

"That means NetScythe's second target probability is your better bet," Price said.

"Murphy's Law," Lyons said.

"All right, Carl." Price looked at the uploaded data feed now scrolling across one of the flat screens of her workstation. "I'm going to pass this to Hunt. I'll get back to you."

"Ironman out."

Huntington Wethers looked up from his workstation. Akira Tokaido, Carmen Delahunt and Aaron Kurtzman were all present, working at their respective stations. "I heard my name," Wethers said.

"Sending you some data now," Price said. "Take a look, see what you can find on the person in it."

"Will do," Wethers promised.

It took some digging and about half an hour, but finally Price was able to place a call back to Lyons.

"I was just about to see if you could call in Hal," Lyons said. "The locals have been crawling over us with a fine-tooth comb for as long as I've been waiting. They've finally decided to believe our story, though the Justice IDs Hal issued us are getting a real workout. He may have to field some verification calls."

"I'm pretty sure he has staff for that." Price laughed.

"Must be nice," Lyons said. "All right, lay it on me."

"We ran the name and the photo through news databases worldwide," Price said. "We also tapped a super-computer database to help us with the number crunching, which allowed us to run an automated search against video-sharing Web sites."

"I don't doubt or question your methods, Barb," Lyons said. "Just give me the bad news, please."

"It isn't really a bad-news, good-news situation," Price said. "Though the situation has become slightly murkier. The man on the tape is a Burmese crime warlord. He goes by the name Than only, and from what we've been able to determine, he is the leader of the Triangle."

"It's not Thawan?"

"Thawan is highly placed in the organization," Price said, "and he is even mentioned several times in the videos we've found online. The videos are almost viral—our search turned them up in some of the oddest places. Their purpose is clear, however. With a lot of drug-addled doublespeak, this warlord, Than, manages to make it known that he is recruiting, looking for operatives. Faithful service to the Triangle, to hear him tell it, is rewarded with cash, with women, with power…with whatever the new recruit desires. All he or she has to do is serve the Triangle. In some cases that's no more than looking the other way. In the case of a few trusted servants, to use Than's terminology, that service might be much more involved."

"I don't get it."

"It's an attempt to create a god figure out of the warlord," Price said. "By building a mythology around himself, he becomes larger than life. The fear and respect people have for such a figure helps make it easier, at least up to a point, for Than to do business. His godlike status discourages assassination attempts and helps provide cohesion to a disparate power structure."

"Barb," Lyons said, "please talk to me like I have no idea what any of that means."

"He's trying to become like a pharaoh," Price explained. "A deified leader on Earth. It helps cement his power and make his people more pliable, while creating a mythology that furthers the Triangle's business. It helps explain why the Triangle has been so hard to stop, so hard to pin down, up to now. It wasn't just violence and intimidation that kept its enemies in fear of it. The Triangle has the advantage of an almost religious terror, spread by their own hand, creating the impression that they are led by a figure who is more than a mortal man. That's this warlord, Than."

"Do we have any data on this Than?"

"There's very little other than the mythology he has created," Price said. "However, by piecing together some of the references, as well as culling through some of the lore surrounding the Triangle and Than, we think there's a connection between him and Thawan that goes deeper than Thawan acting as field commander for the organization."

"What's that?"

"Either biological or adopted, we think Thawan is Than's son."

"Well, they were right," Lyons said.

"Who was?" Price asked, confused.

"The proverbial they," Lyons continued. "They were right."

"About what?"

"It starts in the home," Lyons said.

CHAPTER NINETEEN

Moscow

Yuri Andulov stepped to the podium. In an unprecedented move, the candidate had called an unscheduled press conference and rally ahead of the rally that was scheduled for later that evening. The Moscow and national Russian press were abuzz with the news. Foreign journalists were present, as well. The reporters moved in mobs around the platform set up in Red Square, in the shadow of the Kremlin. Already, Andulov supporters waving signs and holding sandwich boards were moving in a wide perimeter around the platform, chanting Andulov's name.

From his position in the upper floor of another office complex overlooking the square, Rafael Encizo looked through the scope of the SVD rifle. He hoped the 7.62 x 54 mm Dragunov, which had been scared up by Andulov's people somewhere, was sighted in. If not, this plan was about to go horribly wrong, horribly fast. It was Andulov's people who had helped smuggle Encizo into the building, for that matter, before providing him with the weapon. If any of them were not trustworthy, his position was blown and the whole affair was over before it could begin.

Andulov's speech was to be translated from Russian into English in real time. The English translation was projected on a screen behind him; Encizo could read this as he monitored the political theater that was about to commence. His transceiver still linked him to the rest of Phoenix Force, who were circulating among the crowd below. That was very necessary, for should the *mafiya* get wind of the prerally and decide to make their move that much sooner, the only thing preventing them from killing Andulov before Encizo could do the deed would be McCarter and the others, from the ground.

Encizo wiped sweat from his forehead with the back of his forearm. He hadn't been in this position for quite some time. It was eerie, really, to overlook a politician like this, through the scope with the crosshairs on the man. Encizo thought he understood how the world's most famous political assassins must have felt moments before leaving behind bloody footprints as they walked into history.

Andulov was an expert at working the crowd. He moved among them, glad-handing, even kissing a few babies carried by the new mothers in attendance. The Cuban-born Phoenix pro supposed that politicians were politicians the world over. Andulov, at least, was a reasonable man, unlike the president who sought to remove Andulov from the running. To Encizo, that alone was sufficient enough reason for Phoenix Force to get involved, though the stakes were much higher than that.

Andulov finally approached the podium, tested the microphone and waved to the crowd. He waited while they got even more raucous cheering out of their system— damn, the man was popular, Encizo could not help but think—and then settled himself in behind the podium.

"People of the Russian Federation," Andulov said, "I stand before you today, a man who loves his country with all his heart."

There were more cheers. Andulov wisely let these go on for as long as the crowd wished to carry them. When they started to die down, he continued.

"I have been deeply humbled by the many ways you have shown our campaign your support," Andulov said. "You have volunteered for the campaign. You have distributed signs. You have helped us print leaflets. You have donated money so that we may buy media advertising. You have been the strong shoulder, the column on which we have built everything you now see poised to take the presidency!"

The cheering started anew. Andulov waited it out before going on. "What do I offer you?" Andulov said. "I offer you a new way. I offer you an end to needless posturing, needless warring, needless enmity. I offer you peace. I offer you prosperity."

The Russian candidate paused, gripping the podium for effect, bowing his head for a few moments before raising it again. "For wishing to bring you these gifts," he said, "I have endured almost constant harassment. My family has been threatened. My home has been vandalized. My phone has been ringing constantly, and so often when I answer it, I hear nothing, or I hear the vile words of cowards who promise violence while hidden by distance and anonymity."

The crowd murmured at that. Andulov looked them over knowingly, the picture of resolve.

"There are those who have said I should step down for my own safety," he said, "for it is widely known that those who oppose Aleksis Katzev often meet with unfortunate accidents. Terrible sickness. Strange, fatal coincidences.

Outright disappearances. This is what befalls all who stand between Aleksis Katzev and power."

Encizo smiled. Seeing the man speak, even in translation, he understood why the Russian people liked him.

"Do you even know the company your president keeps?" Andulov demanded. "He holds court with murderers. He consorts with terrorists. He takes money from drug traffickers. He would see your nation intertwined, irrevocably, with the cancer that is organized crime in this nation."

Andulov spread his arms wide. "Are you not sick of this?" he demanded. "Do your hearts not ache to see what we have become? Do you not yearn for the freedom of a time when Russia was her own nation, beholden to no one, in league with no evil? Crime is a cancer. International terrorism is a poison. Drugs are a monster. Yet your Aleksis Katzev would let each of these into your nation, into your house, into the rooms of your children!"

The Russian was red in the face now, almost trembling with rage. Encizo was very nearly transfixed by this masterful display. He forced himself to focus on the task at hand.

"Some may wonder how I would dare say all this of the president, how I would dare accuse him of such horrible, capital crimes. I say that I can tell you of them as loudly, and as often, as I wish…for truth is the ultimate defense! These are facts. Aleksis Katzev cannot refute them. He cannot stop us! He cannot defeat us! Truth is not on his side!"

The crowd was going nuts now, chanting again and again the Russian word for *truth* and alternating that chant with repeated choruses of Andulov's name.

"Join me!" Andulov demanded. "Join me now in saving Russia from her enemies, within and without! Join me and become truly great! Join me and be the Russia you were meant to be, free of criminals and parasites! Join me and we will, together, be strong! We will be Russia! We will be Russia! We will be Russia!"

The crowd went berserk. They cheered. They waved their arms. They stomped their feet. They screamed Andulov's name so loudly that Encizo thought he could make out individual voices in the crowd, even from as far away as he was stationed.

"Movement, movement," Manning reported from his spot in the crowd. "I've got possible hostiles moving in from the east."

"And from the west," Calvin James reported. "I've got goons in suits. Repeat, goons in suits. The *mafiya* has joined the party, boys. They're making straight for Andulov, and if it's his bodyguards, they're nobody we've seen."

"Stay with them," McCarter ordered. "Shadow them through the crowd."

Andulov kept speaking, but Encizo no longer heard him. He was maintaining a fix on the politician and the area around him, trying to track multiple moving hostiles at once. It might be the case that the Dragunov and Encizo were the only barrier between a Russian mobster's bullet and Andulov's untimely death. Encizo was not about to let the man, or his teammates, down.

"Rafe, Rafe, come in," McCarter said. "Track right. Repeat, track right. Follow my marker, follow my marker. We need to thin the herd. Go now!"

Encizo didn't need to be told again. He followed the bearing McCarter had given him, locked on to the knot of men moving purposefully through the crowd, and took up the slack on the rifle's trigger.

"I need confirmation," he said.

"Hold one," McCarter said. "You'll have it." As Encizo watched through the scope, McCarter walked boldly up to the group of men.

"You there!" he said, once more affecting an outrageous Cockney accent. "Stand down, immediately, in the name of the Queen!"

The men exchanged glances. They reached into their coats and produced Skorpion machine pistols. The man in the lead shoved McCarter aside and tried to draw a bead on the podium.

Confirmation. They were here to assassinate Andulov; it could only be the *mafiya*.

The rifle bucked against Encizo's shoulder. The head of the lead mobster literally exploded as the Cuban rained death on the men below him.

Pandemonium broke out. When the sound of the shot reached the crowd and those nearest the dead man saw what had happened, they began running, screaming, pushing. It was classic panic, and the mobsters were determined to use it to their advantage. Two of the *mafiya* soldiers in the crowd began firing at the podium on full automatic, chipping away at the wood.

Under the wood was armor plating.

Andulov's people had cobbled together the podium some time before, they had explained that morning, for appearances such as these. It offered a refuge in the event of an assassination attempt like this one. The man was brave, Encizo could truthfully say, but he was also not stupid. He hunkered down behind the podium and let the mobsters' bullets ricochet from it, tearing away the wooden veneer.

Encizo tracked the next target. He drew in a breath, let out half of it, held his breath, and squeezed the trigger. The Dragunov fired itself, taking one of the mob gunners in the chest, knocking him down forever.

The shooters were starting to get wise to the fact that opposition on the ground was not all they faced. One of the mobsters began to run forward, then back, then forward again, obviously unsure, suddenly, of where might be safe. Encizo decided to teach him that, for predators such as the *mafiya,* there was nowhere to go but hell. He put the crosshairs over the man's head and fired, punching a hole straight through the man's brain. The mobster was dead before the bullet even left him. Gravity finally caught up with his corpse.

"Keep clearing, Rafe," McCarter said. "We're taking up defensive positions!"

Encizo watched through his scope as his teammates split into two groups. McCarter and James broke left, while Manning and Hawkins broke right. They took cover behind the engine blocks of the nearest parked vehicles. The *mafiya* shooters, meanwhile, were scrambling to find cover of their own, and failing, caught in the cross fire between the Phoenix warriors.

Andulov popped up briefly from behind the podium, leveled the Makarov pistol he apparently carried when it was not in his desk and put a bullet through the neck of the nearest mobster. He ducked back down behind his podium before the return fire could find him, and Encizo did him the favor of shooting the man who was trying to target him.

Andulov peeked out from behind the podium, looked straight at where he knew Encizo was positioned and mouthed the words *thank you* in English.

Yes, Encizo thought, tracking the last of the moving mobsters and launching a 7.62 mm bullet through his skull, that Andulov was definitely a likable guy.

He actually almost felt bad for what he was about to do.

"All right, we're mopping up," McCarter reported.

"Take it home, lads. Secure the area, make sure the mobsters are all down to stay and then fade. We need to disappear, and fast, before the police show up in response to this whole debacle."

The Phoenix Force members checked the bodies of the Russians and then blended into what remained of the fleeing crowd. They had a rendezvous destination already set, something that Andulov's supporters had helped arrange. Encizo had to hand it to the man; he definitely commanded the loyalty of those around him. Once he was convinced of the Stony Man commandos' good intentions, he had pulled out all the stops in getting Phoenix Force what it needed. He'd moved personnel, changed schedules, angered public-relations experts, drawn resources and gone out of his way to make sure Phoenix Force was properly supported.

Knowing his life depended on it likely had something to do with it.

"All right, we're gone," McCarter said. "Rafe, report!"

"Encizo here," the Cuban said. "I am in position for the main event. Repeat, I am ready for the main event."

"All right," McCarter said. "We'll meet you at the designated location. Good luck."

Encizo watched the Phoenix Force warriors move out of sight. Then he refocused on Andulov below. The Russian was back at the bullet-scarred podium, holding out his arms, as if to say, "I am still here."

Slowly, very slowly, the crowd began to drift back. They moved cautiously at first, some of them half crouched, but their desire to witness something great overcame their fear. The reporters, always desperate for a story, were first to close in. They surrounded the podium with their cameras and microphones. Whomever Andulov was using as an English translator began translating both Andulov's answers and the questions themselves, as the recklessly scheduled prerally turned into a recklessly held press conference.

"Mr. Andulov, Mr. Andulov!" one reporter yelled. "Was this an attempt on your life?"

"I can't see how one could interpret it any other way," Andulov said, nodding. He gestured to the dead men, still lying in Red Square where they had fallen. Security personnel and police were now converging on Andulov's location, but he did not stop his press conference. He invited some of the police up onto the platform with him, explaining to them what had happened and doing his best to ingratiate himself to them.

"Will this cause you to drop out of the race?" another reporter asked.

"Far from it," Andulov said. "This merely strengthens my resolve. It is more important than ever that we stand up to this murderous Katzev and those who help him retain power through force of arms, through terror, through brutality. We are Russia, and we will not be cowed by this blatant act of cold-blooded assassination!"

"Are you accusing President Katzev of being behind an assassination attempt?" another reporter asked.

"Yes," Andulov said. "Yes, I am indeed."

"Surely you must understand how provocative an act that is," the reporter said.

"Provocative? *Provocative?*" Andulov scoffed. "Trying to shoot a man down purely to remove him from the political equation is provocative. I have merely told the truth."

"Do you think there is any truth to the rumors that President Katzev wishes to have you arrested for sedition?"

"Of course I think they're true," Andulov said. "Do any of us truly doubt that he would wish that? Fortunately for me, and for you, the Russian people, he is not yet a total dictator. He does not yet have complete power over every aspect of your lives as Russians. There is still time to fight him! There is still time to defeat him! Join me, Russia! Join me in protecting what is yours! Join me in preserving your birthright!"

"What of those whose ideologies you have rejected?" yet another reporter asked. "Katzev has his supporters. If you are elected president, will those supporters fare no better than you have? Can they expect the same treatment you have been given when the shoe is on the other foot?"

"An insightful question," Andulov said. "I can say, unequivocally, that my administration will take no vengeful actions. We will condone no retribution against those who, out of fear or out of a genuine desire to see Russia succeed, have sided with Katzev against us. Ours will be a regime of peace. We will unify Russia again. We will bring its people together for common purpose. We are not in the business of holding grudges or of taking revenge."

Encizo scanned the crowd. His partners would be waiting at the rendezvous point once he fled this place, but he had to admit that he was nervous about something going wrong. There were a lot of variables. Fleeing alone through a foreign city carrying a sniper weapon that was as good as a death sentence once it was matched to the crime in which it was about to used…that was harsh imagery indeed, and it generated feelings Encizo did not particularly wish to explore.

Andulov, ever the politician for all his decency, again began playing the crowd. Encizo could not fault him for it; it seemed to him that the man could almost never turn off what made him do what he did. It was all or nothing with Andulov, which was probably what made him an effective leader. Certainly "all or nothing" described McCarter, the current leader of Phoenix Force and the man who would be, if Encizo did not show up at the rendezvous point at the designated time, hot on the Cuban's footsteps until he determined what had gone wrong.

"Please, everyone," Andulov said through his public address system. His translator again typed out the words in English on the screen behind him. English was a universal language, of sorts, a common denominator among those who did not speak Russian. This was convenient for Encizo and the other members of Phoenix Force.

"Do you have anything more to say?" a reporter asked Andulov. "Is there some further message you wish to bring to the Russian people?"

"First," Andulov said, his tone somber and genuine, "please, someone, bring blankets or even jackets, anything, and cover up these men." He pointed to the dead men littering the square.

"Jackets!" someone called. "Jackets or blankets!" These were found from among the supporters in the crowd.

"You show compassion to those who would murder you?" someone in the crowd called out.

"Compassion?" Andulov asked. "What compassion is that? I show common decency among human beings. These men are dead. They can hurt no one now. Treating them like garbage, like refuse, this diminishes us all. This has been the central message of my campaign from the beginning. I wish to restore to Russia its former glory, just as does my opponent. But where Katzev would use dishonor, violence and crime in an attempt to force this goal, I will do so genuinely, with a true understanding of what is required of our people."

"What does that mean, exactly?" one of the reporters asked.

Good one, thought Encizo. He was starting to bloviate. Must be a tendency among all politicians.

"What I mean," Andulov said, "is that a renewed Russia cannot be born from fear, from violence, from crime, and from ignominy. A renewed Russia can only be born from the qualities that truly renew her…from the values that made her great in her youth. Does anyone here disagree? Speak out, if you will."

"Do you believe you'll live to see the election?" a reporter called out.

Andulov looked at him for a moment. "Have we become so jaded?" he said finally. "Have we become so cynical that we think of all politics in Katzev's terms?"

"But this is reality," the reporter said. "This is the fact of what we're up against. President Katzev holds great power, and he opposes you. You have accused him publicly of horrific crimes. You do not expect him to react?"

"I would expect any man to react," Andulov said. "And I am quite certain Katzev will react. The question becomes, in what way will he react? Will he react as president? Or will he react as criminal, as terrorist…as murderer?"

Encizo sighted in very carefully. He lined up the Dragunov's crosshairs over Andulov's chest.

"Make no mistake," Andulov said. "I will fight for as long as there is breath in my lungs. I will fight for as long as I have the will to speak, the energy to listen and the brains to—"

Encizo's shot took Andulov in the chest and knocked him onto the platform.

CHAPTER TWENTY

Boston, Massachusetts

Mok Thawan checked the magazine in his 1911 pistol, then shoved the weapon into his waistband. Standing in the basement, he checked the bombs in their casings. The storage rooms above him were full of what was left of the Triangle's drugs, weapons and other resources, meager though they now seemed. But even this last refuge was to be denied him, for the clever surveillance cameras placed throughout the neighborhood had found and alerted Thawan to the presence of the deadly commandos who stalked him. He would recognize the big blond man anywhere. The man haunted his dreams and made him worry that he was less the man he'd once believed himself to be, when he proved himself the best knife fighter in his village. That accomplishment seemed far away, now. Far away and feeble.

He flipped open the wireless phone and dialed the long number from memory. The phone was answered after the second ring, which was very unusual. The man who answered said nothing, which was often a test of the resolve of whoever called. Thawan had no patience for the game.

"Father," he said. "I need to speak with you."

"I am here," Than said.

"I am in Boston, where I said I would go when things became…irretrievable."

"And have they?"

"They have," Thawan said.

"You must be strong," Than said. "There is much left for us to accomplish. We are poised for victory, my son. The international news reports that Katzev is alone in his race for president of Russia. Katzev, or someone in his employ, has succeeded in murdering the rival who was challenging for the office. Our ally Katzev will thus be president for another term, in position to carry out the bargains we have brokered."

"He may be," Thawan said, "but we will not be. We cannot carry out our end of the bargain. We cannot finance him. We have no resources."

"What do you mean, no resources?"

"I have consolidated everything that was left here in Boston," Thawan said. "You once told me, 'Put all your eggs in one basket, and watch that basket.' This I have done. I have withdrawn to our most fortified of safehouses, and I have brought all that we have left, all that we are, all that the Triangle may use to further its goals, here to this place."

"Then I do not understand," Than said. "This is what I wished you to do."

"They are here," Thawan said simply.

"'They'?" Thawan asked. "Who is 'they'?"

"The commandos, Father," Thawan said. "The men who have been hunting me. I do not know how they did it. I do not know how they have found me repeatedly, how they have anticipated my every move. It is like I am stalked by ghosts."

"You have let them follow you!" Than accused. "They have tracked you to the place of hiding and now all is lost!"

"I have not let them follow me," Thawan said. "That is what I do not understand. They could not have followed me."

"Do not lie to me, you wretch!" Than demanded. "Do not try to cover your failures! I will not stomach it!"

"Father," Thawan said, "I do not think you understand."

"Then explain it to me."

"What money and resources we have," Thawan said patiently, "are here. In this building, with me."

"Yes? And?"

"If those resources are confiscated or destroyed, they are of no use to me."

"What is your point?"

"If they are of no use to me, they are certainly of no use to you. You are much farther removed from them than I am."

"So?"

"Father, this is all. There is no more. The coffers are empty. Our banking-house transactions have been seized by the investigating governments, as I feared might happen. Did you not think to look into the aftermath of the breach in Russia? This was reported to me—it should have been reported to you, as well. Did you not care? Do you not grasp that this affects all of us…you, me, everyone we know, everyone who has benefited from your generosity in the past months, at the very least. In some cases, it may instead be years."

"What are you telling me?"

"I am telling you, Father," Than said, "that you are no longer the old man in the mountain. You are no longer the powerful drug warlord, Than. You no longer have the money to pay your soldiers, to buy your food or even to purchase the affections of the cheapest harlot to cross your threshold in curiosity."

"How *dare* you—?"

"How dare I?" Thawan asked. "I dare as a man who has always done your dirty work, like so many before me. I dare because, while you send me and others like me out to hurt, to kill and to die, you reap the profits, or you did. I dare because I no longer feel the need to be…dirty. I no longer feel the need to tolerate the likes of you."

"But…you are my son!"

"Am I? Thawan asked. "And does it even matter? You are the same horror regardless of parentage, mine or yours. You are the same monster who lives in the mountain, never daring to do more, to be more, than to sponge from others, to make demands, to enjoy a lavish, unearned lifestyle. What are you, Father? You are monster. You are evil. And I am both, because of you. I have nothing now, because of you. I could have been anything. I could be poor and living on the streets right now, stealing to survive, but my own man, and happier for it."

"You could be whoring yourself to businessmen in Bangkok for a Euro a throw, too," Than said viciously. "Perhaps I will see to it that this happens."

"I do not doubt that there was a time when you were vindictive enough to do so," Thawan said. "I do not doubt that you are that vindictive now. The difference is, you have no money. Oh, you have some in theory. It is here in the house in the form of your drugs. It will be gone soon, for as I told you, the Western demons are coming. They will destroy everything, or I will. Perhaps I will manage to destroy us all, if I have the courage. I do not think that I do. I think that, despite everything, I love my life and I fear death. But you…you no longer have the ability to make anyone do anything. You have become just a pathetic old man, hiding in a stone house that is too big for him, caring for pets he does not understand how to care for. Your pets, your henchmen, will quickly abandon you when they discover you have no money…or they will turn on you and loot what they can. Heed that, if you survive the day and the night."

"You are dead to me," Than said bitterly. "You are dead to me! Do you hear me? *Dead!*"

"I hear you, Father," Thawan said. "Goodbye."

"OH, WELL, THIS IS just a choice neighborhood," Schwarz complained.

"If NetScythe is correct," Lyons said, "and it's not been wrong yet, this is where Thawan is projected to have fled."

"Well, to be fair, so was the auto shop in Salem," Blancanales noted.

"Think of that as the appetizer," Lyons said. "We're about to hit the main course."

"This is looking pretty…shady, Ironman," Schwarz said.

Lyons had to admit that the electronics expert was correct. This was easily the worst part of the worst neighborhood in Boston. He had no problem believing that this was where Thawan would choose to make his final stand.

They had consulted with Barbara Price and the cybernetics team at the Farm after the hit on the Salem shop. By eliminating that variable, NetScythe had been able to produce a much higher probability analysis concerning Thawan and the Triangle's travels and activities. By including all of the data points thus far, including those locations Able Team had hit, where they had found Thawan, where they hadn't and where Thawan had gone when he escaped them repeatedly, the NetScythe program produced a very explicit profile. The Triangle was running out of resources; it might even be completely out of them. This location was likely Thawan's last bolt-hole, his last place of refuge. Chances were good that the location would be heavily fortified, and that they would meet heavy resistance.

Thermal imagery of the target site once more showed a great deal of thermal activity. That would be the thugs Thawan kept on hand. It was possible that those within were all that he had left. The Triangle had already begun the process of packing up and consolidating its dwindling resources, after all. This was very likely the last repository, the place to which Thawan had fled when there was nothing left to him.

In other words, he would be like a trapped animal.

Dangerous as Thawan was known to be, he would be doubly so now. Desperate, determined not to be caught and more than willing to use booby traps and bombs to his advantage, he would be a very dangerous foe.

The neighborhood began to devolve into a series of alleyways. According to their GPS device, the direction in which they needed to go to reach Thawan was due east. That way was blocked, however, by a crude plywood-and-brick barrier that stretched across the alleyway.

"Fortifications," Blancanales said. "Looks like we have to play it on his terms."

"I try to avoid fatal funnels," Schwarz said.

"So do I," Lyons said. "But it doesn't look like we have a choice in this instance. Grab the gear. We're going in. There's no time to waste. I don't want Thawan getting nervous and jerky and blowing up the entire goddamned neighborhood."

"Good point," Schwarz conceded.

Lyons and Blancanales affixed combat lights to their

primary weapons—Lyons to his shotgun, Blancanales to his M-4. Gadgets had a combat light that he would use in a two-hand grip with his 93-R machine pistol. Each man slung over his shoulder a canvas war bag full of grenades and other surprises. They were going into this fully laden for battle.

"Move very carefully," Lyons warned them. "Given Thawan's penchant for clever explosions I don't want to risk tripping any—"

"Carl," Schwarz said. "Stop."

Lyons froze.

Schwarz bent, using his combat flashlight to illuminate the floor of the alleyway. It was day outside, but the make-shift plywood tunnel in which they traveled cut off almost all light. Now, examining the floor of the tunnel, Schwarz understood its purpose. It was there, at least in this case, to remove light to make the floor harder to see.

This was because the floor was covered with explosives.

Specifically, the hole was a raised sheet of plywood sitting on two-by-four braces. Holes had been cut into the plywood. Land mines with prominent detonation prongs had been placed in these holes, so that only the prongs extended above the holes, and even then they projected only a little. They were very nearly invisible. Lyons had almost stepped on one.

"I think it's an older model Bouncing Betty," Schwarz said. "Very much unfun. Hold on. I'll start clearing us a path."

Lyons had a death grip on his shotgun, clenching and unclenching his fists.

"Easy, Ironman," Schwarz said.

"There's no telling how far this tunnel goes," Lyons

said. "He's got the route to him completely boxed out, and he's filled it with booby traps."

"And you can bet this will be the only way in," Blancanales pointed out. "A job this thorough is not left to chance. If they've concentrated all their interdiction efforts here, they'll have all other avenues of entry blocked. We are likely stuck with this route, gentlemen."

"What are you thinking, Carl?" Schwarz asked. "Pull out? Find another way? We could ask for some air support."

"No," Lyons said. "As fast as Thawan is, we may not get another chance. I'm done screwing around with him— I really am. This time we're going to catch up to him and we're going to take him down. Thawan and his reign of terror end right now, tonight. That's all there is to it."

"I'm with you," Schwarz declared.

"You know I am," Blancanales said calmly. "Shall we?"

"Let's," Lyons said. They continued moving down the makeshift corridor.

The tunnel made an *L* shape and broke right. As they turned, Schwarz stopped them once more. He had been playing the beam of his flashlight across the floor, but now he was looking at something at chest height.

"Right there," Schwarz said. "Look. That's a tripwire."

"It's extremely fine," Blancanales said almost admiringly. "I've not seen one like it before."

"No doubt it is attached to a particularly elegant device," Schwarz said.

"You guys need help." Lyons shook his head.

"Poor Ironman," Schwarz said. "He can't appreciate advanced technology."

"Shut the hell up, Gadgets," Lyons said. "You're seriously creeping me out."

It was Schwarz's turn to ignore Lyons. He busied

himself with the tripwire, following the line to its source. There was no device, just a mounting clip. Using his flashlight to keep the line visible, he played the beam back and forth and followed the tripwire to its other end.

He whistled.

"Take a look at this," he said. "Pol, this one is vintage Russian."

"What is it?" Lyons asked.

"Glass frag," Schwarz said. "I haven't seen one of these in a long time. When it explodes, it showers the target with shards of glass. Some of the splinters can be microscopic. It's horrible to treat. Really vicious stuff."

"Can you deactivate it?"

Schwarz pulled something free. "Already did."

"Then let's keep moving," Lyons demanded.

"Your wish is my command," Schwarz said.

"You get squirrelly when you play bomb technician, Gadgets," Blancanales observed.

"Wouldn't you?"

"Touché." Blancanales nodded.

Lyons muttered something under his breath that was probably about hating them both.

Another twist of the tunnel brought them to what appeared to be a carpet on the floor.

"That doesn't look good," Lyons said.

"No," Schwarz said. "It certainly does not. And I am willing to bet that's the point."

"What do you mean?"

"At this point in the tunnel," Schwarz said, "anyone who has survived it will start to feel a certain sense of dread, of foreboding, whenever dealing with anything unusual. The carpet is certainly unusual—the impulse will be to step over and around it. Look at the board in the floor just beyond the carpet."

"I can see a seam," Lyons said.

"Yes," Schwarz said. "That board is probably built onto a pressure switch. When you jump over the carpet to avoid whatever it might be covering, you land on the pressure switch, and…boom."

Lyons cursed Thawan. "So how do we defuse it?"

"We don't," Schwarz said. "No way to reach it without lifting up the board, and that might set it off. We just have to get past it. Walk on the carpet and then jump over the loose board."

"What if there's another board behind the first one?" Lyons asked.

"Well, now, that's just defeatist thinking."

"What if there is something under the carpet just for good measure?" Lyons asked.

Gadgets sighed. "Then we blow up, Carl."

Lyons reached down and carefully lifted the piece of shag carpet. There did not seem to be anything there. He gingerly put his foot forward, stepped on the carpet and then stepped beyond the loose board.

"Clear," he said when he was on the other side. "Come on."

Schwarz and Blancanales followed.

They came to what appeared to be a dead end in the claustrophobic plywood tunnel.

"It worries me that there are no guards," Blancanales said suddenly.

"What do you mean?" Schwarz asked.

"He means," Lyons said, "that if we haven't seen any guards, it's because they either think these devices are foolproof and there's no way an enemy could deactivate them—"

"Or they're just too scared to come down here and get near them, because they're so powerful and volatile," Blancanales supplied.

"I really enjoy our trips together, guys," Schwarz said.

"Shut up, Gadgets," Lyons and Blancanales said in unison.

"Any ideas?" Lyons said. He reached out to touch the barrier, then thought better of it.

"Here," Schwarz said. "Let me." He began tapping along the surface of the plywood barrier. When he found a metal handle, he grasped it and, holding his breath, moved the door aside by the barest of fractions. Then he did it again and again. Finally, when he was done moving the door, there was a crack through which he could see.

"Oh," he said. "Very much not good."

"What now?" Lyons asked.

"There is what appears to be a very large surplus mine on the other side of this wall. You know, the kind they used to put in harbors. It's big, it's round, it's metal and it's got rusted contacts sticking out in every direction. If I move this door any farther, it will brush one of those contacts, and that giant, formerly oceangoing mine will be activated, and we will explode."

"I would rather not explode," Blancanales said.

"And I share that sentiment." Schwarz nodded vigorously. "Which means we have to very carefully take this door off its hinges, then very, very carefully slip past that very old and very deadly explosive device."

"Well, that sounds easy," Lyons said.

"Right." Schwarz nodded. His grin was less convincing this time.

"Hand me your multitool," Lyons said.

Schwarz snapped open the Leatherman multitool he carried and gave it to Lyons, who found the screwdriver he wanted. He began probing the edges of the hinges on which the sliding door moved. Finally, using the screwdriver, he very carefully popped the plywood, metal-framed door out of its track.

"Here, Pol," he said, easing the door back, "take this."

Blancanales did so. He moved the wall behind him.

"Try not to shove it into mines or tripwires, anything we left behind by dumb luck," Schwarz said.

Blancanales looked back and cringed. "You should tell me these things *before* I do stuff."

"Where would the fun in that be?" Lyons asked without humor.

"All right, slow going, now," Schwarz said. The mine was suspended in the middle of the corridor from a heavy, rusted chain. Lyons held his breath as he, the widest of the trio, managed to just slide past the mine, barely brushing its surface with his broad chest. Once on the other side of the explosive, he looked down at the rust that had brushed off on his shirt.

"That was a little too close," he said.

His partners joined him, having a slightly easier time of it. They found themselves in an empty hallway beyond the mine. The hallway was partly wood, but near the far end, it became plaster. Beyond the plaster segments was the stone foundation of a building, into which a hole had been chopped, cut or simply crumbled into being.

Beyond this hole was the basement—the entrance to Mok Thawan's lair. There was no doubt in the minds of the men of Able Team that this was indeed the case… because Mok Thawan was standing there waiting for them.

"So," Mok Thawan said, "you have found me yet again. I cannot say I am surprised." Some essential quality had left Thawan. Something important, something vital, was missing from his voice. He looked and sounded half-dead. He looked, in fact, like a man who no longer cared if he lived or if he died.

He held another example of the now-familiar dead man's switch in his hand.

CHAPTER TWENTY-ONE

Moscow, Russia

"Are you certain?" Mogranov asked Katzev.

"Of course I am," Katzev replied confidently. "The main threat is passed, just as you wanted. Andulov is dead. These commandos, these angels of mercy, these terrifying specters from the West…what could they do? Clearly our friends in the *mafiya* seized the day. I would take the time to feel mildly despondent for the men the mobsters lost, but, in truth, I do not care about that. The job was done. Andulov is no more. The election is mine. There is no way the opposition can find someone in time to replace him. Certainly they will not find someone with the same charisma, the same popularity. In their great upset, the people will turn to me, and I will be there to reassure them."

"I still do not like it," Mogranov argued.

"You are like an old mother hen," Katzev said.

"But appropriating the rally?" Mogranov said. "Will that not anger Andulov's supporters?'

"Not if I give an appropriately convincing speech," Katzev said.

"Do you think every sin can be absolved through speeches?" Mogranov demanded.

"Please, Mikhail," Katzev said. "Calm yourself. I am about to ascend the podium. You do not wish me to do so agitated, do you?"

"We still do not know what became of the commandos," Mogranov said.

"Does it matter?" Katzev scoffed. "If ever they were here, they must be gone now. Andulov is dead. The matter is decided. We will now assume the victory that is rightfully ours."

"Very well," Mogranov conceded. "I will be among the crowd, attempting to keep you safe."

"You worry too much, my friend," Katzev told him. "We have taken the day. We have victory in our grasp. Do not be so eager to be defeated. I think you have become too accustomed to living in a Russia who has lost her teeth. Do not worry, old friend—we will restore that Russia together."

"I hope so," Mogranov said. "I really do."

The official start time of the rally—Andulov's rally—was drawing close. A new platform and podium had been set up inside the curtained rally hall, which was adjacent to Red Square, not far from where Andulov had met his unfortunate fate. The symbolism was only too obvious. Andulov, the upstart, the would-be usurper, was gone; in his place there was Katzev. Only Katzev remained; Katzev would be the savior of Russian and none would be allowed to interfere.

That was how Katzev saw it, at least.

The crowds were thick, and working to a fever pitch. Katzev watched their faces as he ascended the platform. He saw fear, he saw anger, he saw trepidation, but he also saw a few admiring faces, though these were few enough apart. It did not matter. Soon they would all grow to love him. Soon they would all understand that everything he did, he did for Russia. Soon they would come to regard him as the savior of their nation, and rightly so. Eventually, perhaps, it was possible that some of the more extralegal things he had done to this point would come to light. But by then, he would have accomplished enough great works in restoring Russia that his people would be willing to forgive and forget a bent rule here or a slightly modified law there.

Wouldn't they?

The press were gathered in much greater numbers than they had been for Andulov's prerally. Katzev had to give the *mafiya* credit for reacting so swiftly and decisively to that unscheduled public appearance. It had opened the way for him to appropriate the scheduled rally tonight, and Andulov's assassination had been as spectacular as he had wished the death to be. It was the perfect setup to the manipulation he would achieve through it, in fact. He would appropriate Andulov's tough-on-crime stance, while simultaneously secretly cultivating the support of organized crime. They, in turn, would squawk loudly for the television cameras and speak of how much injustice was being done them as part of Katzev's new campaign against the *mafiya*.

Katzev stepped to the cluster of microphones at the podium, cleared his throat with a flourish and began to speak.

"People of the Russian Federation!" he said. "I come to you tonight with a heavy heart, for we, the people of Russia, have been cheated."

He paused for dramatic effect. "How have we been cheated, you ask? We have seen one of our citizens struck down in the prime of his life, yes. Yuri Andulov was a good man, a dedicated Russian, a patriot. He loved the Russian Federation as I do. But Yuri Andulov was taken from us. With his murder, self-determination was taken from us."

Katzev paused again, turning slowly from left to right, making sure all of the cameras caught him at the proper angle. "We were to have an election. While I did not agree with my opponent, Yuri Andulov, he was a Russian, as I am a Russian. We were Russians together, bound by a common spirit, a common country, a common language and a common drive to see this nation thrive."

He watched the sullen Mogranov moving among the crowd. *Relax, mother hen,* he thought to himself. *Enjoy the victory.*

"With the loss of my good friend and rival Yuri Andulov," Katzev said, "we have lost the opportunity for the election. There is simply no reason to hold it."

There was a loud reaction from the crowd. He spread his arms for quiet. When the crowd continued to react negatively, he raised his arm and slashed it downward. This was a signal, one for which Mogranov was watching. The security chief spoke a few words into a walkie-talkie, and Spetsnaz soldiers in fatigues, carrying Kalashnikov rifles, appeared from the side doors at the front of the rally hall. They took up positions ringing the front and the first few yards of the sides of the rally hall, forming a protective half circle.

The appearance of the soldiers prompted an even louder, even more derisive reaction. Katzev struggled to get his temper under control. How dare they? Did they have any idea how much he had sacrificed? How much he had truly done for them? If they had, they wouldn't dare treat him this way. He would make them see reason.

"I will, in my second term in office," Katzev said, "hunt down the mob killers who took the life of Yuri Andulov. I will see to it that organized crime in the Russian Federation cannot find root. I will destroy corruption wherever I see it."

The crowd was still unruly, though he believed his words were having some effect. He gestured to the soldiers below, conceiving of a way to bring the angry rally-goers back to his side.

"You see these men?" he asked the crowd. "You see? They are the pride of the Russian military. They are well trained, well funded, well equipped. How many of you have lost loved ones to accidents at sea, or in the air, because our military was underfunded and under-equipped?"

That got them. The murmuring turned less hostile as those listening stopped to think about it. They had of course, many of them, lost loved ones in such situations, or at least knew someone who did; this had been life in the Soviet navy, among other things, and the navy's rotting fleet had little more to work with once the Soviet Union collapsed.

"I will fund the military," Katzev said. "I will restore our pride through the projection of military might. I will put us back on top of the hierarchy of nations. Too long have we suffered the arrogance of the United States!"

The crowd cheered. Anti-American sentiment was always a crowd pleaser, and "the world's only super-power," as the Americans were fond of terming themselves after the Cold War, was a common enemy most people could revile without prompting. Katzev had come to regard mentions of the Great Satan, as it were, a bit like a crutch in his speeches, however. Yes, it got a reaction, but just because the crowd could agree on disliking the United States did not mean they truly loved Katzev.

That, he had to admit to himself, was what he truly

craved. He did not want just their fear; he wanted their respect. He wanted their love. He wanted the power that comes from being truly revered.

Perhaps Than has the right idea, after all, he thought. A little piece of godhead here on Earth, the devotion of followers, the power of absolute rule. Katzev did wonder, however, how distorted his sense of self might become were he to spend more than a few years trapped in an echo chamber with nothing but disciples. Perhaps that, too, explained quite a bit about Than.

He would need to get in touch with Than, now that matters with Andulov were settled. He would also need to assess the damage to Than's operation. If the warlord could still help him, Katzev would do what he could to secure the man's cooperation. If the warlord could not help him, did not have the resources to help him, then Than was a liability who would have to be removed. Just how much his network had crumbled would determine whether Katzev deemed it safe to strike out against the feared old man.

It was time to wrap things up. He had given the masses enough to chew on. He had given them promises, had showed them strength. He would close the rally, go back to his office and resume his business. He would continue rebuilding Russia. He would continue pursuing his vision.

History would judge him well, even if some of his countrymen did not.

"It is now time," Katzev said, "for Russia to move forward. We must be stronger than ever. We must be more feared than ever. We must be more willing than ever to take what we desire. Russia is not weak. We will no longer respond to the pressures of the West. We will no longer brook affronts to our sovereignty. We will withdraw from the United Nations and form our own unity organization, where we will set the rules and other countries will come crawling to us because we have the oil they want. We are Russia. There is nothing we cannot do. There is no obstacle too large. There is no goal too far away. We are Russia!"

"No!" a man shouted, his voice amplified by a megaphone. "*We* are Russia. You are a corrupt fool!"

Katzev stopped. He searched for the voice. He found the speaker just as many in the crowd did. A collective gasp went up from those assembled. People moved back and away, forming a clearing around the space where the speaker now stood.

Andulov.

The man's chest was soaked in blood, but he stood as if he had never felt healthier. To the surprise of a shocked Aleksis Katzev, Yuri Andulov walked across the rally hall. The crowd parted to let him pass. Andulov assumed the podium, gently shoving away the dumbfounded Katzev.

"I am Yuri Andulov," he said into the microphones. "I come to you today with a very difficult message." He pointed to Katzev. "This man is your enemy. He is the enemy of Russia. He is the enemy of all decent people everywhere. He was responsible for the earlier attack. People working for and with him tried to kill me. They would try to kill you, too, if you defied them, if you got in their way. That is how they do things. At the rally earlier today, I wore a special vest with a trauma plate, and over that plate I wore a plastic pack of fake blood. I was shot, not by the *mafiya,* who most certainly did wish to kill me at Katzev's request. No, I was shot by an ally, in the hopes that my apparent death would bring Katzev out of hiding. It has done so."

"Hiding?" Katzev demanded, indignant. "I have never hidden anywhere!"

Andulov ignored him. "There are men in this audience tonight. They are men who saved my life. They are here to take Katzev into custody. They have proof that President Aleksis Katzev has taken money from terrorists and drug traffickers, conspired with same to profit from the sales of illegal drugs and conspired to murder me. We may yet uncover evidence of Katzev's other crimes. He has much to answer for even if we do not."

"You have no authority here!" Katzev shrieked.

"I will now show you the evidence," Andulov said.

Phoenix Force had worked their way into the rally house slowly, moving in with the rest of the crowd. Katzev had left all of Andulov's original planning and security arrangements in place, simply appropriating the time and venue for the rally. Thus, Andulov's people had been able to arrange for special passes for the men of Phoenix Force, which allowed them to circumvent security and bring their weapons into the rally hall.

Hawkins had immediately sought out the controls for the sound system and video screen behind Katzev. He had used a USB cable to connect his secure satellite phone to that system, contacting the Farm and establishing a secure link. Hearing Katzev's cue, Hawkins prompted the Farm for the data transfer.

The screen behind Katzev lighted up with names, dates and numbers. These were the financial transfers that had been funneled through the *mafiya* banking house. Simultaneously, audio of the meeting between the Russian generals and the *mafiya* lieutenants began to play. When this had completed, the screen switched to a montage of all the evidence the Farm had managed to acquire in the course of the raids by Able Team and Phoenix Force.

"Aleksis Katzev," Yuri Andulov said, "I hereby remove you from the office of president, for high crimes against this nation and its people."

"Remove me? Remove *me*?" Katzev laughed. "To

whom do you think the military is loyal, you fool? They understand that it is I who will rebuild them, I who will fund them, I who will do anything it takes to make them great once more. You…what do you offer them? Continued mediocrity? A seat at the table of nations who were *once* great?"

Andulov addressed the crowd once more, knowing the television cameras present would be transmitting his message across the nation and, ultimately, around the world for those who cared to know what went on in the Russian Federation. "You see, now, I trust, my fellow Russians, just how arrogant is the man who stands before you. Aleksis Katzev is a monster. You have seen the proof, projected larger than life behind me! You have seen his reaction. He cannot deny his crimes. He can only claim that whatever crimes or injustices he has committed, he committed them for you. Is that the sort of leader you want?"

The crowd roared back, *"Nyet!"*

"Follow me, and not the old regime," Andulov shouted. "Follow me, and not the old ways. Be strong as Russians. Stand up to evil! We can have more than an endless succession of dreary days bemoaning what was and what might have been. We are strong, we are smart, we are capable…why are we not building more that we require? Why are we not employing more of our own? Why are we attempting to antagonize the West, when the West represents one of the world's best consumer markets for goods and services manufactured abroad? We, Russia, could be on the forefront of that development…if only we let go of the old ways. If only we stopped the rattling of sabers, the pursuit of folly."

"Strength is not folly," Katzev screamed. "Russia will always be persecuted by its enemies. We cannot afford to be neutered. Do we want the West dictating to us what weapons we will and will not have? Do we want the West controlling our economy?"

The crowd appeared confused. Some of them did shout, *"Nyet!"* but it was no longer clear if a response was expected or not. The energy of the rally had changed, leaving its attendees confused as to what they were supposed to be feeling. The intent was there, but not the function; proper form had not been pursued.

"Mr. Andulov! Mr. Andulov!" a reporter began yelling near the stage. He was standing next to a man with a television camera. The light mounted on the camera was very bright. "Are you wresting control of the government away from Katzev? Is this a coup, as was attempted by the Soviet hardliners?"

"This is no coup attempt," Andulov said.

"But you've demanded the president step down."

"That is true," Andulov noted. "I have made that demand. But I have made it because his crimes are self-evident. He is corrupt, and a murderer. He consorts with the enemies of every civilized nation, and antagonizes those civilized nations in the belief that this makes him powerful. I consider these the actions of a man who is incompetent. I consider these the actions of a man who cannot do the job that is asked of him. As such, he should indeed step down, and right away."

"What of our nuclear arsenal?" Katzev demanded. "Do you really want Russia's nuclear weapons in his control?" He pointed to Andulov again. "He is weak. Weak, I tell you. He can do *nothing* for Russia. He is not fit to lead it!"

"Katzev," Andulov said, pity evident in his voice, "it is time you stepped down. Your crimes have become public. You have no more allies, no more means of hiding what you have done."

"I have the military!" Katzev shouted. "I *am* the

military! You cannot stop me! I will kill every man, woman and child within a fifty-mile radius if I must!"

Andulov looked at Katzev, shocked. The man was practically foaming at the mouth, grabbing the corner of the podium.

"Security." Andulov pointed. A pair of guards attached to the rally house staff approached, looking apprehensively at the Spetsnaz soldiers.

"Do not interfere," Andulov told the Spetsnaz men. "Your leader is obviously not well. Would you truly follow him over me? Or do you wish a leader who can be rational, who is capable of rational judgment? A reasonable man who will bring reasonable ideas to the military and listen to you and your concerns? I will not merely make a show, political theater, of the soap opera that is my daily journal of activities. I will not demand that you respect me for the great sacrifices I am making as you give me wealth and power. I will simply serve you, the people of Russia."

"Wow, David," Encizo said, watching Andulov deliver the goods. The data the Stony Man teams had managed to acquire was being projected on the screen. "He's really letting them have it."

"He's quite the fire-and-brimstone type, at that," McCarter said. "All right, lads, look sharp, and keep your duffel bags handy." All the men of Phoenix Force carried bags in which their folding-stock AKs were stowed. Manning also had his grenade launcher.

"David," James said over the transceiver link, "this is starting to get ugly." James was very close to the podium platform and had a good view of the Russian president. "I don't like the way Katzev is drifting. If I had to guess I'd say he's working his way up to something. And all those Spetsnaz soldiers…well, this looks like it's going to turn sour.

"I agree," McCarter said. "All right, lads, time to put it where it needs to be. Spread out farther, establish your positions and make sure you're lined up to take out as many of those special forces troops as you can."

"What do you think, David?" Encizo asked. "Will he really do it?"

"I think Katzev's several clowns short of a circus, is what I think," McCarter answered. "He'll do it, mate. The bloke is stone-cold insane. James is right on. Katzev looks unhinged. We've taken away everything he had in minutes, thanks to the wonders of digital television and that sort of rot."

From his position in the crowd, McCarter could see Encizo looking around. "David, all these people," he said. "It will be a bloodbath. We can't let that happen."

"Nor will we," McCarter said. "Everyone, follow my lead. Choose your spots carefully."

The Briton, working his way through the crowd, leaned in to the nearest bystander, an attractive blonde woman.

"Excuse me," he said, "but do you have a boyfriend?"

The woman said something in Russian. Clearly she didn't understand him. McCarter tried the tactic twice more until he got a woman who looked as if she might slap him for being forward. McCarter raised his hands and explained that he simply needed someone who spoke English reasonably well. When the woman said she did, McCarter asked her to translate a single sentence for him. That sentence was, "Excuse me. There is a fire in this building. Move very efficiently to the exits."

McCarter repeated the phrase until he was sure he could pronounce it. Then he asked the woman to move through the crowd telling people just that.

She nodded and went on her way.

"All right, lads," McCarter said. "You know what to do.

Spread the word. We need to get as many people gone as possible. Their lives depend on it."

The men of Phoenix force circulated among the rally attendees, spreading the rumor. It was not long before people started to flee.

Katzev saw what was happening. "Stop! Stop!"

McCarter, close to the stage now, decided that it was time to put a stop to all of this.

"Aleksis Katzev," he shouted. "Aleksis Katzev. Surrender now. You are hereby removed from office."

"You fool!" He pointed to the Spetsnaz soldiers. "Shoot! *Shoot into the crowd!*"

CHAPTER TWENTY-TWO

Boston, Massachusetts

"Throw down your weapons," Thawan said. "I hold in my hand a switch you will recognize."

"Uh-oh," Schwarz said.

"Indeed," Thawan said. "And, yes, we have danced this dance before, as you put it. But this time you know I am not bluffing. This time you know I am prepared to kill us all. And while I would quite like to live, still, I think, there is no reason I will not blow myself to pieces. I have lost everything. My future. My father. My hope. You have beaten me. But that does not mean I still cannot beat you."

"It doesn't have to go down this way!" Lyons said. Just a quick jerk to put the USAS-12 to his shoulder, a few pounds of pressure on the trigger, and Thawan would be dead. But the dead man's switch would have the last word. This time, the fact that Thawan was not bluffing was more than evident.

The basement in which Thawan stood was one gigantic bomb. The rectangular bomb casings were placed in every corner of the room and in the center of the room. They were packed with plastics explosives; the room reeked of a smell almost like almond.

"Semtex," Lyons said.

"You see," Thawan said. He carried an AK-47, which he made a show of placing on the ground. Next he took a 1911-pattern .45 from his belt, emptied it and placed it, too, on the ground.

"Come in here!" he shouted. The door leading to the house above opened, and several of Thawan's thugs came down the steps, dressed in their castoff military clothing. None carried firearms, but they carried an assortment of clubs and other weapons.

"You see the dilemma." Thawan grinned. "Shoot at me, and you risk killing me, setting off the bombs. Shoot my men, and you risk hitting the bombs themselves. This, I assure you, will also make them explode. You have only one choice. Fight us as men."

Lyons ejected the magazine from his USAS-12 and jacked the shell out of the chamber. Holding the massive automatic shotgun like a club, he took a step forward.

"Then come and get it, you little asshole," he said.

Thawan motioned his henchmen in. The first wave came down the stairs and threw themselves at Able Team. The three Able Team fighters were terribly outnumbered, but the cramped quarters of the basement would help to neutralize that; Thawan's Triangle thugs would be getting in their own way.

"Split up!" Lyons ordered. "Gadgets, get those bombs! Do it fast!"

Lyons swung the barrel of the USAS-12. The heavy stock of the weapon crashed into the side of a man's head, crushing the bone. The Triangle goon collapsed on himself, twitching.

"That's one," Lyons muttered.

Schwarz ran to the nearest of the bombs. Blancanales and Lyons formed up on either side of him, fighting off the Triangle goons. Lyons cracked another man's skull with the Daewoo shotgun. The sound was gut-wrenching.

Schwarz quickly evaluated the bomb. It was a major one, all right. There was a string of daisy-chained detonation wires running from top to bottom, and unless he missed his guess, another false fuse was wired from bottom to top, which was in turn connected to a live detonation wire. There were several chambers of plastic explosives wired in sequence. Each chamber had a special electronic switch, similar to a USB hub. Schwarz realized that the bomb's chambers would have to be deactivated if the bomb was to be successfully neutralized.

"Wow," he said out loud. "What a gigantic pain in the ass."

"Gadgets!" Lyons roared. "Hurry!" He slammed a brutal side kick into the knee of one of the Triangle goons, who screamed and folded on the destroyed joint.

Blancanales had relieved one of the Triangle thugs of a machete and was using the blade to good effect, slicing away at the enemy, at the very least keeping them at bay. Schwarz knew that both men were at a disadvantage, unable to move very far from the spot they occupied to protect him. All he could do was work as fast as possible without screwing up. Blowing them all up in his haste to prevent Lyons and Blancanales from taking a beating wasn't going to be doing anyone any favors.

The idea of anyone beating up Carl Lyons struck him as funny, anyway. Blancanales was no slouch in hand-to-hand combat, but Lyons was the Ironman; he was larger than life, and he brought a lion's sensibilities to any fight in which he engaged.

"You are not doing badly," Thawan taunted from the stairs. "Not so very badly after all."

"Gadgets," Lyons said, throwing a palm strike into a man's face, crushing his nose and folding him over, "if you don't hurry so I can beat the living tar out of that little punk, I'm going to be very irate." He slammed his unloaded shotgun across the legs of another thug, knocking the man sprawling. As the would-be killer struggled to rise, Lyons kicked him in the head. Hard.

"Yes, I would really hate to see you irate," Schwarz said absently. "Remind me of what that looks like again."

"It's pretty much like this." Lyons elbowed a thug in the face, then punched a second one in the throat. Both men hit the floor, one of them out cold, the other choking to death. "Only it's more violent."

"Oh, good," Schwarz said. With the blade of his folding Leatherman tool, he started clipping out wires that had no purpose. The bomb was full of decoys, but they were relatively amateur decoys. The bomb maker was a by-the-book type. Schwarz decided Thawan had rigged it himself, and decided he had; the man had the look of someone who researched topics like these and then just cobbled an explosive device together to see what he could do. These bombs had the look of an amateur's masterpiece to them; no doubt Thawan thought he'd outdone himself with the complexity of these devices.

He clipped one wire, then another, throwing them this way and that while the hand-to-hand fight raged around him.

"Gadgets!" Lyons roared. "What the hell are you doing? Stop pruning the thing and deactivate it already!"

"There are a lot more to go after this one," Schwarz said. "I'll have to do each one individually."

"Wonderful," Lyons said. "Either we're going to run out of steam or we're going to run out of thugs, but either way, I don't think we have that kind of time."

"I'm on it, I'm on it," Schwarz said.

Thawan watched from the stairs, content to play whatever was his perverted game. Had he gone insane? Had the stress of losing his organization, of fighting Able Team time and time again only to escape the loser, taken its toll on a mind already twisted in nature? There was simply no way to tell.

"Now," Thawan said, laughing, "let us see if we cannot make this more interesting." He walked to the top of the stairs and flipped a series of light switches.

The basement was plunged into darkness.

Schwarz swore. He could still hear fighting around him, though Lyons was reducing many of his fights to fairly one-sided beatings that favored him. He was fairly certain Blancanales had been doing okay before the lights went out, too. He fished in his pocket for his combat light, switched it to always-on mode and shoved it in his mouth, holding it with his teeth. He normally didn't like to work that way, but there was little choice right now.

Playing the beam over the bomb, Schwarz found, at its base, a series of DIP switches corresponding to the number of chambers in the explosive device. He memorized the sequence. Holding his breath, he disconnected the first chamber of the bomb.

No explosion came.

Emboldened, he disconnected the next chamber in the DIP sequence. Then he did a third. Finally, satisfied that he was performing the procedure correctly, he continued through the chambers, until he had disconnected them all.

The final stage in deactivating the bomb was removing the RF trigger. This was delicate; it was connected to what looked like a mercury switch of some kind, but there was no guarantee that switch was even truly connected to the device. It might be a decoy, sitting there to prevent a technician from completing the deactivation.

It was risk time. Schwarz knew that if he screwed up and the bombs detonated, not just their lives would be forfeit. There was enough plastic explosive packed into this room to eliminate buildings in a two-block radius. There was no way to know how many people might be packed into the tenements around Thawan's homemade fortress. A blast of the size these bombs could create would be no good to anybody.

"Second bomb," Schwarz announced. "Let's move!" He used the flashlight to find his way. Lyons and Blancanales followed him. He could hear them hammering away at the enemy in the darkness. It was absolutely surreal.

"Do you think you can deactivate them all in time?" Thawan mocked them from the stairs. "In the dark? I have set a timer. You will have to manage to defuse them all before that timer runs down. I will not tell you how much time you have, however. No, I think it is better if you guess."

"Thawan!" Lyons shouted. "Give it up! This won't do anything but make it worse. We fight through this, we take you in. We blow up, you die. Maybe we die, too. But you know we can't just let you go. You know we have to take you in, seize your weapons, charge you with drug trafficking and murder. You understand that's the minimum. You can't walk out of here and we can't let you! We crossed the line a long time ago."

Thawan laughed. "Then what is it you think you offer me?" he said. "There are no benefits, only pain. Why should I not amuse myself?" He laughed again.

Schwarz was busily disarming the next bomb. He checked the DIP switches and found they were different, which meant he had to use a different pattern of chambers.

"You build a really, really annoying bomb," he said out loud.

"Thank you." Thawan laughed. "Perhaps we could collaborate on a future device."

"Won't happen," Schwarz said. "You'll be dead, and I don't do séances." He finished ripping out wires and deactivating the second bomb, using his flashlight to guide him to the third.

"I think you must be gaining on them," Thawan said. "I do not like that. I wish it to be a challenge."

"I don't like the sound of that," Blancanales said.

Suddenly, Thawan realized that he was no longer hearing the sounds of his men exchanging blows with the three intruders.

The Triangle leader flipped the basement light switches back on. He was astonished to see all of his thugs lying on the ground.

Schwarz blinked. "Hey," he said. "Warn a guy when you do that."

"You did not kill me when you had the chance," Thawan said accusingly. "You will not kill me now."

"He must be talking to you, Gadgets," Blancanales said. "Because he sure isn't talking to Ironman."

"Such colorful nicknames you use," Thawan said. "Very amusing."

"Yeah, we're interesting that way," Schwarz said, defusing the next bomb in sequence. "You might try having a personality sometime, as opposed to being a psychopathic, murdering drug dealer."

"You tempt fate," Thawan said from his perch on the stairs. "I could activate the bombs by releasing my dead man's switch."

"But you won't," Lyons said. "Or you would have done it by now, you gigantic pussy."

Thawan looked as if he'd been struck.

"That's right," Lyons said. "I'm talking to you. You

know, I meet a lot of 'tough guys' in my line of work. Most of them are pretty tough. Some of them aren't nearly as hard as they think they are. But you, you're a pussy."

Thawan motioned with the dead man's switch.

"Well?" Lyons demanded. "Go on, then! I'm so heartily sick of jacking around with you, I can't stand it. We've chased you across half the Northeast and still you're whining about your fate, or some such utter crap. I've never met a thug as whiny as you, in fact. You want to run a drug-trafficking ring, you tool? Then butch the hell up! Because nobody respects a drug lord who can't stop yammering about how his mommy didn't hug him enough as a child!"

Thawan stood on the stairs, white as a sheet, his fists balled and his knuckles white. The dead man's switch trembled in his clenched hand.

"Uh, Ironman," Blancanales said, "I'm not so sure that poking him with a stick is the right—"

"Shut it, Pol," Lyons said. "I've had it up to here with this guy." He gestured with the shotgun. "Come on down here, you little scumbag. Put your money where your mouth is. Come on. Face me. I owe you a couple of times over. Maybe we'll give you a tire iron to make it fair. How would that be?"

Thawan was still standing there, but he no longer saw them. His eyes were glazed with fury and he seemed to be focusing on something far away.

"Uh-oh," Blancanales said.

"Uh-oh nothing," Lyons said. "Gadgets, how you coming with those bombs?"

"Working on bomb number four," Schwarz said. "Still annoying, but fortunately he didn't innovate much."

"Not exactly the tortured genius when it comes to bombs, eh?" Lyons taunted. "Maybe you should stick to shooting out the window of a car as you do drive-bys, the way your lowlife kind always does. Can't shoot for shit and can't be bothered even to get out of the car to kill somebody."

Thawan blinked. "I have never in my life—"

"Save it, Mary," Lyons said. He was pushing hard, trying to find Thawan's breaking point. It was keeping the Triangle leader occupied mentally. All that mattered was giving Schwarz time to work, time to deactivate the bombs.

"Gadgets," Lyons said softly, knowing the transceiver would amplify his speech to an audible level, "if just one of those bombs goes off, will it trigger the others?"

"Carl, if just one of those bombs goes off, it's not going to matter. Any one of them is going to vaporize us and a lot of the surrounding landscape. All of them together are probably going to get in each other's way doing the exact same thing. Either way, they're scrubbing us out of the lawns for the next year and a half."

"Well, tough guy?" Lyons demanded again. Thawan turned toward him. "You going to come down here and find out what you're made of?"

"I owe you nothing," Thawan said. "I have nothing to prove."

"Don't you?" Lyons said. "Could have fooled me."

Blancanales turned to Lyons. "You're right," he said, picking up Lyons's lead. "I can see what you mean. You'd think he'd notice."

"What are you talking about!" Thawan demanded, shouting. "Stop! Stop mocking me!"

"That's your name, isn't it?" Blancanales said. "Mock Thawan?"

"Shut up! Shut up!"

"I've seen some sorry examples of manhood before," Lyons said, "but this pathetic little weasel… Well, one for the record books, really."

Under his breath, Blancanales muttered, "Exactly why are we taunting this guy like we're grade school?"

"Work with me here," Lyons said.

"Enough!" Thawan said. He walked down the stairs. Grabbing either side of his shirt, he pulled it open.

There was another bomb strapped to his chest.

"I am holding the dead man's switch," he said. "Once it is grasped, it can never be let go. If it is released, the bomb goes off. This switch is also connected to the bombs in this room."

"Not anymore," Schwarz said, tossing the last of the RF receivers aside.

"This bomb is still more than powerful enough," Thawan said.

"So we're right back where we started," Lyons said with disgust. "Here we are, surrounded by a big pile of your bully-boys, and there you are."

"You do not understand."

"Why don't you explain it to me?"

"You…" Thawan said. "Who are you? Who are you that you appear from nowhere, smash our operations, pursue relentlessly? How do you know where I will be? How do you know where I will go? By what power do you haunt me so? Who *are* you?"

"You want to know who we are?" Lyons asked. "All right, you little piece of garbage. I'll tell you just who we are."

Blancanales looked at Lyons. Schwarz, meanwhile, was standing just far enough away to get a good look at Thawan's chest bomb. It looked to him as if a cell phone was wired into the mess that was mounted to a backpack worn backward around the front of Thawan's body. Chiding his inner dialogue for describing it so inelo- quently, Schwarz began circling, trying to get up and around Thawan. Lyons, meanwhile, was doing plenty to give the Triangle leader something to think about.

"We're the people who stand up to predators like you," Lyons said. "We fight for your victims. All those helpless people you victimize? We're them. We're every one of them."

"You make no sense," Thawan said.

"No?" Lyons said. "Think it over. Even a piece of crap like you understands the concept of revenge."

"Revenge is the purview of the strong!" Thawan said.

"Yeah, well, we don't deal in revenge," Lyons told him. "We deal in something related, something better, called justice."

"Justice?" Thawan scoffed. "There is no justice in this world. There is only the taking of what one wishes. The weak suffer. The strong conquer. That has always been the way. Do not tell me of your justice, American. You let killers roam your streets. You let celebrities get away with murder simply because they have fame. You let drug addicts hold high political office. Your leaders shame you at every turn. And you wish to talk to me about justice?"

"Now, what makes you think I have anything to do with any of that?" Lyons said slyly.

"You are an American, aren't you?"

"You're damned right I am," Lyons said. "And do you know what that means?"

"I am quite sure you will tell me."

"Being an American," Lyons said, "means that even though you're not always in the right, you do your best to be. Being an American means adhering to a set of principles worth fighting for. But most of all, being an American means being willing to fight. For liberty. For what's right. And most important, for people who can't fight for themselves."

"That is sentimental rubbish," Thawan said dismissively.

"Is it?" Lyons said. "Look around you. Who's on the floor? Who's standing up? Where were your goons when you needed them, and why did they fold so quickly?"

"They are…decent enough fighters," Thawan said defensively. "You have special training."

"Not really," Lyons said. "What we've got is heart. You can learn a lot of things, Thawan. You can learn tactics. You can learn strategies. You can train and practice until you're blue in the face. But unless you've got heart—" he looked up at Thawan, his gaze hardening "—you'll never know what you're good for."

"Why are you telling me all this?"

"To keep you busy," Lyons said. "Gadgets?"

"That bomb has no RF receiver," he told Lyons. "It'll go off if you shoot it, but that switch he's holding won't do jack."

"Oooh," Blancanales said. "That's going to hurt."

Lyons smiled.

"I'd kill him," Schwarz said.

The big cop snapped open the *navaja* knife he'd recovered. The blade opened with a menacing crack-crack-crack of the ratchet mechanism.

"You know," Lyons said, "so would I."

CHAPTER TWENTY-THREE

Moscow, Russia

"Do it!" Katzev screamed. "Fire into the crowd!"

"Interdict!" McCarter shouted. "Interdict!"

The men of Phoenix Force pulled their Kalashnikovs from the bags concealing them. They snapped the weapons to their shoulders. The Spetsnaz soldiers looked ready to fire on the fleeing crowd. McCarter lined up a shot on one of them and squeezed off a full-auto burst, folding him in half.

The hellstorm began.

The Spetsnaz soldiers began firing to deadly effect. There was enough random concealment in the rally hall for the men of Phoenix Force to spread out and continue fighting. McCarter was pleased to see that the civilians were emptying out rapidly. His men kept the Spetsnaz soldiers pinned down so they couldn't take decisive aim on the fleeing civilians.

The Russian special forces operatives continued to go down as Phoenix Force's aimed fire whittled away at their numbers. Some of their number apparently realized that they were on the receiving end, losing the initiative. They countered by throwing grenades into the hall.

The conflagration that erupted overwhelmed the rally hall as the flames caught the draperies. The entire building went up like a funeral pyre, casting the space in a flickering orange-and-yellow blaze that was nearly blinding to the naked eye.

"Masks!" McCarter directed. "Masks on!" The Phoenix Force fighters donned their masks.

"There are still civilians in here!" Encizo shouted. "I've got one down. I'm attempting to extract!"

"Andulov is clear," Hawkins reported. "Repeat, Andulov is clear."

"Katzev!" McCarter yelled at the Russian president, who was still running madly about the stage amid the flames. "Katzev!"

Gunfire sounded almost at random now. The flames, the smoke, the shooting from what was left of the Spetsnaz contingent made for one of the most hellish environments the Phoenix Force warriors had ever encountered, and they had seen more than their share.

"We need to get these people out of here," Encizo said.

"Rafe, Gary, T.J.," McCarter ordered. "Form up and perform rescue detail. Find any civilians you can, drag them out, do it fast. Masks on at all times!"

The three Phoenix fighters acknowledged.

"Calvin, police up the Spetsnaz," McCarter said. "Search and destroy. Eliminate any still moving in the building. Do it fast! The place is coming down around our ears. I'm going after Katzev."

In the smoke and flame, McCarter did not see the dogged media crew, coughing through handkerchiefs held over their mouths, filming the blaze and the action within. Had he seen them, the Briton would have dragged them screaming from the mess and to hell with them. He did not, however, and so the film crew, heedless of the danger and desperate for this incredible story, kept the lens of its camera trained on McCarter even as he marched through the burning, smoking, reeking rally hall.

"Katzev!" he shouted again.

"Here!" Katzev shouted. He had jumped from the platform and retrieved an AK-74 and a bayonet from one of the fallen Spetsnaz soldiers. Half-crouched, he fired, emptying the weapon's magazine in McCarter's direction. The smoke and flame made it impossible for him to see exactly where his target was, however.

McCarter returned fire, but in the haze he could not even see the muzzle-blast from Katzev's weapon. He kept moving, closing in on the podium platform, ever closer, ever closer, until—

Katzev leaped and tackled him. Both men hit the ground. McCarter lost his weapon, tried to draw his Browning and lost that to a wild swing from Katzev's Kalashnikov. The Briton managed to grab the weapon and jerk it free, flinging it away, but there was the bayonet, and Katzev, as former KGB, was well trained in its use.

McCarter, breathing heavily under his mask, couldn't understand how the mad Russian president could even breathe. He went for the knife he had been issued for the operation, only to find that it wasn't there. For a split second he thought Katzev had managed to catch him weaponless.

His hand, reaching into his pocket, found the pearl-handled switchblade.

He snapped the knife open. It was small, but not too small to be deadly. Katzev laughed and lunged.

"Sitrep!" McCarter managed to scream through the smoke, through the strain of the fight, through the impossible brightness of the flames.

"All clear!" Encizo shouted. "All clear, David! Get out of there!"

That was all McCarter needed to hear. He began retreating, headed toward the nearest exit. Katzev fought him all the way. As he finally reached the door and managed to back out of it, Katzev almost falling on top of him, he realized that the both of them were being followed by a bloody camera crew.

Doesn't that, he thought, just take the cake?

He fought the urge to rip off his mask and drink in the cool Moscow air. They were adjacent to Red Square; he could feel the incredibly intense heat of the burning rally hall at his back.

"It's over!" McCarter shouted.

"I am President Aleksis Katzev!" the Russian shouted. "You do not tell me when it is over. I am the president of the Russian Federation! My word is law!"

"You've been exposed!" McCarter shot back, slashing and parrying, his support hand blocking and warding as he did his best to compensate for the short length of his blade. Katzev's style was very direct, very military. It had no finesse because none was required. He stomped forward, lunging, trying to put the blade of the bayonet deep into McCarter's ribs. The Briton fought back, hard, slashing the air with the keen, quick little blade, going for Katzev's face and, failing that, trying to score disabling cuts on the man's knife hand and wrist.

"I say when it is over!" Katzev said again. "I am going to build a new Russia! No one can stop me! My vision is all! All who oppose me will be removed!"

Christ, McCarter thought. *He's gone completely around the bend.*

Katzev was very good, but McCarter was also very skilled. The two of them could probably fight like this for half an hour without scoring a hit. McCarter, however, was feeling winded. The mad Katzev did not even appear affected by the massive smoke inhalation he had suffered. He was wheezing deep in his throat, yes, but it did not seem to be slowing him down at all.

"You can still cut a deal," McCarter ventured, though he knew trying to reason with the man was probably hopeless. "You have information about the corruption at the highest levels of your government. Cooperate and it can go easier on you!"

"Who are you?" Katzev demanded. "Are you Mogranov's phantom commandos? Do you think you can come into my country and tell me how it is run, how it will be? Do you honestly believe you have that kind of power?"

McCarter slashed and then stabbed. He managed to score a deep cut across the knuckles of Katzev's knife hand. The Russian screamed but transferred the knife to his left hand. He came back swinging harder and thrusting faster than ever before. McCarter was hard-pressed to keep up with him.

"For the last time," McCarter said through his breathing mask, his words distorted but audible. "You're the leader of this entire country. Think of your people. Think of what they'll go through!"

"My people?" Katzev shrieked. "What are they to me? Sheep to be led! The people exist so that men of power may rule! It has always been that way, and always will be. Weak men like Andulov have no place in power, and will forever be swept away! Any of the sheep who get in my way will be sheared! I am the leader! I am the master! You will know my will!"

All the while, the television crew, coughing from the smoke and nearly singeing themselves in the flickering flames from the burning rally hall, recorded every word and every moment of the duel.

"You're going to die now," Katzev said to McCarter. He lunged with the knife.

"This can still end!" McCarter said.

"Oh, it's going to!" Katzev screamed. "Mogranov! Now!"

Reacting on instinct, McCarter threw himself to the ground. The gunfire passed over his head and ripped into Katzev. The stunned Russian president looked down at the bloody wounds in his chest and stomach, put his hand to them and toppled forward.

"I…" he said. "I am…" The light left his eyes, leaving on the dancing fire from the burning building looming over the body.

The man called Mogranov threw down his Kalashnikov in horror and turned to flee.

McCarter pursued. After everything he'd been through, his lungs were screaming at him. His ribs felt like he'd been mule-kicked.

Mogranov ran across the square. McCarter followed, doing his level best to stay with the other man. It was not easy, but he hung in there, pumping his legs with every last bit of willpower he could muster, thinking back to his Special Air Service days. It was just like the physical training back in those days, he told himself. Tough, but nothing he couldn't stomach. He was, however, almost delirious from the run by the time they reached a business district adjacent to Red Square. He could see the Moscow river in the distance. Colors, sights and sounds took on a surreal quality as he ran. There was nothing in the world but running, nothing that mattered except staying in pursuit of his quarry.

When Mogranov finally went to ground inside a small coffeehouse, McCarter was on the verge of collapse. Mogranov, too, had run as far as he was going to be running. He looked like he wanted to throw up.

The Russian ducked into the kitchen area of the coffee shop. The workers screamed. Mogranov drew a Makarov pistol and shooed them out. McCarter came up behind him, saw the weapon before the Russian could bring it to bear and slapped it away. It landed on the floor underneath a counter.

The two exhausted men squared off. Mogranov lashed out with a vicious front kick. McCarter willed his leaden arms to fight the man back, slapping away the kicks, doing his best to counter with low, sharp strikes of his own booted feet as they danced back and forth in the crowded kitchen area.

The Briton realized, as they fought, that they were dead-locked. Either they were very evenly matched, which was rare but did happen even in real-life combat such as this, or the two men were simply so tired that their exhaustion negated their personal skill levels. It came down to will. McCarter fought with all the fury he could bring.

Huffing and puffing, both men were reluctant to waste words during the fight, but McCarter could not help himself. He had to know. As he kept his guard up, deflecting blows from the Russian's attacks, he managed to choke out his question.

"Why?" he breathed. "Why help Katzev? The man was insane!"

"He understood that Russia needs to be strong." Mogranov backed up a pace. Both men stood panting, trying to catch their breath, guards up, alert but unwilling to move forward, unwilling to reengage. It was now a waiting game. Who would be first to regain enough strength to deliver a decisive blow?

"Russia can't be strong if it's forever locked in conflict with its neighbors and the rest of the world," McCarter said through his mask. He was grateful for the mask, even now.

The filtered air it provided him was no doubt better than the polluted atmosphere of Moscow itself, or of the kitchen in which the two men stood.

"What would you know of it?" Mogranov spit. His English had almost no accent at all. "You have not felt what it is like to have a once-great nation torn from under you by foolish policies and more foolish politicians. The Russian bear was neutered by the idiots in charge. We were feared the world over. The United States lived with the knowledge that one day we would be there and we would assert our will. The Americans once built their entire military plan around what we would do, or not do. That was fear. That was respect. That is what Russia deserves."

"To what end?" McCarter asked. *Keep him talking,* he thought to himself. *Get your breath back and then take him out. Keep him talking…but know that while you're recovering, so is he.*

"Why do the Chinese build missiles that do not always go where they are supposed to?" Mogranov asked. "Why do they shoot rockets at the moon? Why do they bother with a space program at all, while begging for the Olympics to assert their national pride? Do you not see that a nation needs pride? It needs identity. A nation that is not the best must know that it can become the best. Otherwise, why is it? The Americans suffer right now because they once were the best but have fallen on harder times. They are unsure of themselves. That lack of confidence, that lack of identity, causes them to do stupid things. It makes their government do stupid things. They project weakness."

"You sound like you've given it a lot of thought," McCarter said. His chest rose and fell, the ache in his ribs ebbing somewhat.

"Of course," Mogranov said. "It is the same thing that has happened in Russia! We became unsure of ourselves.

We wanted your jeans and your tape decks and your television. We wanted to be like you, not like us. And so we lost our way. We projected weakness. And when that started, we collapsed from within."

"It doesn't have to be that way," McCarter said.

"No," Mogranov said. "We can instead be stro—"

McCarter struck. He lunged out with the switchblade while Mogranov was engaged in his little inner dialogue. Some part of McCarter wondered if the Russian hadn't always longed to give that particular speech to somebody. Now it was not his problem. His knife danced in and out; Mogranov snatched up a paring knife from the counter next to a pile of sliced apples. He struck back, but the two men were again deadlocked. The close confines of the kitchen meant they could move forward and back, but that flanking maneuvers and position changes were nearly impossible.

McCarter lunged, then withdrew. Mogranov did the same. McCarter, however, had fencing experience, and suddenly the exercise felt very familiar. He began to execute fencing lunges with the little knife held before him. Mogranov's eyes went wide; he hadn't been expecting that tactic. McCarter slashed and parried, stabbed and parried, moving in and out, gaining his second wind and moving faster and faster with the pearl-handled blade.

He could only hope they'd managed to outdistance the camera crew. He was probably going to catch hell for that. Ah, well, he thought to himself. Spilled milk and whatnot.

Mogranov's considerable strength was fading fast. McCarter, by contrast, felt as if he was gaining a second wind. He finally scored a major hit, shoving the small pearl-handled blade into Mogranov's abdomen before ripping it back out again. The Russian groaned in surprise and shock, putting his hand to the grievous wound that had suddenly opened in his belly.

He swore in Russian. "You... You have..." He turned white as a sheet.

Shock, thought McCarter.

The Russian, bleeding copiously from his wound, staggered out of the kitchen into the coffee shop proper. McCarter was appalled to see that there were still customers milling about, perhaps not realizing just how serious the sudden invasion of the two men truly was. Before he could do anything, Mogranov had grabbed an aging woman by the neck and was holding her in front of his body with the paring knife to her throat.

"You will...let me go," Mogranov said. "You will stay here. I will leave."

"You're not going to make it more than a few steps," McCarter warned him. "You're fading fast, Mogranov. If the shock doesn't lock you down, the blood loss will have you numbed and useless."

"You let...me worry about that," Mogranov said. "I want you to stay here. If you follow me...I will kill her."

"All right," McCarter said. "She's all yours. Go on."

Mogranov looked surprised at that. A flicker of doubt flashed across his eyes. Was it a trick? Or was it true that he would not get far? McCarter could see the Russian debating it with himself. Finally he threw the paring knife down and left the woman. He staggered out into the street, managed four steps away from the door of the coffeehouse and collapsed. Blood pooled around him.

McCarter checked the woman. "Are you okay?" he asked. She looked at him uncomprehendingly. Probably did not speak English, and McCarter's Russian was not particularly good. He motioned for her to sit down and stay in the shop, and went outside.

Mogranov's breathing was shallow.

"I...killed Katzev," he said.

"You did." McCarter nodded. "Saved me a pretty spot of trouble, too. Better that he die by your hand than mine."

"Who…are you?" Mogranov asked.

"Sorry, chap." McCarter shook his head. "Can't tell you that."

"I…will take it…to my grave."

"Not even then," McCarter said. "But I can tell you that we're here to help you. Katzev had a few screws loose."

The Russian looked at him, confused.

"Katzev was insane," McCarter corrected himself. "It is best that he not hold power any longer. I know you thought he was the right man for the job. I even understand that you had your country's best interests at heart. But Katzev wasn't the man to do that."

"I…do not know you…" Mogranov said, "and you have killed me…but the fight…was fair…"

"Sorry, mate," McCarter said. "I don't get into fair fights. But I know what you're getting at."

"I must ask…something of…you." Mogranov struggled for breath. "It is perhaps not best that you…do it, but…there is no one else…"

"Go ahead, mate, I'll try."

"I have…a wife…" he managed. He recited the address haltingly. "I want her to know…I want her to know that…my last words…my last thoughts…were for her…."

"I will do that for you," McCarter said. "And I'll see to it your body is squared away. Your family will live with the knowledge that you died for your country, doing your job."

"I…cannot change…the past…."

"No," McCarter said with compassion, "and you're not going to be doing too much changing in the future. But know this. Things will be better here in Russia. They'll be better, and your people will be better off."

"It is...strange to...thank my killer, but...I...thank you," Mogranov said.

"Bloody hell," McCarter said under his breath.

Mogranov stared upward, blankly, into the beyond. McCarter reached out and closed his eyes.

He stood then. "David to Phoenix," he said. "David to Phoenix."

"Encizo here," came the response. "David, your signal is weak."

"Yours, too," he said. "I'm getting out of range."

"Where did you go?" Encizo asked.

"Had to pursue a loose end," McCarter said. He began to drag the body, looking for a suitable hiding spot, eyes alert for police. It wasn't likely there would be much in the way of law-enforcement presence here, not with the huge fire near Red Square and the figurative self-immolation of the nation's president to keep them busy. Still, he did not want to be caught.

He tried to tell himself that the stinging in his eyes was from exposure to the smoke.

"Bloody hell," he said again.

CHAPTER TWENTY-FOUR

Boston, Massachusetts

Carl Lyons moved in with the knife. Thawan had withdrawn a *balisong*. Unfolded, it glittered in his hand, the blade flashing in a pattern of intricate movements.

"So," Lyons said. "Not so weak after all."

"I will kill you!" Thawan screamed.

He lunged with his blade. Lyons, who was larger and slower but also had longer reach, managed to rake the blade of the *navaja* across Thawan's forearm. The smaller man screamed and backed up, but then immediately lunged again. He began slashing the air, turning the blade this way and that, cutting elaborate patterns in the air.

"Let me take him," Schwarz said, bringing up his 93-R.

"No," Lyons said between cuts. "He's wearing the bomb. One stray shot is all it takes."

"I can get him, Carl,"

"I," Lyons said, ducking as Thawan came in again, "know you can. But it's a risk I can't warrant."

"Stop talking as if I am not here!" Thawan shrieked.

"Stop talking as if the blade of my knife is not about to cut you deep, you miserable bastard!"

"Well, that's certainly unequivocal," Schwarz said.

Lyons shot a painful front kick into Thawan's shin. The small man backed up, howling, and Lyons followed him with a lunge, stabbing the large *navaja* toward Thawan's face.

"You cannot best me, American!" Thawan shouted. He slashed and stabbed, describing figure-eights in the air, his footwork lightning fast. He had some training in blade work; that much was for certain. Given his origins, it would have been unlikely for him not to pick it up somewhere. "You will die! You will die screaming, and your friends will watch you bleed out on this basement floor!"

"It's going to be a real pleasure," Lyons said, "to finally shut you up."

Thawan seemed to take that as a challenge. He stopped talking, pursed his lips and focused all his attention on one, single-minded goal: kill the big man in front of him.

The two men were locked in combat for a time, but Lyons knew that no knife fight could go on forever. That was the nature of the knife; its use was nasty, brutal and short, to employ a famous saying. One mistake and someone would be, as Thawan had said, bleeding out. Lyons began making bold, powerful thrusts and slashes, moving diagonally across his body, slashing X patterns into the air. He drove Thawan back, and back, and still farther, pushing the man into the far wall of the basement.

The *balisong* came out and Lyons caught the inside of Thawan's knife arm. The slash was bad; it was so deep he could see muscle tissue. Thawan howled and dropped his knife.

Lyon was on him then. He let the *navaja* fall to the ground and grabbed Thawan with both hands, tossing him over his hip in a judo throw. Thawan hit the concrete floor of the basement in a rush of air as the wind was knocked out of him. Lyons landed on top of him, digging one knee painfully into the middle of the smaller man's back.

"The knife, the knife," Lyons said urgently. "Somebody get me the knife!" Schwarz retrieved Thawan's *balisong*, made sure it was open, and handed it handle-first to Lyons. The big ex-cop got the clip-point blade under the straps of the backpack Thawan wore. He tore the knife through the straps, lifting the bomb off the struggling Thawan. When Thawan tried to rise, he threw a vicious palm strike into Thawan's face, knocking him onto his back.

"Stay down," he growled.

He threw the backpack onto the floor of the basement and pulled open its tabs. The bomb inside had a mechanical clock attached to it. It was like nothing he'd ever seen.

"Pol, sit on him," he said, pointing to Thawan without looking away from the bomb. "Gadgets, I need you here."

Schwarz handed Thawan off to Blancanales and got a good look at the clock mechanism. "Holy crap, Carl," he said. "That's an Omicron Eight. It's like the holy grail of complicated tabletop clocks."

"What does it mean?" Lyons demanded.

"It means that he's probably got the wiring all meshed up with that clock," Schwarz said. "It's exactly the sort of harebrained thing an amateur bomb maker who fancies himself the next IRA master destroyer would do."

"Why is it moving?" Lyons asked.

"Because it's counting down," Schwarz said. "And I don't know how long we've got, because I can't see the clock internals."

"Can we pry off this cover?" Lyons asked.

"If we want to set off the bomb, sure," Schwarz said. "It's bound to have an antitamper."

"I need options!" Lyons said.

"We call the Farm," Schwarz suggested. "Akira can bring up the schematics and walk us through disassembly of the face and the guts. It's the only way to disarm it without setting it off."

Lyons dialed the Farm on his secure satellite phone. The reception was poor, underground like this, but he was still able to get through thanks to the advanced technology the Farm used in its communications units. He once again thanked his lucky stars that the Farm wasn't limited to commercial, off-the-shelf Iridium satellite phones or some other such device.

"Price here," Barbara Price answered.

"Barb!" Lyons said quickly. "I need Akira, now!"

Without comment, Price put Akira Tokaido on the line. "Akira here."

"Akira," Lyons said, "I've got a bomb here built out of a—"

"Omicron Eight," Schwarz said.

"Omicron Eight clock," Lyons continued. "It's an intricate all-stainless-steel design."

"I am familiar with its use in this way," Tokaido confirmed. "Stand by." There was a pause as he accessed the data. "Is the clock ticking?"

"Yes."

"Are the hands moving?"

"Yes."

"How far from the twelve-o'clock position?" Tokaido asked urgently.

"About four minutes."

"All right," Tokaido said. "That means you have roughly four minutes to disarm it, if the configuration of the wiring within is the most typical of bomb types."

"And if it isn't?" Lyons asked.

"Less," Tokaido answered. "Act now."

Schwarz unfolded his Leatherman multitool and positioned himself above the Omicron Eight. Lyons held the phone up to his ear.

"I'm ready," he said.

"First," Tokaido directed, "unscrew the four screws in the top corner of the face, but not the bottom screws."

Schwarz did as he was directed.

"Next, peel the face down, from the top. It is flexible. Do not bump the hands or change their motion as you do so. You must avoid the hands as you peel the face. Cut it if you must."

Schwarz had the face off in a few seconds. He was forced to slice it open to do so. This revealed the guts of the intricate clock, as wires connected to the moving clockwork traveled in and out and next to each other.

"Damn," Schwarz said as he got a good look.

"That's not a good thing," Lyons said. "That's not what I want to hear, Gadgets."

"There should be a wire wrapped around the minute hand," Tokaido said. "Unfold this wire and remove it. Be careful not to touch it to the clock housing."

"Done," Schwarz announced.

"There will be two wires moving in opposed directions, connected to corresponding opposed portions of the clockwork. Do you see them?"

"I do," Schwarz said.

"You must remove them simultaneously."

Schwarz used the pliers to grab one wire by its insulation. He was able to grab the other with his fingers. He lifted them both out.

"The bomb should be neutralized provided those wires never touch," Tokaido said.

Schwarz put the clock down very, very carefully.

He let out a breath.

The clock began to buzz. Time was up.

No explosion came.

"Well," Schwarz said, "that was exhilarating. Let's see if he's got any more to take apart."

Lyons blinked at him.

"What?" Schwarz said.

"I hate you, Gadgets." He remembered to sign off with Tokaido before hanging up and replacing his satellite phone in its place on his belt.

"That, I think," Blancanales started to say, "should be just about—"

Mok Thawan surged to his feet.

He slammed into Blancanales and drove him back into the wall, next to the hole leading out to the makeshift corridor. Throwing himself through this, he barreled down the hallway.

"Oh, hell, no," Lyons said.

"Careful," Schwarz said. "That's where all the land mines and such are."

"Yeah, thanks, Gadgets," Lyons said caustically. He scooped up his shotgun and reloaded it. "I'm not about to go through that again."

Stepping out through the hole in the foundation, he pointed the barrel of the Daewoo automatic shotgun at the plywood roof of the corridor. Now that they knew where the corridor began and ended, and what the layout was, this was an option. Lyons was about to take the high road.

He held the trigger back. The shotgun sprayed double-aught buck pellets in roughly a circular pattern as he moved it around. Splinters and then halves of the plywood hatch he'd just cut fell on his head. He cursed and brushed these off, spitting out a few that had landed in his mouth.

Pulling himself up, he pushed out and onto the roof of

the corridor. Testing it to make sure the rickety structure would hold his weight, he took a few tentative steps and then broke into a run.

His combat boots boomed on the plywood as he ran. There was no telling how far along Thawan might have gotten, or how familiar he was with his own booby traps. Whether they would slow him down at all was not something Lyons could know. He pushed himself, running as fast as he could, the Daewoo at port arms. When he got to the termination of the corridor, he leaped down and to the side. Then he pressed himself against the outer wall, to the left of the mouth of the corridor, and waited.

As he listened, several times he thought he heard someone approaching, but it was his imagination. Eventually, however, he heard the heavy breathing of a man trying to hurry while being careful at the same time—a formula for failure every time. Finally, Thawan broke free of the corridor. Lyons judged the distance and the arc and hurled his now-empty Daewoo at Thawan's legs, tripping him up. He landed in a flat sprawl on the pavement, smashing his nose.

"Nnnggg!" Thawan grunted.

Lyons was on top of him then, going for a choke to take the man's lights out. Thawan was incredibly fast and much stronger than he looked, as Blancanales had discovered. He rotated, swiveled his hips and fired a round kick into Lyons's ribs that staggered the big man.

Never one to "celebrate the hit," as one of his old instructors had said to him, Lyons simply dived right back in, throwing spear hands and punches at Thawan's neck and midsection, respectively. He connected with at least one of the punches and was rewarded with a whoosh of air from Thawan's already bruised lungs. Thawan was reaching for a hidden weapon—it turned out to be a tiny

North American Arms minirevolver in his pocket. Unable to grab the diminutive weapon from his position, Lyons did the only thing he could; he stepped in and stomped the Triangle leader, driving his combat boot into Thawan's stomach. The smaller man shuddered, turned and vomited onto the pavement. He dropped the tiny revolver.

Lyons bent, picked up Thawan and threw him against the plywood wall. He bounced off it and hit the pavement, sprawling on his stomach.

"I owe you for a tire iron to the face," Lyons said. "And a whole bunch of other things, probably. It's over, Thawan. You're going away. You're going away for a long time."

"No," Thawan said. "I am not."

The switchblade came out of nowhere. It was a small out-the-front automatic. Thawan burst upward with the blade in his fist, driving the knife toward Lyons's eyes.

"I really don't want to know where that was hidden," Lyons said. "What the hell is it with you, anyway?" He belted Thawan across the face. The smaller man, instead of going down with the blow, rolled and started to run down the street.

Lyons charged after him. As a big, burly man, sprinting was not his strong suit, but he was in good shape and highly motivated. He wasn't normally one to run flat-out without good cause…but he was highly motivated in this case. He burned up the pavement, hustling as fast as he possibly could, hot on Thawan's tail and determined to bring him down.

Thawan began throwing obstacles in his way as he ran through the burned-out neighborhood.

There was no way Lyons was going to let Mok Thawan escape. The man was a menace and, left at large, there was no telling what he might do. Drug trafficker, amateur bomb maker and all-around scumbag, Thawan was a mission priority. Plus there were the murders of quite a few FBI agents to answer for, including one woman that the bastard Thawan had shot in cold blood, execution style.

Lyons stopped and drew the Colt Python. Cocking the hammer back, he took careful aim right between Thawan's shoulder blades.

The piece fired itself when it was ready. Lyons waited and watched Thawan go down. Then he walked to where Thawan lay prone on the pavement.

He stood over the Triangle leader and toed him over with one combat boot. Thawan gasped and screamed in pain, looking up at Lyons with fear and terror.

"Please…" he gasped. "Please…"

"Tell me, Thawan," Lyons said. "In New Jersey, did the woman ask you, 'Please'?"

"I…" Thawan began.

Lyons stood over Thawan. He positioned the shiny barrel of the Colt Python right over Thawan's face, right between his eyes.

"Nothing," he said, "would give me more pleasure than to put a bullet in your brain, Thawan," he said. "It would be a fitting death for you. To die as you've killed others."

Thawan gaped and gasped like a fish. No sound came out of his mouth.

"Goodbye, Thawan," Lyons said. "When you get where you're going, tell them I sent you there."

Thawan died. The light left his eyes. The look on his face was one of sheer terror.

EPILOGUE

Stony Man Farm, Virginia

"Tell us again, Hal, what did the Man have to say?" Barbara Price asked Hal Brognola's larger-than-life image on the plasma screen.

"The Man was exceptionally pleased with the operation overall," Brognola said. "He did say, however, that in the future, our operatives should try to refrain from engaging in knife duels with world leaders in the middle of burning buildings while high-definition video of the event is televised internationally."

"He said that, did he?" McCarter managed to say with a straight face.

"He seemed to think it was important." Brognola nodded. More soberly he added, "In all seriousness, this was the closest we've come to a very real breach of international relations thanks to our activities. It's no laughing matter. Given the scope of Katzev's confessed crimes, however, a lot is being forgiven. The mysterious foreigner who dueled the mad Russian Katzev is becoming something of a folk hero in Moscow, I'm told."

"Who do they think I am?" McCarter asked.

"There are a lot of rumors," Brognola said. "Everything from CIA to space aliens to everything in between."

"Space aliens?" Schwarz asked.

"We, of course, have denied all involvement, as have the other members of the world intelligence community. This one is going to be chalked up to a mystery man or men. Whether the Russians choose to believe it was their own firefighters or military is their business." Brognola shook his head.

"Thank heavens for masks," McCarter said.

"We've tried to put forward the rumor that it was Spetsnaz—that some of Katzev's special-forces operatives were not completely coopted and that they fought him and those who were." The big Fed went on. "That version of events is getting a lot of play, particularly here in the U.S. media, and we think it has a good chance of sticking. It helps that Katzev was ultimately killed by one of his own people, his head of his security detail, a Mikhail Mogranov. Mogranov, whom David eliminated, is officially listed as missing. The spin we've tried to help put on that is that he went back into the burning building to rescue people he thought might still be inside, and never came out again. Mogranov's been elevated to the status of national hero as a result."

The members of Able Team and Phoenix Force were gathered around the long table in the conference room. The debriefing had included clips of the video shot by Russian media outlets during the conflagration at the rally hall in Moscow.

"What is the fallout in Russia?" Carl Lyons asked.

"As you can imagine, the country is taking it pretty hard," Brognola said. "It's the talk of the media worldwide, of course. It's not every day that an elected president is revealed to be in league with terrorists and drug traffickers, then goes insane, for all practical purposes, before fighting to the death on international television. Between that and the fact that Katzev was caught on tape ordering his special forces operatives to shoot into the crowd—and they did it—and you've got something they'll be hashing out culturally and sociopolitically for a long time to come. That was part of the motivation for our version of events, to give them some kind of out. It's hard to believe a man like Katzev could have coopted his country's armed forces so totally, but we know that at least in certain units, he did. The Russians are cleaning that out, too, using some sort of polygraph-and-loyalty test. I didn't ask because I didn't want to know."

"I don't blame you," Price said.

Somber nods all around greeted Brognola's serious gaze.

"The question on all our minds should be," Brognola said, "did we avoid an international incident? Given that the Russians suddenly have serious internal problems to deal with, I think it's safe to say we did, especially because newly elected President Andulov, who promises to clean up that mess, seems very favorably disposed to the West. He seems to be under the impression that he owes his life to some of our operatives, though of course we denied everything."

"Of course," McCarter said.

"Officially, we're getting some static from abroad. Thailand, Burma and elements within Russia have all made certain inquiries, wondering if we've been polluting their ponds with our business. That, too, we've denied, though not too strenuously. It doesn't hurt for them to realize that, the longer they kick the dog, the sooner it's going to turn and bite them."

"I love it when you use homespun metaphors, Hal," McCarter said.

Brognola ignored that. "Now, as to the Triangle, and on a larger scale, the NetScythe operational testing. The DoD, and the boys and girls at NASA, thank us very much, whoever we might be, for our input in the testing of the satellite and imagery system. Officially they think we're some kind of consulting firm, and we've done nothing to disabuse them of the notion. There's the possibility that NetScythe will see use in the future, though I gather there are some bugs they want to work out of it, some refinements they want to make."

"Beats me what those would be," Schwarz said. "It seemed to work pretty great for us."

"Yes, well, they don't tell us everything," Brognola said. "They don't even tell me everything."

"So where do we stand with the Triangle?" Calvin James asked.

"The Triangle," Brognola said, "is effectively smashed. Their troops have been largely wiped out, thanks to all of you. Their connections to the Russian *mafiya* have been exposed and rooted out. There's some talk about what President Andulov will do next in regard to assigning special task forces to deal with organized crime. As you can imagine, his administration already has the powers that were in a snit in Moscow."

"So the stateside distribution network, as well as the links in Thailand and Burma…?" Blancanales asked.

"Effectively neutralized," Brognola said. "It will be a while before we have confirmation of that through official channels. Interpol is working something up for us and they promise it by next month."

"The wheels move slowly," Encizo commented.

"Interpol does thank us for the safe return of Agent

Nguyen," Brognola said. "Though the agent himself seems to have suffered some very minor hearing loss as a result of an entire house being blown out next to him."

"Can't make an omelet…" Schwarz said.

"Shut up, Gadgets," Lyons whispered.

"Speaking of Interpol," McCarter asked, "was there any word on Peng? Does Interpol or maybe the CIA have anything they can tell us?"

"We do not know where Peng ended up, unfortunately," Brognola said. "I'm afraid he'll have to be listed as a casualty of the mission. Obviously, if any of our sibling intelligence agencies get word, there'll be a notification flagged in the networks, and we'll be told."

"I suppose that's the best we're likely to do." McCarter nodded.

"What about Than, the warlord who was the real man in charge of the Triangle?" Lyons asked.

"We've never had a location on him," Price said, "and NetScythe was able to provide nothing. Not enough data points."

"Maybe that's one of the bugs," Schwarz said.

"Is it worth tracking him down? Taking him out?"

"It's not a priority," Brognola said. "Not for one man. His network is smashed and his resources cut. I doubt very much a figure like that, who has doubtless made many enemies, will survive long once he no longer has the protection of his criminal organization behind him."

"The king is dead," Blancanales said. "Long live the king."

"If some new group or figure does arise to fill the considerable vacuum left by the destruction of the Triangle," Brognola said, "you can rest assured that we will follow up."

"My one regret," Schwarz said, "is that I didn't get any bootleg MP3 players or designer jeans."

"About that," Brognola said. "Interestingly, FBI reports a measureable decrease in retail piracy. It's too soon to know, but that may have something to do with our operation against the Triangle."

"That's us," Lyons said. "Making the world safe for name-brand DVD players and leather jackets."

"At any rate," Brognola said, "I want to thank you all. Good work, people. I know we ask a lot of you, and you always come through for us. The Man extends his personal thanks. The souls of those FBI agents, among many others, can rest a little easier now, thanks to you."

"Thanks, Hal," Price said. "We appreciate it. I think that's all any of us want. Justice for those who've suffered."

"That is why we do what we do," Brognola said. "As long as there are men and women in the world like you, people willing to put it all on the line for their country, for civilization and for what is right, we will always be a step ahead of the predators."

"Amen," Blancanales said.

Somewhere in Burma

THE MAN ONCE KNOWN as the warlord Than sat in his ornately carved throne, watching cockroaches scuttle across the stone floor. He was quite surprised at how quickly the vermin had appeared. The sudden encroachment of the insects had matched the speed with which his court of hangers-on had left him when the source of his wealth and power dried up.

A few of his thugs, the ones with no prospects, had lingered for a few days. Even these, however, left when it became clear he had no money to pay them. They had ransacked the temple before leaving, and Than realized he was powerless to stop them. In the years living like a king, he had grown soft. He could not even bring himself to pick up a gun and defend his property. It all seemed so pointless.

He began to feel hungry, but he realized there was no food. There was also no water. Those men in his employ who had stayed the longest had raided what stores remained before leaving. There was nothing he could do about it. They all laughed at him, too. The once-powerful old man in the mountain. Warlord Than, now… nothing Than. A sad shadow of his former glory, doomed to die of starvation and dehydration.

He could leave the temple, he supposed. But where would he go, and what would he do? He had no prospects. He had nowhere to go, no other hiding places, no further contingencies. Thawan was gone—he regretted now what he had said to his son, but it was far too late to do anything about that—and everything had crumbled around him. He even considered suicide, but he was afraid; he did not want it to hurt, and he did not know what waited for him on the other side, if anything.

He was sitting like that, contemplating the same thoughts that had run endlessly in his mind for days, when the small man with the mangled hand came to him.

The man wore leg irons that dragged behind him. They scraped the stone floor as he shuffled. He held his hand awkwardly, pressed against his breast. He had been badly beaten and appeared to have been tortured. Something about him was vaguely familiar, but Than could not place it.

The little man looked on the former warlord sadly.

"You do not remember me," he said.

"Should I?" Than asked.

"I am Peng," the man said. "Does that name mean anything to you?"

"Should it?" Than asked again.

Peng paused for a long while. "No," he said finally. "I don't suppose it should."

"Were you one of my soldiers?" Than asked.

"No," Peng said. "I was not one of your soldiers."

It was then that Than noticed what the man who called himself Peng carried in his hand.

"You have a grenade," he said.

"Yes," Peng said. "One of your soldiers left it behind. I found it after I managed to pull my chains from the wall. The stone is old, the chains old, as well. It took a long while, but I managed it."

"You were in a cell?"

"Your men, after they beat me and mutilated me, left me there to die," Peng said. "I think they thought it too much trouble even to kill me before fleeing this place."

"Perhaps," Than said.

"Do you know why I am here?"

"I wish you would tell me," Than said. "I know very little anymore."

"My family," Peng said. "You killed my family. I grieve for them. I have worked against you for a long time now, but this does not fill the hole in my soul. My grief knows no end. It never will. I am here to end it. I am here for revenge."

"Revenge?" Than said. "It does not sound like revenge."

"No?" Peng asked. He pulled the pin from the grenade.

"No," Than said. "It sounds like…justice. Yes, that is the word. Justice."

"I think you are right," Peng said. He let the grenade fall from his fingers. The spoon popped free and the grenade rolled under the throne.

"Thank you," Than said.

The light was very bright.

TAKE 'EM FREE

2 action-packed novels plus a mystery bonus

NO RISK

NO OBLIGATION TO BUY

JAMES AXLER
DEATH LANDS

Blood Harvest

Welcome to the dark side of tomorrow. Welcome to the Deathlands.

Washed ashore in the North Atlantic, Ryan Cawdor and Doc Tanner discover two islands intact after Skydark, but whose inhabitants suffer a darker, more horrifying punishment. When the sun goes down, mutants called Nightwalkers manifest to unleash a feast of horror…which Ryan and Doc must struggle to survive.

Available March 2010 wherever books are sold.

AleX Archer
SACRED GROUND

The frozen north preserves a terrible curse…

For the Araktak Inuits, the harsh subzero tundra is their heritage. Now a mining company has purchased the land, which includes the sacred Araktak burial site. Contracted by the mining company, archaeologist Annja Creed is to oversee the relocation of the burial site—but the sacred ground harbors a terrible secret.…

Available March 2010 wherever books are sold.

www.readgoldeagle.blogspot.com

GRA23